# Dragon Village
# FIREBIRD

## RONESA AVEELA

BENDIDEIA
PUBLISHING

# Contents

# Characters

**Theo**: Almost thirteen-year-old boy who has connections to Dragon Village.

**Pavel**: Theo's best friend who invents gadgets.

**Diva**: Samodiva girl who lives in Dragon Village. Diva's name means "wild." *Samodiva* means "Wild alone." From Bulgarian mythology, Samodivi were wild creatures who shied away from humans.

**Baba Yaga**: Witch from Slavic folklore who lives in a house with chicken feet.

**Boo**: A magpie.

**Bor Stobor**: A Karakonjul. *Bor* means pine in Bulgarian, and *stobor* is a strong person (strong like a big pine wood).

**Ejko Bejko**: Kikimora's pet. A term used in Bulgarian for hedgehogs.

**Firebird**: In Slavic mythology, a bird that can be both a blessing and a curse. Its feathers glow brightly, and some say the bird can see the future.

**Hala**: Lamia and Zmey's mother. Female dragon who is associated with the wind and bringing storms.

**Harpy**: Half-woman, half-bird creature from Thrace and found in Greek mythology.

**Ispolin** (plural, Ispolini): Bulgarian word for "giants."

**Jabalaka**: The Keeper of Secrets. A man Lamia turned into a frog creature. *Jaba* is the Bulgarian word for "frog."

**Jega**: A Kuker (mummer) who wields fire. The word *jega* means "hot" in Bulgarian.

**Karakonjul**: Half-man, half-horse creature.

**Kikimora**: Creature who lives in the marsh, where she brews beer.

**Knights of Darkness**: Knights of Light who were corrupted by Zlo.

**Knights of Light**: Zmey's special guards who remained faithful.

**Kosara**: Guardian of the Znahar Tree.

**Kotka**: Baba Yaga's flying cat. *Kotka* is the Bulgarian word for "cat."

**Kuker** (plural, Kukeri): A man who wears animal skins and huge bells that scare evil spirits. The tradition dates back to Thracian times.

**Lamia**: Zmey's sister. Female dragon with three dog-like heads. She is cruel and brings hail to destroy crops, as well as stopping the flow of water.

**Lesnik**: Kikimora's husband. A guardian of the forest.

**Lord Vodnik**: Leader of the water creatures.

**Manol**: In folklore, the master builder of the Kadin Bridge. He built his wife into the bridge, so her shadow would keep it safe.

**Mraz**: The oldest of the Kukeri brothers. The Bulgarian word is for "cold."

**Nia**: Theo's twin sister.

**Old Lady Witch**: Old woman in Selo whom people think casts spells.

**Oristnizi**: In folklore, they are the three sisters of fate, who visit the home of a newborn during the infant's first hours of life. They circle the child's crib, and each one predicts the child's future.

**Pazach**: Another name for Jabalaka. The Bulgarian word for "keeper."

**Rusalka** (plural, Rusalki): Bulgarian word for water spirits, often called mermaids.

**Ruslana**: A Rusalka who's friendly toward Theo.

**Samodiva** (plural, Samodivi): Woodland nymph in Bulgarian lore. You may be more familiar with one of their other names: Veelas, like in the Harry Potter stories.

**Sava**: Diva's oldest sister.

**Shar**: Theo's deer companion. *Shar* means "colorful" in Bulgarian.

**Slugi**: Red, slimy, octopus-like creatures. *Slugi* means "servants" in Bulgarian.

**Struma**: Spirit of a woman built into a bridge wall.

**Sur**: Diva's deer companion. *Sur* means "gray" in Bulgarian.

**Tangra**: Thracian god of light and the sun.

**Ula**: Diva's sister.

**Uroki**: Evil spirit.

**Vodnik** (plural, Vodni): Slavic water creature that looks like an old man.

**Whirl**: Pavel's deer companion.

**Youda** (plural, Youdi): Evil Samodiva who lives in forests and mountains. She has the power of witchcraft.

**Youda Stana**: The leader of the Youdi.

**Zima**: A Kuker who has the power of freezing. The word *zima* means "winter" in Bulgarian.

**Zlo**: Lamia's lord and mentor. The word in Bulgarian means "bad" or "evil."

**Zmey**: Theo's birth father. Villages throughout Bulgaria have invisible patrons who protect their villages.

**Znahar**: Woman who heals with herbs. People sometimes call them witches because they are often clairvoyants as well.

**Zunitza**: A Samodiva. Theo's birth mother. The word comes f":rom *zuna*, the Bulgarian for "rainbow."

# Glossary

**Cherna Mountain**: *Cherna* is the Bulgarian word for "black." This is where the dragon castle is found.

**Chutura**: An old Bulgarian word for "mortar."

**Cold Marsh**: Home of the Vodni, Jabalaka, and Kikimora.

**Eniovden**: Midsummer's Day, celebrated on June 24.

**Forest of Souls**: The place where the souls of Dragon Village's ancestors reside in globes.

**Forest of Whispering Bells**: Forest where Baba Yaga lives. The bells jingle when someone approaches.

**Kadin Bridge**: Called "Bridge of the bride" (*Kadin most*) in Bulgarian, or "Bride bridge" (*Nevestin most*), the Kadin Bridge is a stone arch bridge that spans the Struma River at Nevestino in southwestern Bulgaria. It was constructed in 1470.

**Kaleto**: The Forgotten Land, home of the Ispolini. In Bulgarian, the name means "fortress."

***Lamia's Bible***: A book that contains secrets about those living in Dragon Village.

**Pavel-o-paraylzer**: Pavel's device that temporarily stuns creatures.

**Paveltron**: Pavel's multi-purpose gadget.

**Ribotron**: Pavel's fish-catching invention. *Riba* is the Bulgarian word for "fish."

**Selo**: Fictitious place along the Black Sea. Bulgarian word for "village."

**Vida**: Village where Youdi live.

**Zmeykovo**: Bulgarian name for "Dragon Village." Mystical land where mythological creatures live. Said to be at the end of the world.

**Znahar Tree**: A fictitious World Tree connecting the three realms: heavens, earth, and underworld.

**Zuna**: Name for the rainbow in Bulgarian folklore.

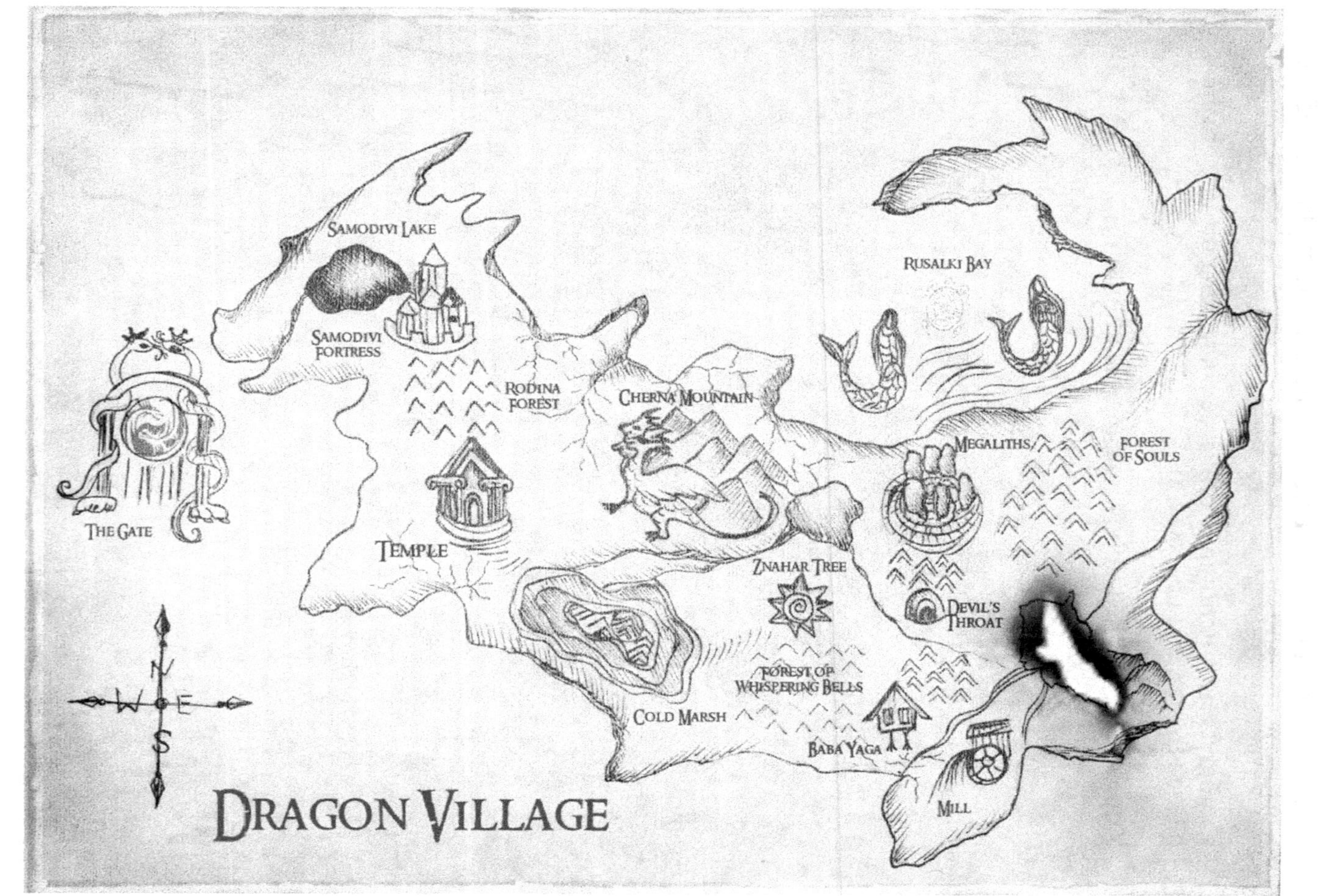


# DRAGON VILLAGE

# Chapter 1
# Call for Help

**JUNE 17**

SOMETHING WAS WRONG. The sea should have been full of fishing boats on a mid-June morning. Instead, they were all docked at the pier or pulled up onto the beach. The small crafts bobbed as waves licked their sides. And where were all the fishermen? Even after the day's work, they usually hung around the wharf telling their tales. Today, it was completely empty.

Waves smashed against the rock barrier, and a torrent of spray soaked Theo's T-shirt and shorts. Shivering from the chill, he dipped his bare toes into water that had pooled in a gap in the breakwater. That was as much of his body that he cared to immerse in the Black Sea.

The wind nipped his cheeks as he stared at the abnormal sight a while longer. He'd had a feeling something unusual was going to happen and hoped that meant today was going to be his lucky day. Not just for fishing, although he had caught nothing yet, and he'd been fishing for a couple of hours. Maybe he'd finally—

"Theo, Theo, help!" Nia's shrill cry shattered his concentration.

*Not again. Not THAT!* He dropped his fishing pole and jerked his head, looking up and down the beach for his twin sister.

There she was. In the sea.

The waves surged and crashed against the shore. Screeching and flailing her hands, Nia struggled against the onslaught as she hastened away from a creature covered with green algae.

Theo was too far away to see the monster clearly. He raced along the sharp breakwater until he reached the shore. Breathing heavily, he scrambled down the remaining rocks and rushed along the beach toward his sister. He tripped over his feet as his toes dug into the hot sand, but he righted himself before he fell. He called, "I'm coming!" as he scrambled closer.

Where was Pavel? Theo's best friend should have been watching Nia, protecting her. Unless … Did the monster already devour Pavel?

"Theo!" Nia screamed again, followed by laughter as the monster tackled her.

*What?*

Theo stopped short, staring at the scene. The algae-covered monster had transformed into a ruddy-complexion, dark-haired boy with seaweed clinging to his head and clothes.

*Pavel.* It was only his friend. Not a monster.

"It's all right. Nia's not in danger. It's all right." Theo repeated the words until his heart stopped racing.

"Come on in, Theo. The water's awesome." Nia tugged seaweed from her clothes and swatted Pavel, pushing him away.

Her dark curls and tanned skin glistened in the sun. She raised her voice against the roar of the waves. "Stop being like a lizard under the sun. Come in for a splash."

Theo's relief turned to anger. "I'm not a lizard. And why were you screaming like that? You scared me."

"Did you think a dragon was kidnapping me?" Nia laughed, but looked around warily.

"It's not funny." Theo stormed back to the rocks and retrieved his fishing pole. He might not catch any fish, but the motion of the waves tugging against the line soothed him, so he cast into the turbulent water.

How could Nia even joke about a dragon taking her? Last year, Theo had told her he wished a dragon would seize her, and one had carried her off to Dragon Village. Never again would he use words so carelessly.

Pavel forced his legs through the waves and climbed the breakwater. He plucked seaweed from his hair and the rim of his glasses and threw the plants into the water like an offering. "St. Nicholas, master of the sea, send a fish to my friend."

"Go away. You're dripping all over me." Theo tossed a towel to his friend without looking at him. He stared at his fishing line, willing Pavel to leave.

Pavel wiped the moisture off of his glasses and draped the towel over his shoulder. "Don't be such a wuss." With his bare toes, he nudged Theo. "Come have fun. You don't have to go into the water. We can fish together tomorrow. I'll bring my newest invention, the Ribotron. I designed it so we can catch fish and crabs."

"You and your gadgets." Theo huffed as he waved a dismissive hand behind him. His friend was always creating something new. Few of these inventions worked the way Pavel planned. "You have too many ideas and too much free time. Unlike you, I have to work to support my family. A rod, a hook, bait, and luck are enough for me."

Pavel stepped in front of Theo. "Why are you so mad all the time?"

Theo looked up, clenching his fists as he did so. *Because I want to leave!* he shouted in his mind. *I want to return and live with my birth father, Zmey, in Dragon Village.*

But then, he didn't know if Zmey wanted him. His father hadn't returned to get Theo, and it had been almost a year. On top of that, Theo had lost his connection to his birth mother, Zunitza, the queen of the Samodivi, the woodland nymphs. Zunitza had died before he'd ever had a chance to meet her, but her spirit had guided him on his mission. Now, since his return to Selo, her voice was silent. A sob choked Theo's throat. He needed them so badly, but didn't know if they wanted him back.

But how could he tell his best friend that? And how could Theo even think about leaving? He couldn't desert his adoptive mother and Nia. He was responsible for them and had to make sure they were protected and safe. His family and Pavel were still the dearest people in the world to him. He couldn't tell them he wished to go. Besides, apparently, he couldn't depend on his friend to protect Nia. Not that it was Pavel's obligation. But Pavel was like a brother to him, a part of the family already.

Instead, Theo said, "You told me you'd make sure nothing happened to Nia."

"Nothing has. Come on, Theo. Lighten up. Have some fun."

Theo shook his head. "You shouldn't have let her go into the water. My mom didn't want us to come to the beach at all. Did you forget about the red tide that's been invading other places? You promised Mom—and me—that you'd stay on the sand."

"You worry too much for nothing."

"We have to be careful. I don't want Nia—or you—to get sick."

"I promise you. There's nothing in the water. I checked before I let her go in. Only this green stuff floating around." He snatched a remaining piece of seaweed from his swimsuit and flicked it at Theo. "Besides, I don't think it's—"

"Hey, guys, stop bickering and come on in." Nia tiptoed around the sharp rocks. When she reached the boys, she grabbed Theo's hand and tugged him up onto his feet, making him drop his fishing pole.

"Leave me alone. I don't want to swim. Not today. Not here."

Nia let his hand go. "I thought you weren't afraid of the water anymore."

"I'm not." Even though he had learned how to swim the previous summer, the thought of swimming in the Black Sea made him queasy. It was the place his adoptive father had disappeared while fishing; a storm arose and swallowed him on the night Theo and Nia were born.

"Then why—"

"You know he doesn't like to swim," Pavel said.

"Actually, I like it now. I really do." Theo bent and picked up his fishing pole. "You two go have fun. I promised Mom fresh fish. If I don't catch any, we'll have to buy horse mackerel from the fish market."

*If they have any.* Maybe the men had all been out to sea earlier than normal. An approaching storm could have forced them to return early.

"All right." Pavel sighed. "But first I wanted to tell you about the red—"

"Come on, geek boy." Nia laughed as she grabbed Pavel's hand and pulled him back down the rocks and into the bluish-green water. Theo knew they'd forget about him while they became engrossed with their games.

Theo was torn about leaving for another reason. If he lived with Zmey in Dragon Village, would his family and friends in Selo forget he ever existed? He'd probably become part of the legends the old folks told.

"Okay, princess." Pavel twisted his body and waved to Theo. "I'll tell you later."

Despite his apprehension, Theo smiled. He was glad to see Nia and Pavel getting along. A year ago, everything was different. Back then, they'd hurled "geek boy" and "princess" at each other as insults. Nia's traumatic experience of being captured by a dragon had changed her, changed them all.

His sister no longer acted like a princess. Well, not as much anyway. She still had her moments. Mom said it was a part of growing up, since they were both only a week away from their thirteenth birthday. Even so, Nia willingly helped Mom around the house and had volunteered at an animal shelter.

Pavel had changed, too. Now, he was more willing to set aside his staunch scientific beliefs and accept that strange and magical incidents were possible. And Theo himself was different, and continued to change, in more ways than one. Those who knew what happened last year called him a hero. He still didn't feel like one. He couldn't even—

The tip of his fishing pole dipped. Theo jumped up and jerked the rod, trying to snag the fish. The rod pulled left and right as he struggled to wind in the spool. Slowly, he brought in his catch. To his disappointment, only a pile of green algae hung on the hook.

*Luck's not on my side today. I guess I'll have to go to the fish market after all.*

The sun had almost reached the top of the sky. Theo folded the line, tucked his gear into his backpack, and started down the breakwater. Wings fluttered above his head. He looked back. A cormorant landed in the water and thrust its head under the waves. When it emerged, it held in its long, hooked beak a wiggling fish, struggling for its life.

*I guess you're the lucky fisherman today, not me.*

The bird lifted its head, gulping as it swallowed the fish whole. Waterlogged from its fishing expedition, the cormorant flew onto the rock Theo had been sitting on. Facing the sun, the bird spread its wings and shook them, releasing a flurry of water. The warm sunlight reflected on its feathers as the bird stood still, giving the pitch-black wings a smooth, goldish-blue shimmer. With its dark plumage drying, it looked like a sparkling cross. The fishermen in the village told stories about how this symbolized nobility and sacrifice.

*Maybe that's a sign for me. I just hope it doesn't mean more troubles.*

A dazzling gleam and a splash in the sea on the other side of the breakwater caught his eye. Lost in thought, he hadn't seen the bird disappear. It had a voracious appetite, so maybe it was fishing again.

A second splash produced a rainbow of spray that scattered in the air and sparkled like pearls. Several droplets, carried on the wind, touched his face.

Theo looked through his backpack and found his phone. If he was lucky, he'd be able to get a video of the bird. He wished he'd thought of that earlier.

He gazed down the beach. Nia and Pavel were lost in their fun, splashing in the water. They wouldn't notice he was gone. He scrambled down the other side of the rocks and followed the black shape moving under the waves. He'd never been on this side of the beach before. The shore was rockier, and he stepped around jagged rocks as he made his way along.

Another splash sounded behind a boulder at the head of a second breakwater, and a fountain sprayed into the air. Theo breathed in the smell of salt and drying seaweed. He hurried to the rocks, slipping on the wet, green-patched stones, but kept his balance. At the top, he looked down. Two seagulls squawked as they quarreled over small snails. But that's not what intrigued him. The receding tide had exposed a rocky cavity in the middle of the barrier. A carved stone arch about half his height marked the entrance. The path inside sloped toward a tunnel.

*I wonder what's down there.*

He wanted to explore it, but not alone. He'd promised his mother to be sensible and think twice before heading off on any more adventures. She'd been overprotective all his life, because she'd lost her husband. After everything that happened the previous summer, she became more frantic whenever they were gone too long. With a sigh, he turned to leave.

A splash and a glow within the cavity piqued his curiosity.

*I'll look quickly. After that, I'll go back.*

He removed a flashlight from his backpack and left the bag and fishing pole on the rocks. To avoid hitting his head on the arch, he hunched over as he lowered himself into the tunnel. Stepping stones descended into the darkness like a staircase. At the cave's entrance, salt water and algae had pooled into niches carved into the stone over time.

He flashed the light into the dark hollow. "Is there anybody down here?"

*Here ... here,* the echo answered.

Another splash came from deeper within the cave. Theo ventured inside.

"Theo ... Theo ... help!"

"Nia?" He twisted around to look up the tunnel.

A fragment of blue sky peered through the opening, but no one was there. His sister hadn't followed him. The sound came from farther away, deep inside the cave. It was impossible that Nia had entered before him. Someone else was in trouble. Someone who knew him. He stepped forward, but then drew his foot back.

*I should get Pavel.*

"Theo." His name echoed around the cave.

His breaths increased, and he bit his bottom lip. He shuffled forward a step, then stopped.

*What should I do? I can't help by myself. I don't have my pow—*

"THEO! Can you hear me? HELP!"

Despite the chilling urgency of the cry, that voice was familiar. Melodic. Enchanting. For a moment, Theo went back in time to another underwater cave in Dragon Village he'd been in last year.

That experience had been terrifying, too, but in a different way. Even so, he'd made a friend, one who showed him the beauty and wonders of the sea, and the joy of swimming. Could it be her? How did she manage to come here, to Selo, before the portal between her world and his had opened?

He made up his mind. His friend was in trouble. She'd saved his life—more than once. He had to find her and help. Now. Without Pavel. Without Nia. He couldn't put either of them in danger again.

He followed a rushing stream deeper into the cave. The farther he went, the mustier, earthier the cave smelled. His flashlight uncovered glimpses of broken shells and lichen-covered boulders, but no living beings. A strange azure light glowed in the distance. That must be where she was. He crept along the slippery rocks, pressing his free hand against the damp wall to keep his balance.

*Bang. Splash.*

A chunk of rock from the ceiling exploded against a boulder in the frothy river, hurtling a spray of cold water toward him. Chilled and momentarily blinded, he stepped onto something sharp. Pain pierced his bare feet, and he slipped, falling onto his knees. His flashlight banged against the rocks, flickered, and went dim.

"No, not now, not now!" he screamed.

*Now, now* the unmerciful cave threw back at him.

Theo shook the flashlight. It emitted a weak light, enough for him to avoid stepping onto any more broken shells. He reached a junction. The angry river flowed down another tunnel. What he wanted was straight ahead. In a few more steps, he reached the back of the cave where the blue glow and voice beckoned him.

The place held only a large conch lying by a still pool. A stream of light radiated from the water onto the shell. Theo kneeled by the pool's edge, peering into the clearest water he'd ever seen. His reflection stared back at him. His red hair tussled, a frantic look in his pale-blue eyes, and his mouth wide open.

*Who called me here and how?*

"Theo …" The voice had faded to a whisper.

"Where—" His gaze rested on the conch again. The light was coming from the shell, not from the pool.

He picked up the conch, cradling it in his palms. Brown carved symbols spiraled along the pearly surface, reaching to the shell's golden peak, which shone like Poseidon's spear. He'd seen those marks before, an ancient, mystical language written on pieces of parchment. Riddles. Nature's clues. Friends had translated the inscriptions for him. He'd needed the clues when he'd been in Dragon Village.

"Theo, please help …" The words slipped from the conch.

He opened his eyes wide. When he was little, his mother told stories about how Rusalki, mermaids, used shells like sea phones. All he'd ever heard before was the roar of the sea. The voice must be his friend. Using both hands, he held the conch to his face.

"Ruslana?" he said.

Instead of waves, a pleading female voice moaned, "Theo, can you hear me? We need your help. Zmeykovo and Selo are in grave danger. Come back, Theo …"

"Danger!" Zmeykovo was the name his friends called Dragon Village.

He stepped back to lean against the damp stone wall but slipped on the slimy stones. The shell flew out of his hands and slammed into the pool, and the water engulfed it in seconds. The glow from the shell extinguished, leaving Theo with only the fading light from his flashlight.

*I have to get the conch back. Find out what's going on.*

He kneeled by the pool and reached into the water with both hands. Slippery red algae tangled in his fingers, stinging them. He pulled out his aching hands.

"What is that?"

The water had been clear moments ago.

The tip of the conch poked its golden peak out of the water. Theo grabbed for it, but two red tentacles twisted around the shell, hugging it. Two more slimy tentacles wrapped around Theo's arms, digging into his skin and binding him like a metal rope, creating a white line that ran down his arms.

Rage clawed at Theo's skin, demanding release. It pulsed stronger, stranger than any emotion he'd ever experienced. The fury within him took form, emitting orange-red sparks that crackled and smoked. Their sulfuric odor tainted the air and gagged him, filling his mouth and nostrils. He grabbed a handful of the offending sparks and squeezed. Their prickly jabs oozed a fiery ichor in his fist.

He returned his attention to the creature holding him captive. "LET. ME. GO!"

The veins in his arms swelled, pain tightened his chest, and he emitted a loud hiss.

The creature jerked its tentacles away from Theo and slithered back into the water, but the other two held the shell with an unyielding grip. The creature pulled away and disappeared into the now-murky reddish water, carrying the shell into the depths.

Theo shook. *What just happened?*

His anger subsided, and his breathing calmed. Afraid he'd turned into a monster like the one in the water, he stretched out his arms in front of him, examined his hands and chest, and touched his face with his slimy, trembling palms.

*I seem to be normal.*

What was that creature? It most definitely wasn't a result of red tide. It was no eco-accident. Despite the danger, Theo had to bring Pavel here to show him. His friend was one person who would know what those creatures were. Not only was Dragon Village in danger, the Rusalka had said Selo, their home, was, too. Theo needed his friend's help to save both places he loved.

With that terrifying thought, Theo sprinted out of the cave, not caring that broken shells cut into the soles of his feet.

# Chapter 2
# Invasion

THEO STOOD at the cave entrance, with Pavel and Nia by his side. They all had put on their flip-flops, because Theo had warned them about the dangerous creatures and broken shells. His own feet and arms ached from his encounter with both hazards. The boys set their backpacks onto the rocks, while Nia clutched her beach bag.

In the short time Theo had been gone, the scene had changed. Now, small, red, coral-shaped creatures teemed in the pools of water, twisting their slimy, octopus-like tentacles at the intruders.

One approached Pavel, and he pushed it away with his foot. "I thought you said there was only one inside the cave."

"When I left, there was."

The creature returned and crawled onto Pavel's toe. He shook his foot, but the tiny thing adhered like glue.

"That won't work," Theo said. "The one that attacked me had stinging suction cups. Do you know what they are?"

"No, I— Ouch. It bit me." With his other foot, Pavel crushed the aggressive creature that had crawled up his leg and clung like a leech to his skin. "That little thing hurts like a jellyfish."

"Tell me about it." Theo rubbed his arms from elbow to armpit, the areas streaked with swollen scratches.

"You really should go home and have Mom put salve on your cuts," Nia said. "That stuff she got from Vela's mother works miracles. You'll feel better in no time."

Pavel snickered. "Not sure I'd trust anything from Old Lady Witch."

A suffocating pressure built up in Theo's chest, and he coughed. It felt as if something was trying to get out, rip itself out of his body like the creatures in the movie *Alien*.

Theo shoved Pavel against the tunnel wall. "She's not a witch."

"I don't want to argue. Just saying …" Pavel rubbed his shoulder. "What's the matter with you? Ever since we've come back from Dragon Village, you've been moody and angry."

"I don't like you calling her names. Vela's mother helped me. She's kind." Theo coughed to get rid of a tickle in his throat. "She heals everyone in the village for free or almost nothing."

He coughed again and bent over double as a severe pain wracked his chest. His body spasmed. "Ohhhh …" A terrible taste like ashes filled his mouth, and he spat out a black substance.

"Theo!" Nia patted his back. "What's wrong?"

"Nothing. I'm fine. Don't worry about me."

"Spitting out black gunk is *not* fine."

He straightened and wiped residue from his lips. "Must be infection from that creature's bite."

"You should go home and—"

"No!" He glared at Nia, and she shrank away from him. "We have bigger problems to solve."

"Theo, man—" Pavel started.

"Enough. It's just a cough."

The pain receded. His heart ached as he looked at his sister and friend. Nia clung to Pavel, her lips trembling and her eyes bright with tears. Pavel's mouth was open, and he shook his head slightly as he stared at Theo with a blank look.

"Sorry … I …" Theo hung his head. "I don't know why I got so angry."

Sniffling, Nia shuffled closer and hugged Theo. "It's okay."

"I … we have to figure out what these *things* are." Theo stomped in the pool of water, crushing several of the slimy things as he tried to get rid of the aggression still raging within him. Puffs of red spores shot out of the creatures and filled the air with a foul odor.

Nia scrunched up her nose. "Oh, that stinks like rotten eggs."

"Yah, it does." Theo coughed and waved his hand to clear the red residue from the air. "You don't know what these things are, Pavel?"

"Yes and no. I tried to tell you earlier." Pavel pulled out his phone from his backpack. He fiddled with his glasses as he scrolled. "You know my father works for the Oceanology Department in the city, right?"

Theo nodded.

"Well, I was looking up 'red tide' on Google earlier today, since that's what everyone was calling it." He showed Theo and Nia pictures and articles.

"These creatures are red tide?" Nia asked.

"No, I overheard my father talking—"

Nia laughed. "Using one of your inventions to listen to him, I suppose."

"As a matter of fact, yes. It was a—"

"Later, please?" Theo gestured with his hand for Pavel to continue. "What did your father say?"

"He and his co-workers are stumped. They've never seen such creatures—"

"He said 'creatures' and not 'red tide'?" Theo clenched his fists and squeezed his eyes tight for a moment, trying to control the anger bubbling up again. "And you're just telling me now?"

"I tried earlier when you were fishing." Pavel shrugged. "I didn't think they were these alien things. My dad didn't describe them. All he told my mom was that they were an unknown species, nothing that's ever been seen in the Black Sea before. Or anywhere in the world even."

Nia opened her eyes wide. "Did he say they came from outer space?"

"Nah." Pavel shook his head. "My dad believes only in science. They've been experimenting on the samples they collected. He's bound and determined to find an explainable solution. If nothing else, he'll say it's a mutation caused by global warming."

"I'd be okay with aliens coming to kill life on Earth." Nia laughed nervously. "I'd even rather face the Gorgon Medusa. Anything. As long as it's not that horrible, ugly, sinister Lamia."

Theo cringed at the mention of the three-headed dragon that had kidnapped Nia last year. He and Pavel had found a way to get to Dragon Village—to rescue his sister. He'd never, ever forget *that* adventure.

Pavel took off his glasses that had fogged up and wiped them against his bathing trunks. "My dad said people from the village are saying it's an invasion of demonic beings. The fishermen won't even row out to sea."

"So that's why no one was out today," Theo said.

"Yah, you know how superstitious the adults are, especially the old folks." He put his glasses back on and fiddled with them until they sat a bit below the bridge of his nose. He leaned closer and whispered, "Dad said everyone's terrified. One of the beaches was covered with dead fish. Not only dead, but their insides, all the meat and juices, had been eaten clean away. All that was left was dried up skin and skeletons."

Nia gagged and covered her mouth. "And you let me go into the water?"

"That place wasn't anywhere near here." Pavel rolled his shoulders, as if unconcerned. "Do you think I would have gone in myself if I thought it was unsafe?"

"I suppose not," Nia replied. "I'm surprised Mom let us come down here, though, if that's what people are saying."

"You know she doesn't go out much," Theo said. "If she'd heard it was more than a red tide, she'd have locked us in the house."

"You're right." She nodded. "I'm glad our beach has been clear, so we can enjoy our summer vacation."

"Not likely. If the creatures are out here," Pavel said as he nodded toward the puddles, "and there was only one before, then the problem's getting worse. If these things take over the water, it'll be an ecological catastrophe. Humans won't survive. Dad says people are saying this disaster has happened because Selo lost its protector when the statue of Zmey disappeared."

Pain stabbed Theo's heart. He had met his birth father only last summer on the rescue mission to Dragon Village. Zmey had promised to come back and teach Theo about his origins and abilities, but Theo hadn't seen the dragon since that day. Every day, Theo felt changes, power, but didn't know how to harness that energy. He exploded with anger for no reason, and he experienced moments of helplessness. He had to discover a way to get back there and find his father.

"Nobody believes me that Zmey's alive and in Dragon Village," Pavel continued, "only the old witch."

Theo clenched his fists again. Friend or not, Pavel had better not say that again. "Stop. Calling. Her. A. Witch!"

Pavel held up his hands, palms out, in front of his body. "Sorry, sorry. Bad habit. Chill out."

Theo breathed slowly. *Why is my anger getting out of control?*

"Theo?" Nia squeezed his arm.

"I'm okay. Now we know what these creatures are, or aren't, but we still need to find out what's happening in Dragon Village. And we can't do that unless I find the conch and talk to the Rusalki." He put on his backpack. "Are we ready to go into the cave?"

Pavel and Nia nodded.

Pavel removed a flashlight from his backpack and handed it to Theo. "Use this since the batteries in yours are low."

*I just hope we're not already too late to help.* Theo led the way. "It's not that far, but be careful not to slip on the wet rocks."

Nia followed Theo, and Pavel entered last. They remained quiet, the rushing of the underground river and the crunching of shells underfoot the only sounds. The cave now had a rotten-eggs odor, the same as the smell of the creatures he'd stepped on outside. Theo flashed the light onto the river, hoping they didn't swarm the water down there as well. Streaks of red flashed past, and several dead monsters lay crushed, caught in seaweed by the large boulder. Theo groaned. They were here, too. And these were much larger than the ones at the entrance. At least the fast water kept them from climbing up onto the path.

Skidding came from behind him, and Nia yelled, "Ahhh!"

Theo whipped around and grabbed her by the elbow to keep her from falling. "You okay?"

She nodded. "Sorry. I thought a shell was one of those nasty things. I slipped when I kicked it away."

"Hold onto me. We're almost there. Just a few more steps."

When they entered the pool area, he focused the flashlight onto the water. It crawled with the red beasts, larger than any of the ones they'd seen so far.

"The shell fell down there?" Nia whispered. "You can't go in. They'll kill you."

"I agree with Nia," Pavel said. "It's not safe. We'll have to find another way to get the shell."

Theo replied, "We don't have time. I have to try now. Our friends are in trouble."

"Wait, then, if you insist. I have something you can use." Pavel pulled an item from his backpack. "Take this." He handed Theo a narrow, brownish-orange brass capsule about the length of a pencil.

"What's this? A bullet?" It certainly was shaped like one. "You want me to shoot them?"

"No, it's a knife, in case you get stuck in nets, ropes, or anything else while you're underwater. Press the button, and the blade will appear. It looks like a needle but can cut through anything."

"How's that going to help him with these nasty things in the water?" Nia asked.

"But wait, there's more." Pavel grinned.

He dug in his backpack again and took out a small lantern-like object and aimed it at the creatures in the water. When he flicked a switch, a stream of violet sparks shot out. The red algae froze mid-squirm. Paralyzed, they floated to the edges of the pool. A clear circle formed in the water like a cave opening.

"This is my Pavel-o-paralyzer. It's a miracle worker."

Nia shook her head. "How many of these gadgets do you carry around with you?"

"All my latest. I never know when I'll need one." Pavel turned back to Theo. "I'm still not sure it's a good idea. You don't know how far down the conch fell, or if the creature took it away."

"I'll use my mermaid belt. It'll let me breathe in the water."

"You brought it with you?" Nia asked.

Theo nodded. "Always, whenever I'm near water."

"Drat," Pavel said, "I didn't bring mine. I don't like the idea of you going down there alone."

"I'll be fine." Theo removed his backpack and shuffled through items, retrieving a fishing net belt interlaced with algae and colorful shells. It was fancier than the original one a Rusalka had given him, which he'd lost in Rusalki Bay. That one had only ferns woven around the net. Nia had added the shells to the new ones they received before they left Dragon Village last year, saying it made them look more authentic. A human version of a mermaid belt. Not wanting to refuse, after her terrible ordeal, he accepted the decorations.

He removed his flip-flops, tightened the belt around his waist, and gulped as he looked at the infested water. This was important. He could do it.

"Okay, if you're sure you want to do this. Alone." Pavel gave the stunning device to Theo. "Take this with you in case you come across more of these things down there. I think it should work in water."

"You *think*? You never tried it in water?"

Pavel shook his head. "Better than nothing, right?"

"Okay, Einstein. Do you have any more 'miracles' I need to take with me?" Theo crossed his arms and tapped his foot. He wanted to leave before they discovered his real goal.

"No, that's it. You can go now if you still want to." Pavel shrugged and pushed his glasses up his nose. "Good luck. Hope you find the conch."

Nia hugged Theo. "Be careful. I love you."

"You better hurry, Theo." Pavel looked at his phone. "The paralysis will hold for no more than fifteen or twenty minutes."

Theo gripped the gifts from Pavel in one hand while he used the other to tighten his belt, making sure it was secure. He squatted by the pool, looked at his sister and friend, and dove into the water. Once under the surface, he glanced back.

He almost laughed as his splash created a fountain of salt spray and foam that covered Pavel and Nia. The paralyzed red algae flew out of the water like leaping salmon, before dropping to the stones. Pavel and Nia both jumped. Nia scurried back to the damp wall, while Pavel pushed the creatures into the water with his foot. Theo's view of Pavel and Nia became clouded with white foam and red creatures.

By the time the water calmed, Theo had descended farther into the depths of the pool. The cold liquid encased him as he pushed with both legs to explore. He'd been afraid to tell Nia and Pavel he was going to look for a portal to Dragon Village, then come back later when he was alone. They would try to stop him or, worse, say they wanted to come with him. The Rusalki had called to him for help. Theo couldn't put his sister and friend in danger. If the conch came from the Rusalki, then there had to be a way back to them this way.

Farther and farther he went down, looking for anything that might be a way to Dragon Village. The darkness made it difficult to see, his ears hurt from the cold, and his hands shook. He kept a tighter grasp on the gadgets Pavel had given him.

At last, his feet touched the bottom, and sand squished under his bare toes. Shells lay scattered all around, but he didn't see the Rusalki conch. He pressed forward until he reached a large smooth rock. With his fingers, he pressed all around, searching for a niche that might open a portal. He looked to the left. He looked to the right. He dug his fingers underneath to lift the rock, but it was too heavy. Taking the knife Pavel had given him, Theo poked around. Nothing worked. He felt as if he'd been trying for an eternity.

*How can I possibly help my friends if I can't even move a rock? I should be strong and powerful like Zmey.*

Theo shivered. Something or someone was watching him. A red blur floated past. Another drifted around his legs. He tucked up his feet and swam away.

*Where did they come from?*

A glimmer of light lay farther ahead in a tunnel. Kicking his legs, he swam down the passage. The water grew colder and more turbulent. Red creature after red creature appeared. Theo stayed close to the edge of the tunnel, away from the monsters. Onward he swam until the light grew brighter, and the creatures grew more numerous.

He had reached the end. It wasn't a portal to Dragon Village. The passage led him to the sea.

An enormous patch of red glided toward him. His racing heartbeat echoed in his ears. He reversed direction and kicked his feet as hard as he could.

*Don't look back. Don't look back.*

He did. The red blob of squirming tentacles had gained on him. He kicked harder and swam faster.

Finally, the rock he'd thought was a portal lay beneath him, but only darkness stretched overhead. The pool—and safety— were up there. With all his strength, Theo launched himself upward. The darkness crept away, and the smaller creatures by the edge of the pool became visible. But now they were squirming. They had revived from Pavel's earlier shock treatment. Theo pressed the switch on Pavel's paralyzer.

Violet sparks spluttered.

*No! No! Work!*

With a whoosh, a stream of light shot out. Theo sighed with relief and pointed the light at the mass of creatures. They became still once more. He kicked past them and broke the surface. Foam from the water covered his face. Gasping, he reached out his hand, and Pavel pulled him out of the pool. Theo flopped onto the rocks. A creature clung to his shoulder. Too exhausted to flick it off, Theo zapped it with the violet light. It dropped onto the rocks, and Pavel kicked it into the water. Theo hadn't found the portal, but he was glad to see friendly faces again. Well, anxious looking ones.

"Theo!" Nia shrieked. "I thought I lost you. Are you all right? Your face is blue."

At the same time, Pavel said, "What happened? We were worried. You were gone for so long."

Theo held up his hand, palm out, hoping they understood he'd tell them as soon as he got his breath back. He lay on the rocks, wiped seafoam from his face, and pushed his wet hair out of his eyes. When his heart stopped racing and he could breathe normally again, he sat up and wiped salty drops from his face. He handed Pavel his laser device and knife.

"No, keep them. I have more. Tell us what happened."

"I failed. I didn't find a portal …" Theo covered his mouth. It was too late. He'd said what he'd meant to keep secret.

His sister's and friend's worried looks turned angry.

"Portal?" Pavel shouted.

"I thought you went to look for the conch," Nia said.

"I … I … wanted to find another way to Dragon Village."

"And you'd go without your best friend?"

"And your sister?"

"Yes. No, I just wanted to find a new way there for now." Theo hung his head and muttered, "It doesn't matter. There isn't an underwater portal ... nothing ... just sand, darkness, rocks, and shells." He hesitated. "And a lot more red creatures."

Pavel looked at the red tentacles moving in the water, thirsty for prey. "We'll try something else tomorrow. There has to be a way to get to Dragon Village before the normal portal opens next March."

His brow furrowed and his mouth set in a firm line, Pavel paced the cave. He stopped. His eyes brightened. "Oh, wait. I have an idea."

# Chapter 3
# The Power of the Megaliths

BACK AT HOME, Theo stood in front of his bedroom mirror, waving his arms like a bird. He spun in a circle with closed eyes until he became dizzy, but wings never appeared.

*What am I doing wrong? I should be able to fly. I'm part dragon.*

The boy with skinny chicken arms looked at him from the mirror and seemed to be saying, *Theo, what's the matter with you?* He'd grown more muscular while traveling around Dragon Village, but it wasn't enough. He had to get stronger, be more confident. How else could he save his friends? Maybe he could invoke his dragon abilities when he was in Dragon Village again. Everything there was magical, mystical, so different from the human world.

But what if Zmey didn't want Theo to return? Something had kept his father away for so long. *Has he decided he doesn't want me because I'm a failure? What about my birth mother? Has Zunitza deserted me, too?*

Maybe trying to go back to Dragon Village was a mistake.

Theo shook his head. The Rusalki had begged him to come. If no one else wanted him there, at least they did.

With hunched shoulders, he paced the room. *My parents wouldn't abandon me, would they?* His breathing became heavy and shaky. *No. There must be another reason, but what?*

His stomach clenched, and he wanted to scream. *Lamia. Has the beast returned?* The three-headed dragon was the one who wanted to destroy Zmey, her brother. The same way she'd murdered Zunitza.

How could Lamia be there? Theo had killed her, seen her dead body transformed into its human form. Even so, he felt the beast's presence with him always, following him everywhere, taunting him.

An explosion of hate bubbled beneath the surface of his being. *I'll make her pay if she's harmed my father. I'll—*

His skin itched, and a burning sensation crept toward his armpits. Theo patted the area and lifted his T-shirt, twisting to see what was happening. He couldn't feel anything, so he returned to look in the mirror.

The same pale, weak-faced boy watched him. The light of the moon reflected off of his red hair. Nothing had changed.

He sighed. After his unsuccessful attempt at finding a portal to Dragon Village earlier today, Theo hoped Pavel's plan, whatever it was, would work. His friend had an idea for everything, brilliant ideas, but often unsuccessful and impractical. Like the wings he'd made last summer when Theo wanted to fly. They were heavy, clumsy, and ineffective. All that Theo had accomplished that day was getting a lot of scratches and bruises.

His desire to fly had been the catalyst to Nia being kidnapped by Lamia. Wrong place, wrong time. Or was it? Lamia had said it had been no mistake. Capturing Nia had been the dragon's way to get Theo to go to Dragon Village.

Now Pavel's idea was to return to where that all happened. The Stone Forest. The place where they'd found a portal to Dragon Village the first time. Pavel hadn't explained what his plan was, and Theo was apprehensive. If he could fly and use his powers, he might be useful and get them to Dragon Village. Instead, he was forced to rely on his friend to do that.

It was time to get going. Everyone in the house should be asleep.

Theo reached into the back of his closet and drew out a quiver of arrows and a black bow engraved with a golden snake. He lovingly stroked the bow, a gift from the priestess Kosara, but that's not what made it so precious. It had once belonged to his Samodiva mother.

He searched in his closet again until he found a crystal dagger shaped like a lightning bolt. This one was Nature's gift to help him in his quest. It had served its purpose. Perhaps it would be an adequate weapon if he needed one in close quarters.

These two weapons—along with whatever gadgets Pavel was bringing—should be enough to defend them. They'd had less than that the first time they arrived in Dragon Village.

He slipped on his jacket and quietly opened the door to Nia's bedroom. She slept deeply, no doubt tired from the sun, the sea water, and the day's troubling events. He left a note on her nightstand and looked back once more before stepping softly to the front door.

Mom would be devastated. He hated sneaking away, but she'd try to stop him if he waited until morning. And Nia would be angry and disappointed. Even though he was sure she wanted to come along to prove that she could be helpful, he was certain she was still terrified of Dragon Village. And Theo wouldn't put his sister in danger again.

He stifled a laugh. Maybe Nia wanted to see a certain boy she'd met there, someone who had treated her like the princess she once thought she was.

He left the house like a shadow, locked the front door, and waved to Pavel, who waited for him hidden under the eaves of the house next door. They walked in silence, following the silver moonlight along the cobbled street on their way to the Stone Forest. Only the cry of an owl broke the lonely sound of their footsteps.

"Are you ready for the trip?" Pavel whispered.

"Ready or not, I have to help my friends. You—"

"They're my friends, too, don't forget."

"I know, but you don't have to come. I don't want you to get hurt."

Pavel stopped and looked Theo in the eye, a glimmer of determination in his own. "Friends help each other."

"What about your parents? They'll worry."

Pavel snorted. "They're *always* worried about me, just like your mom. Even when I'm right outside the door or in my own room. Parents."

"True." Theo nodded. "So, what's your plan? A new invention?"

"I'll explain when we get there." Pavel glanced to the side. "How'd Princess Nia take it when you told her she couldn't come with us? I bet she was mad."

"She's sleeping. I wrote her a note."

"Coward."

Theo tapped Pavel's shoulder with his fist. "And did you tell your brother you were going?"

"Umm, no," Pavel said. "But I can just imagine Nia's face tomorrow morning when she wakes up and finds you gone. And *she* has to explain it to your mother. 'Cause I'm sure you didn't tell your mom either."

"No more than I'm sure you told *your* parents," Theo replied. "I know Nia wants to go with us, but I … just can't let her. Someone needs to take care of Mom. When everything is back to normal in Dragon Village, Nia can come. She's only ever been in the castle, never had to trek across the island. As you know, there are a lot of dangers."

"You protect her too much," Pavel said. "Your sister's tougher than she looks."

"Hmm. If you had a sister, you'd protect her, too, no matter how tough you thought she was."

Pavel laughed. "Touché."

They walked the rest of the way in silence. Black tree branches seemed to hold out grasping hands. Gleaming eyes in the forest blinked like fireflies, and popping and crackling sticks resounded through the veil of night as animals scurried about. Only a lonely cat looking for her prey crossed their path and disappeared into the darkness.

At last, they arrived at the base of a hill. Chiseled stone steps ascended through a narrow tunnel to the Stone Forest at the summit.

Theo broke the silence. "It's no less scary now than it was when we first found it." Each time he came here—to try to fly, the tunnel reminded him of a dark, musty dungeon. "Well, let's do this." He stepped inside, and Pavel followed.

After a long walk through the tunnel, they arrived at the top. The crisp air held only a tinge of the sea. In the distance, lights flickered in the village houses. The wind was asleep, so the high altitude remained mild this summer's night.

The majestic marble statue of Zmey, the village guardian, had once stood to the side of the site. Now, grass, moss, and weeds had grown wild around the only part of the statue that remained, the dark limestone slab. Tonight, it held something more. Fresh flowers and herbs lay on the ground.

Pavel crouched and touched the bouquet, and a few petals dropped from the stems. "I wonder who left them."

"Since the statue disappeared, a lot of older people come here to pray for the village's protection," Theo said. "They think Zmey's abandoned us."

*Just like he's abandoned me.*

Theo had to stop thinking that. His father wouldn't have deserted him unless the dragon was in trouble.

Theo continued, "They're afraid Lamia will stop our water from flowing, steal the children for sacrifices, and destroy our crops and fish."

Pavel cringed, looking into the dark trees around them. "Just mentioning that demonic creature makes me sweat and shiver. No one believes me that we—you—killed her."

"I just wonder …"

"What?"

Theo hesitated. "She really was dead, wasn't she?"

"Of course. We all saw her lying there."

"Then who can be causing problems in Dragon Village now?"

"Don't know." Pavel shrugged. "Let's see if we can get there to find out."

"Will you tell me now how you plan to do that?"

"By using the natural energy of the megaliths."

While Pavel dug through his backpack, Theo turned to look at the circle of stones that gave the Stone Forest its name. There was the broken one he'd jumped off of when trying the wings Pavel made him last summer. The remaining six marble columns, each with a carved horse head on top, stood intact in a circle like a sanctuary.

Every time he came here, energy filled him, the anger throbbing within his chest abated, and he felt like himself again: a boy with a dream. If the energy from the megaliths could do that, then Pavel's idea might work.

The urge to fly overtook him. He closed his eyes and held out his arms, making small wavy motions. The air around him felt soft. In his mind, he became a bird. Free. Flying high into the night sky, up among the stars. Someday, he *would* know how to harness his powers and soar through the air—as a dragon, not as a make-believe bird.

He opened his eyes and checked on Pavel. His friend was assembling numerous parts of his invention that lay on the ground. Theo cleared a spot on the former statue's slab, set his backpack, bow, and quiver onto the cold limestone, and sat beside them.

Pavel chatted while he worked. "Do you know about the earth's whispering energies?"

Theo shook his head, even though Pavel couldn't see. "No, but I think I'm going to learn now."

"Ancient megalithic architects knew that standing stones, large blocks like the Stone Forest, generated various forms of free energy."

"Uh-huh." Theo listened, but didn't understand everything Pavel said. All he cared about was having the new invention work.

"Many studies in England and other countries that have megaliths say these places have a band of magnetic force that forms a spiral." Pavel made a swirl in the air, then continued attaching pieces to his device. "It starts on the outside and flows toward the center where it forms a rabbit hole."

"Like the story of Alice?" Theo asked. "But we don't want to go to Wonderland."

"We won't. These rabbit holes can take people to other worlds, too."

"How do you—?"

"There, done."

Two devices lay on the ground beside Pavel. He stood, holding one that looked like a Geiger counter. It rattled and sent out a shrill pitch as Pavel walked around the megaliths. "Can you feel how the circle of stones pulsates with concentric rings of alternating current, like the ripples in a pond?"

"Einstein, I don't have a clue what you just said," Theo said. "What are you doing?"

"I'm trying to locate the entry point."

He continued at a slow pace, holding a probe close to the rocks. When he reached the easternmost stone, the device set off a series of steady beeps.

"This is it. Can you get me a stone to mark the exact spot?"

Theo stood and brushed off dirt from his pants. He picked up a stone and set it where Pavel pointed. "Now what?"

Pavel walked around the inside of the megaliths in a spiral motion, following the steady beeping of his device, until he reached the center. "Here. Place another stone in this spot."

Theo did. "What next, boss?"

"Did you know," Pavel continued, apparently still lost in his own mind, "according to Tesla's research, the Earth and the universe create energy that we can use to fly, to create electricity, and more. Many scientists have tried to open a portal to other dimensions, but unfortunately, they still don't know how to use this energy."

"And you do?"

"Well … the megaliths were built and placed here for a reason."

Theo groaned. Pavel was side-stepping the question. He obviously didn't have a clue. Of course, he didn't. He'd never tried this invention before. "How are you going to make it work?"

Pavel looked over the rim of his glasses. "It's simple. The idea is to harness the power of static energy from the megaliths, which will activate my invention's magnets, copper coil, and crystal. This, in turn, will open an energy tunnel to another dimension, specifically to Dragon Village."

"How do you know we'll go there?"

Pavel was silent. "I guess not everything in science is precise. If I made a mistake, we could go to another world. Then we'll rely on your superhuman abilities to survive."

Theo looked from Pavel to the megaliths, then back. "What?"

"I'm joking." Pavel laughed. "I know because …" He glanced toward the slab where Theo had left his backpack and weapons.

"I'm waiting."

"Uh, because … Oh. You have magical items from Dragon Village. Their energy, combined with that of the megaliths, will send us to the right place."

Theo shook his head. "You just made that up."

"No … yes, you're right. But it makes sense, doesn't it?"

"I don't know anymore." Theo wrapped his head in his hands and paced.

"How about this idea?" Pavel said. "It'll work because the energy of the megaliths will be combined with the fact that you're the son of a dragon and a Samodiva. How powerful is that?"

"I don't—"

"No, wait. Let me finish." Pavel waved Theo's words away. "You have sensors unknown to humans. You could likely just *think* about Dragon Village, and we'd be guided there."

"Pavel, I—"

"I wonder what I should call you. Since you're not human, what kind of species are you?"

"Pavel." Theo raised his voice, knowing it was no use. His friend was on one of his rambles.

"Drakowild? Dracosam? Dracovil? Dragowild?" Pavel circled Theo, staring at him, as if trying to imagine the creature he was naming.

"Stop." Theo grabbed Pavel's shoulder.

The wild stare dissipated from Pavel's eyes. "Huh?"

"I'm not a *species*. I'm just a boy who knows nothing about himself and his abilities."

"I know, but—"

"Wait. My turn to speak." Theo remained silent until Pavel nodded his agreement. "If I knew how to use my abilities, we'd be in Dragon Village now or at least on the way there by air. I'm not a full-blooded dragon. Maybe someday I'll become one if I ever see my father again."

"Okay, sorry. I got carried away." Pavel got another faraway look. "If you don't want to try my invention, maybe we can try Plan B."

"What's that?"

"We could ask the wit— Vela's mother if she can open a portal with a spell."

"She's—"

"I know. I know. Not a witch spell. You said she's an honorary Samodiva …"

Theo thought about it. Vela's mom had told him the Samodivi made her like a blood-sister to them and taught her their secret arts. "She knows their healing power, not how to open portals. If she knew how to do that, she wouldn't have needed my help to get Vela back from Dragon Village. She would have gone herself."

Pavel sighed. "You're right."

"How about Plan C? We try my medallion instead," Theo said. "We know *that* opened a door to Dragon Village. It's still a week until my birthday on Eniovden, but maybe it'll work like the last time."

"It can't hurt. It's good to have another option." Pavel took his phone out of his backpack, swiped it, and looked at the time. "It's close to midnight. I guess we could try that first."

Theo removed a chain holding a seven-pointed silver star from around his neck. He always wore it now, a gift from his Samodiva mother, meant to protect him. His fingers tingled with a burning sensation when he touched it.

*Yes, it still has power. It might work.*

He paused. Something felt different on the back. He turned it around. A tiny bump protruded from the center. How had he damaged the medallion?

"Ready to try, Theo?" Pavel asked.

"Yes, sorry." He'd worry about the bump later. He couldn't do anything about it now.

He walked into the center of the megaliths and kicked away moss that had once again overgrown an engraving that matched his medallion. Each point of the star on the ground aligned with a megalith. This time, he didn't uncover the mosaic of colorful stones that spiraled like sun rays around the engraving. All he needed was a place to set his medallion.

He laid it against his cheek, cherishing the memories of his Samodiva mother, then pressed the medallion into its mate on the ground. It snapped into the hollowed star.

He walked a little distance away and sat with Pavel. "Do you think it'll work?"

"We'll see in a few minutes."

Theo sat with eyes glued to the spot, counting off the seconds to himself. Each one felt like a minute, each minute like an hour.

The absent wind made an appearance and chilled him, but still no portal opened. A moment later, the forest stilled, and Theo tensed, waiting for a flash of white from his medallion. That had been the first sign when they'd opened the portal before. As he stared at the medallion, a bright light flooded the sky, and a distant rumbling broke the silence.

Theo jumped and bumped into Pavel. His friend stared back with his mouth wide open.

*I must look the same to him.* He snapped his mouth shut.

They waited. No more lights flashed. No whirlwinds blew. No portal opened.

"It was only thunder and lightning," Pavel said.

"It didn't work." Theo retrieved his treasure and placed the chain around his neck. "We can't wait a week to try again. I'm worried about our friends. The voice from the conch was clearly distressed."

"Well," Pavel said, "do you have any other suggestions?"

Theo shook his head. "No, I guess we're back to Plan A. We'll have to rely on your genius idea to open the portal."

"Great. Let's get started."

"Do you need help?"

"Yes. Take this crystal." Pavel handed him a large, pyramid-shaped crystal wrapped in copper wire, resembling a spring.

"Where'd you get this? From the school lab?"

"Don't ask," Pavel said. "When I say so, put it in the middle of the spiral, at the same spot where you placed the medallion."

Pavel retrieved the other device he'd placed near their backpacks. It was made from a cut PVC pipe and shaped like a sun, with seven arched rays attached to a center circle. A magnet was glued to the end of each half-arc beam. Each piece was about two inches high. A metal bearing in the middle allowed the sun to rotate.

"Are you planning to blow us to Dragon Village with your new fan?" Theo couldn't imagine how such a simple-looking device could work.

"No, this is my Heliomagnet. The magnets will attract the energy of the megaliths and create our portal. I set it to stay open for only a short time, so we don't let beings from the other realm into our world."

"What?" Theo froze, with the crystal in his hand. "It'll do *that*?"

Pavel shrugged. "That's how doors work. It'll be fine. Get all your stuff together, so we're ready when it opens."

They both retrieved their gear, and Theo followed Pavel into the center of the megalith.

"It's time to put the crystal in place. Make sure the flat end is in contact with the stone," Pavel instructed.

Theo placed the crystal into the carved area so it pointed up like a pyramid. The blue light of the moon refracted through the crystal and illuminated the stone.

Pavel kneeled beside him. "Now hold the crystal steady while I slip the Heliomagnet on top."

Theo grasped it with both hands to keep them from shaking.

Pavel spun the sun-like spiral and stood beside his friend. "Now, we both have to touch the marker." He set his foot on the stone Theo had placed there earlier, and Theo followed suit.

"Why do we have to do that?" Theo asked.

"The energy from the entry point will travel around the megaliths like a spiral." Pavel demonstrated with his hands. "This is the final point. The force of the energy generated will suck in everything in its path when the portal opens."

A thunderous boom made them jump. Light spread out from the crystal, circling around until it reached the location outside the portal marked with a stone.

Theo gripped his bow and quiver, keeping an eye on Pavel's invention.

The solar spiral spun faster and faster. The outlines of individual rays were lost and merged into one, resembling the movement of a fan. Rays of light the color of the rainbow shot out from the crystal, forming an inverted small pyramid. The pyramid grew larger, and the rays touched the pillars, illuminating the horses' heads and making their eyes shine as if alive.

Theo took Pavel's hand and squeezed it tightly, the two boys looking at each other with wide eyes. Two fiery serpents appeared in the middle of the pyramid, their heads touching and forming an arch. With a great whoosh, the light outside the megaliths spiraled back.

The next moment, Theo was plunged into the pyramid's bottomless arch. Pavel's cry was the last thing he heard before complete darkness descended.

# Chapter 4
# Return to Dragon Village

A BRIGHT LIGHT replaced the darkness, momentarily blinding Theo. Spots flashed before his eyes, and he blinked, trying to regain his sight. He felt light as he drifted through a tunnel like a water slide but one filled with fluffy, warm air. He breathed in a strange odor. *Hot metal and charred meat?* He sniffed again. *No, more like sulfur or gunpowder.* Pavel would know.

He turned to ask his friend, but Theo's hand grasped empty space. He'd gotten separated from Pavel again when traveling through a portal. *Please, let him be okay.*

Theo gripped his backpack and bow tightly to his body. As the spots diminished, a sea of colors emerged: stars mixed with stardust. He was swimming in the universe; he was swimming in time.

He had no idea *where* in the universe he was or where he was headed. Or *what* universe it was. It couldn't be the one he knew. With no protective equipment, he wouldn't be able to breathe, and he'd freeze to death.

Pavel's earlier words returned to him: "You could likely just *think* about Dragon Village, and we'd be guided there."

*Will that work?*

He closed his eyes and imagined Zmey, the regal white dragon, standing in front of the castle waiting for Theo. Next to him was Theo's Samodiva friend, Diva, dressed in her white tunic. She held a bow in her hand, and her curly hair the color of moonlight swayed in the breeze. At her side was Sur, her six-winged deer companion, his magnificent antlers bathed in a pink-violet glow coming from a fireball that floated between his antlers—the color a sign of friendship, welcome, and good feelings.

Everything in Dragon Village was blooming: the rivers were filled with golden water, and the grain crops were full of ears. Fertility, light, peace, love—

*Slam.* He stifled a cry as severe pain rifled through his back and shoulder. His floating had come to an abrupt stop. Seconds later, another body pounded the ground next to him.

Moaning, Theo opened his eyes and sat up. Pavel had made it, but where were they?

Silence. Darkness. And terrible cold. Had they arrived in Dragon Village or on Pluto? He patted the ground to locate his bow. It lay beside him. At least he had his weapon if any danger approached.

"Ouch." Theo rubbed his leg where something kept biting him. "Pavel, are you okay?"

In a weak voice, his friend responded, "Yes, I think so. I'm all ... Wiggle your leg."

Theo did.

"Try the other one."

Theo moved his other leg.

"Oh, good. That's yours. I didn't feel anything when I pinched it. I thought mine had gone numb." Pavel groaned as he moved to a sitting position. "Where are we? Did we make it out of the Stone Forest?"

"I don't know. I thought you'd be able to tell me."

"What happened to the golden chariot drawn by a snake? The one you rode in last time." Pavel dusted off debris from his jacket and pants. "You're the son of the ruler. I expected a better welcome ceremony, with fanfare and a red carpet."

As Theo's eyes adjusted to the darkness, metallic gray forms emerged. A circle of stones surrounded them. "Maybe we're still in Selo."

Something didn't feel right. The shapes cast two shadows.

"Look, the moon … two moons." Pavel pointed toward the sky. "Can you see what I see? Or am I hallucinating because I bumped my head?"

Theo peered upward. The sky indeed held two full moons: one blood red and the other metallic blue. They touched each other, forming a figure eight. "I don't think we're in Selo anymore."

"Not in Kansas, either," Pavel said. "Although I've never been there, so who knows."

"Do you know any planet that has two moons?"

Heavy footsteps and torch lights interrupted the conversation and blinded them. Two hands gripped Theo like a vise. Before he had a chance to scream or pick up his bow, the creature slung him over its shoulder, knocking his breath away, and carried him like a sack of potatoes. The wet-dog odor of its pelt gagged him. He reached for an arrow from his quiver but lacked the strength to pull one out. He ached too much to resist being carted away. The light from the moons disappeared as the creature entered a cave.

"Pavel? Pavel?" Theo finally managed to whisper. His voice echoed, but his friend didn't answer.

The creature's footsteps clomped as it walked down a musty passage. Torchlights along the wall sputtered and created strange shadows on the ground. Finally, a heavy door clanged shut. Warmth. A crackling fire. Theo dared to twist his head to the side to see where he was. In the room's dim light, he saw meat cooking over an open fire, the fat sizzling as it dripped onto the flames. His stomach growled.

A rumble sounded in his captor's body.

Theo struggled to get away. *Is he going to cook me next?*

The rumble turned to laughter as the creature laid Theo onto a wooden platform facing the stone wall.

*Maybe he's going to eat me raw?*

Even though his back ached from the fall, Theo wasn't going to give up without a fight. He didn't have his bow, but he could still defend himself. He inched his body around to face into the room, hoping his captor busied itself with other matters. *Like how to slice me up.* He sprang to his feet and made fists, ready to go on the offensive.

"Welcome back, Theo."

In front of him, covered in animal skins, stood a towering being, grinning instead of growling. Before Theo could say a word, he found himself in a suffocating embrace.

"Theo, my friend. We're glad you got the message."

"Jega, let me go." His words came out muffled.

The other boy released Theo. "I was wondering who had invaded our home. I wouldn't have been so rough if I'd known it was you. I didn't recognize your bow until I brought you inside." He handed Theo the weapon.

Theo breathed a sigh of relief. They'd made it to Dragon Village. He was happy to see Jega, the youngest of many brothers, who lived here with Zima and their oldest brother, Mraz. They were Kukeri, an ancient race of magical men who protected not only Dragon Village, but also the human world. They normally wore a belt of large bells, which created discord as the men danced to chase away evil spirits.

A moment later, a terrifying-looking being entered, clothed in animal skins and wearing a mask with blood-red eyes, long fangs, and curved horns. The creature carried Pavel over his shoulder.

*That must be Zima.*

The being tossed Pavel onto the bench Theo had vacated. His friend landed with a *thunk*.

*Yes, definitely Zima.* Jega's brother wasn't known for his compassion. He was cold like the magical power he possessed, manipulating ice. This ability had earned him the nickname "Ice" when Theo had first met him. But Zima was also rational and practical, a person who wanted to get straight to the point. Theo had dubbed Jega, however, with the nickname "Fire," not only because he could control its heat and flames, but also because he was warm, caring, and a romantic, often overly poetic.

Theo waited, but Pavel didn't sit up on the bench. "What's the matter with him?" He rushed over. "Did you knock him out, Zima?"

"Not intentionally. I likely tossed him over my shoulder harder than I thought."

Jega lifted Pavel's limp hand and pressed a finger to his wrist. "His pulse is fine. He'll be up in a little while, I'm sure." He turned back to Theo. "Everyone's been anxious, wondering if you'd make it. Let me go get them."

Jega dashed out of the room. Moments later, hasty footsteps echoed in the corridor, and the shadow of a broad, powerful man filled the doorway. Dim light heightened the creases in his careworn face and danced through his white hair, making it look as if it was on fire. He stepped inside the room, and a huge grin brightened his somber look.

"Theo, we're happy you're here."

Theo fell into the man's embrace. "Mraz, glad to see you again."

Two beautiful women, Samodivi, filed into the room after Mraz: Diva's sisters, Sava and Ula. The eldest, blond-haired Sava was serious like Zima, but gentle and kind. Brunette Ula had a playful air, always ready to bubble over with gaiety.

Everyone laughed, talked loudly, and hugged Theo. Greetings merged with each other, until Theo wasn't sure who was saying what.

"Zunitza's son has returned."

"Theo, welcome back."

"How have you been?"

"We didn't know if you'd get our message."

Theo, his cheeks feeling flushed, finally freed himself from the last embrace. When the chaos settled down, everyone sat around a wooden table, with Mraz at the head.

Theo asked a barrage of questions. "Why did the Rusalki call me here? Where is everyone else? Diva? Zmey? Why is it so cold? Why are there two moons?"

"Whoa. Slow down." Mraz chuckled. "You'll get answers. First of all, we asked the Rusalki if they could get a message to you. The sea creatures in Rusalki Bay aren't restricted to when they can travel between our worlds. They can easily get to yours any time of the year. It was our only hope of reaching you."

"Why did they deliver the shell so far away?" Theo asked. "I've never been to the cave where the … messenger dropped it off."

"I can answer that." Sava, sitting across the table from Theo, leaned closer. "A new threat, red monsters with poisonous tentacles—we don't know exactly what they are—chased their carp messenger."

"Those things came from here?" Theo's stomach clenched. The situation was getting worse. "They're in Selo, too. Killing our fish. They've turned beaches into tombs."

"Yes, they're designed to kill," Zima noted.

"Was that why you called me here? I-I don't know how I can help."

"No," Mraz said. "After you left, someone kidnapped the Firebird and Kosara."

Theo gasped. Kosara, the guardian of the Znahar Tree was gone? And the Firebird, the messenger to their deity, too? The holy tree contained the essence of all life in Dragon Village. Without Kosara's protection, darkness, sickness, and famine would occur as the tree slowly died, and life in Dragon Village would cease to exist along with it.

"We have to get him back." Jega got up and paced the room. "The Firebird was the sun and soul of the tree. When he flew around, his eyes sparkled, bringing happiness, prosperity, and positive energy to our land."

"Why—?" Theo began.

"There's more bad news," Mraz continued, grasping Theo's hand. "They're not the only ones who have disappeared."

Theo looked around the room. Grim faces met his glance. He again noted who was missing. "Diva? And my father?"

Each person nodded once.

"What happened? What's the connection? Who took them?"

Mraz responded, "Zlo's army returned. It was so sudden we didn't have time to prepare for battle. They stormed the castle and abducted Zmey."

"We've heard rumors that Zmey's alive, but chained in some prison," Sava added.

"Who's Zlo?" Theo asked.

Everyone started talking at once.

"He's Lamia's lord and mentor," Sava said.

Ula added, "He's avenging Lamia's death."

"She was his spiritual slave," Jega said, "following his orders and drawing her power from him. Every evil thing she knows, she learned from him."

"Not only that. Zlo's guards are everywhere," Zima concluded.

Theo's head spun, with all the words, with all the terrible implications. He paced the room. "Why didn't you let me know earlier? I've been gone almost an entire year."

"We tried," Sava said. "Zlo's army barricaded Rusalki Bay, and we had no way to contact the Rusalki until recently. We sent word as soon as we broke through."

Mraz raised his wrinkled hand to quiet the room. "Although the others have been taken a while ago, Diva's only been missing for a few days."

The pain in Theo's chest returned, making its way up his throat, choking him. He coughed, and a bile taste coated his tongue. "Water," he croaked. Someone handed him a jug, and he drank deeply. Still, the pain didn't lessen.

"You okay, Theo?" Sava's gentle voice soothed him, and she made circles on his back, murmuring words he didn't understand.

Soon the pain eased. "Better, thanks." Theo inhaled deeply, then slowly released his breath. "Does Zlo have Diva? And Kosara and the Firebird, too?"

Sava shook her head. "We're not certain who has Kosara and the Firebird, but Boo told us the Youdi took Diva."

"The magpie's been her constant companion since you left," Ula added.

"Boo." Theo scanned the niches in the stone walls, hoping to see the magpie take flight and surprise him. He carried a packet of the bird's favorite seeds in his backpack. "Where is he now?" He missed his little friend, even the raucous *waak* noise he made.

"No one's seen him since he told us," Sava said. "We think he's gone to keep watch over her."

"Do you know where the Youdi took Diva?" Theo dreaded having to face them and their wolves. Unlike the Samodivi, the Youdi were wicked nymphs, witches, who had worked for Lamia.

"Yes." Zima stepped forward. "They have her in their fortress in the village of Vida. All my brothers and I and many Samodivi tried to storm the tower where they're keeping her. We thought it would be easy, since the walls are crumbling, but the Youdi have powerful magic fortifying the place; it's too strong, too secure. Not only that, but numerous monsters guard the interior of the fort—bats, Harpies, wolves—and those red monsters overflow the moat. We almost died from their sting."

"This task requires cunning, not force," Jega added. "Something my brother's not good at. But, I, on the other hand—"

Zima slapped Jega on the side of his head. "Knock it off. We don't need you serenading those witches. That's not the way to rescue Diva."

"Ohhh, my head." Pavel sat up. His body swayed as he tried to stand. "What happened? Where am I? Theo?"

"I'm here." Theo walked over and helped Pavel up. "We made it. You got us to Dragon Village."

"I did? Wow! I knew my invention would work." Pavel looked around the room. "Hey, Mraz. Jega. Zima. Sava. Ula."

Another round of hugs ensued. Pavel approached Zima, but the Kuker stepped back. "Aw, c'mon, Zima."

Zima rolled his eyes and crushed Pavel in a tight embrace.

Pavel wheezed. "Let me go. Can't breathe."

When Zima released Pavel, he pulled away. "Okay, okay. I won't ask you that again."

Sava asked, "Pavel, what kind of invention brought you here? We were worried you wouldn't find a way to open a portal."

Pavel explained in detail how he used the power of the megaliths, and how he had come up with the idea when he and Theo had visited the Kukeri before. "I thought—hoped—I could map a connection between our megaliths and yours," he said in conclusion.

"What a relief it worked better than your last invention," Zima remarked. "That one almost got us killed."

"All quite ingenious." Mraz tapped his hand against the table. "But now can we get back to planning how to save everyone?"

"What's going on?" Pavel asked. "Did someone mention Diva?"

"Yes," Mraz said. "The Youdi have her." He filled Pavel in on the details.

Pavel's eyes went wide. "We have to save her!"

"We will," Mraz said. "We need to make a plan."

"Diva first," Pavel shouted. "No matter what else is going on here, we need her with us."

"I agree," Zima said. "She's proven to be a mighty warrior. We can use her abilities."

Jega winked at Pavel. "Don't worry, we'll save your lady love."

Pavel's face turned red. "I told you before, she's not. What's going on with those two moons? There was only one when we were here last year."

"Ah, yes, the moons. That's a bit more complex." Mraz closed his eyes for a moment, then began to speak as if telling a tale. "When I was a child, I often used to play in the room where my father, Pazach, worked. You remember, he's the one now called 'Jabalaka'?"

Theo and Pavel both nodded. Theo's heart ached. The last story Mraz had told them was about Theo's parents, a story that didn't end well.

"Well, this time, Pazach went suddenly quiet. His body stiffened, and his eyes glazed over. He was having one of his many visions of the future." Mraz paused and cleared his throat. "I was young, but I clearly remember him saying 'two moons,' 'destruction,' and 'unborn hero.'"

"That's why I'm here?" Theo asked. "Because I'm the unborn hero?"

Mraz nodded. "We don't know exactly what your role is, but it seems you have to be here if we have a chance of stopping this disaster."

"Can't you ask Jabalaka? Wouldn't *Lamia's Bible* have the answer?" How could he help? He was the son of a powerful dragon and fearless Samodiva, but beyond that, he didn't have a clue about himself. So many people kept telling him he was special and had a gift, but he had no idea how to tap into his own powers. Without his father's coaching, Theo was helpless.

"I'm sure the book would have answers, but it's so cryptic sometimes, it's likely to make us ask more questions," Mraz said. "Anyway, Pazach is terrified and has gone into hiding. I don't blame him, after everything else he's had to go through."

"Everything else we know about the moons comes from an ancient poem." Jega stood, bowed, and recited:

" 'Two moons in the sky,
Portend all will die.
One blood-red, the other icy-blue
Release evils you never knew.
When they meet, the end is near,
And a time for all to fear.'
But if—' "

Zima covered Jega's mouth. "I think that's enough, brother. They get the point that the moons are a bad omen predicting the end of Zmeykovo. No need to recite all sixty lines of the poem. We have better things to do with our time."

"How long do we have until it's too late?" Theo asked.

"The moons appeared on June 1, and have been slowly moving toward each other," Mraz said. "These last few days, their rate has been increasing. From my calculations, the moons will merge in four days, on the twenty-first."

"How're we going to possibly solve all these problems by then?" Theo raked his hands through his hair.

"I propose we form teams," Mraz said. "You and Pavel will join Zima and Sava to rescue Diva. I'll take Jega and Ula with me, and we'll join forces with my other brothers and the rest of the Samodivi. We'll see if we can help them discover where Zlo is hiding, and where everyone else has been taken—and why."

Mraz and his team went to the other side of the room. Theo reached into his backpack and pulled out his map of Dragon Village. "Zima, can you show me where the Youdi fortress is? I can't read the map."

"It's named after the Vida River." Zima moved his finger over the parchment. "It's here, by the curve of the river. What we really need to know is the layout of their fortress. Let me ask Mraz if he has a map."

He went to speak to his eldest brother. Mraz left his group huddle and retrieved a rolled-up piece of leather from an alcove in the room and gave it to Zima.

Zima returned and stretched out an old, faded map onto the table. "This is Vida Fortress. The layout should still be accurate. I don't think they've ever renovated the place. The inside is falling into ruin just like the walls."

"We'll need a miracle to get into that place," Pavel said.

"Or a trick." Sava grinned. "And I know just the person to help."

"Let's get those nasty witches." Pavel pounded his fists together. "They can't kidnap Diva and get away with it."

"Do we have time to get there?" Theo asked, still looking at his map. "It'll be a long walk, and probably dangerous."

"Don't worry." Sava put her hand onto his shoulder. "We have a better way of traveling."

# Chapter 5
# Flying High

**JUNE 18**

THE NEXT MORNING, after Theo had eaten food that Mraz must have set on the table, he went outside. Darkness still overcast Dragon Village, despite the late hour. The two moons had begun to cross paths, now looking like googly eyes. The sun tried to burst through the dense clouds, but it was as if the moons had erected a defensive shield to keep the light at bay. At least the extreme chill from the previous night had abated. The air remained cool, not frigid, but it felt heavy, suffocating. Theo listened for birdsong, but only a few brave souls heralded sad greetings, as if the joy of a new morn had been torn from them.

Theo understood their pain as he stood at the cliff edge, staring out toward the land's destruction. When he'd left Dragon Village, it had begun to flourish, to heal itself from the damage Lamia had inflicted. Now, once again, burned trees and landscapes filled the scenery before him as far as the muted light allowed him to see.

The ruined scene made him long for home and family. Mom was probably angry and worried. Nia, too. Even so, he was glad he and Pavel had returned. He had a mission; his friends needed help, and he'd do whatever he could to restore the land to its former beauty. He'd deal with the problems at home when he returned.

He wondered where Pavel had disappeared. His friend wasn't sleeping in the room when Theo awoke, and Pavel's backpack was missing. In fact, no one had been around. Where had everyone gone?

The ground shook, and Theo turned to see what was happening. Zima led two black buffaloes up the steep hill path to the Kukeri sanctuary.

*One down, five to go.*

Next, Jega stepped out of the cave, pulling a rumbling cart. It was full of woolen blankets, bags, wooden sticks, shovels, ropes, metal brackets, and wedges. Mraz, Sava, and Ula followed, their hands filled with weapons, shields, and supplies that they placed inside the cart.

*Almost everyone accounted for.*

"Has anyone seen Pavel?" Theo asked.

"No, but he better return soon. We're almost ready to leave." Jega patted the pile of woolen blankets.

The blankets moved, and Pavel, yawning, poked out his head.

Theo laughed. "What are you doing in there?"

Pavel crawled out of the cart. "It was so cold on the bench last night, and all these warm blankets were piled up here. I think I found my new room."

"Of course." Zima sneered. "Puny human that you are. It doesn't surprise me."

"Zima …" Mraz gave his brother a scorching look, before he turned back to Pavel. "I'm afraid you're going to lose your comfy room. It's going with Jega, Ula, and me. We're ready to meet up with my other brothers and the Samodivi to see what they've discovered."

"That's fine." Pavel stretched, then turned toward Zima. "This *human* doesn't need to sleep now."

"Enough, you two." Mraz crossed his arms and spoke with a sharp tone. "We need to work together." With a slight shake of his head, he added, "Jega, will you hitch the buffaloes to the cart?"

As Jega did this, Sava said, "We're ready, too. Theo and Pavel, do you have everything you need?"

"Yes." Theo picked up his bow and slung his backpack and quiver over his shoulder.

Pavel nodded and removed his backpack from the cart. "We don't get a cart? You said we didn't have to walk."

"You don't. We have a better plan. Just wait and see." Ula covered her mouth, but barely stifled her laughter. "Shall we, Sava?"

"Yes, it's time."

The two Samodivi pulled long, curved, pins from their belts. The silver tip was hollow.

"Are those hat pins?" Pavel asked.

"No, silly," Ula said. "They're whistles."

"You gonna call us a taxi?"

"Something better."

Sava and Ula walked toward a meadow. They put the larger end of the pin to their mouths and blew. The whistles emitted no noise, but soon the birds appeared to wake up, and they sang melodic tunes. A few darted from hiding places in the depths of the forest to fly around the women.

"It won't be long now." Ula looked toward the sky.

A thunderous noise filled the air, followed by high-pitched whistling.

Pavel crept closer to Theo and whispered, "I hope that's not Zlo, or we're doomed." He took out his Pavel-o-paralyzer and pointed it toward the sky.

Theo nocked an arrow in his bow, preparing to attack.

A herd of six-winged flying deer blotted out the dark clouds as they approached the meadow. Diva's deer, Sur, led the pack. The amber fireball between each animal's antlers glowed bright, creating an illusion of dozens of small suns. The deer's hooves sparkled from the light. When the animals landed, the ground shook like an earthquake.

Sur, a large, muscular gray deer with a white star on his forehead, bowed his head before Sava and snorted his greeting.

"Welcome, my dear brave friend." She stroked his neck. "We need your help and that of your herd to try again to release your mistress from the Youdi."

Sur's hair bristled, and sparks shot from the fireball, now swirling with purple and green flashes. He snorted while he dug deep grooves in the ground, tossing dirt far behind him.

"Yes, I know you want to tear them and their wolves apart. We'll let these others," Sava said as she gestured toward the Kukeri and boys, "do that, but they need to get to Vida Fortress quickly. Will you convince the herd to accept strangers?"

Sur tossed his head, crowned with magnificent fifteen points that spanned well past his ears, and stomped toward the herd like a king.

Pavel's eyes bugged out and his mouth hung open. "Where's Rudolph?"

"None bear that name," Sava said.

Grinning, Ula turned toward Theo and Pavel. "Anyone know how to ride a deer?"

Pavel cast a quick glance at Theo before answering, "I tried a horse once, never a deer, but I'd love to learn. Do I get to pick mine?"

"No, the deer will choose you," Sava said. "They might challenge you first to test your worth. If they respect you, they'll accept you."

"How will we know we've been accepted? Do they speak?" Theo asked.

"Their fireball will glow amber, and you'll connect with the animal. You'll be able to hear his thoughts," Sava said. She looked toward the herd. "Sur's indicated they're willing."

Jega heaved a heavy sigh. "Mraz, maybe you could take Zima instead, and let me—"

"No way, brother." Zima strode toward a massive white deer that had shot him a glance.

He grabbed the animal by the antlers and leapt onto his back. The stag bucked, but the Kuker held on. Lying low, Zima appeared to be speaking into the deer's ear. The animal relaxed, his fireball turned amber, and the deer sprinted across the meadow toward the cliff edge. Zima lifted his arms in victory and let out what sounded like a war cry as the deer flew into the murky sky.

Pavel shoved Theo toward the herd. "You try next."

"How do I know which one?" he asked.

"Find one that makes eye contact," Sava told him.

He gulped and approached a motley deer, his back freckled with white spots like stars.

The animal stared at him.

"Easy, I'm not going to hurt you."

The deer stepped back, and the fireball sparked purple. Snorting, the animal lowered his antlers toward Theo. "*My mistress is gone. I'll never choose another.*"

"What?" Theo rubbed his temple. "Are we connected already? The fireball's not amber … and that didn't sound promising." He turned to look for another deer.

Pavel yelled to him, "Hurry up. I want to try."

Grumbling under his breath, "You don't have to wait for me," Theo held his hands out and took small steps toward the deer. His gaze never leaving the antsy animal, Theo stroked the creature along his shoulder and flank.

The creature drew back, pawing at the ground. The sparks died down, but the fireball remained purple.

"Let's be friends," Theo said. "I've lost people, too. I never even knew my birth mother. Lamia killed her. Now I need someone to help me save my friend Diva."

The purple streaks turned pale, and the animal lowered his head.

Theo slid his hands toward the antlers and clung tight.

The deer snorted and shook his head, tossing Theo from side to side.

"Please, stop," Theo screamed. "I need you. I'm scared of what's going to happen to Diva. Sur would want you to help us."

The deer stood still as Theo pulled himself onto the creature's back. In a flash, the deer sped across the meadow, then gave a push and was in the air as swift as an arrow.

Theo lay flat on his stomach against the deer's warm body. He caressed the animal's tight neck muscles and ran his fingertips along the feathered wings. Remembering how Zima appeared to relax his deer by speaking to it, Theo said, "You're so noble and brave. I wish I could be like you."

The deer thought nothing back, but the movement of the animal's muscles and the beating of his powerful wings invigorated Theo. The feeling was different from when he'd flown on Zmey's back on his return to Selo. This was like being on a giant roller-coaster.

The deer increased his speed, and Theo's ears rang with the whistling wind. The air split against his face, rolling down his cheeks like a cold blade. Far below, his friends looked like chess pieces, and the castle on the distant Cherna Mountain like a doll house.

The fireball swirled between the deer's antlers like a hurricane, scattering purple, then emerald sparks into the gray sky. The pulse in Theo's throat beat wildly, and pain tightened his chest. As the deer climbed higher, Theo shivered. He grasped the animal tighter, fearing he'd fall. His warm breaths panted against the deer's neck.

"You're so amazing." Too afraid to release his grip, Theo rubbed his cheeks against the deer's neck, hoping the contact calmed the animal.

The deer slowed its frenzied climb. It glided downward into the clouds, then lower. The whistling in Theo's ears faded. Green and brown spots below turned into forests, bushes, boulders. Soft amber light replaced the emerald sparks in the deer's fireball.

Theo loosened his grip on the antlers and hugged the deer's neck. "You've accepted me."

They soared through the air a while longer. Slowly, gently the deer veered toward the ground. When they landed by Sava and the others, Theo grinned as he slid from the deer. His legs wobbly, Theo leaned against the creature, stroking the deer's side.

"Your turn, Pavel, and hurry," he said out of breath. "It's great to fly like a bird."

Pavel took a few steps forward toward a chocolate-brown deer munching what little grass he could find. The stag lifted his head and came closer, sticking his pinkish nose into Pavel's face. The fireball glowed amber.

Theo laughed. "Looks like you have a fan."

"Will he bite?" Pavel asked, leaning backward.

"He's not a dog," Sava said. "The deer don't bite, but they do kick. But that one's passive. Go ahead. He's accepted you."

With trembling hands, Pavel grabbed the deer's antlers and grunted as he tried to pull himself up several times. He turned back toward Theo. "Will you help me up? This one's taller than yours."

Theo gave Pavel a boost, then backed away.

"Come on, deer. I'll call you 'Whirl.' " Pavel patted the animal on the side. "Giddyup. Let's fly."

Instead, the deer bent to eat more grass.

Pavel slid up the deer, lying on the back of the animal's neck. "Help! Make him go."

Ula covered her mouth, giggling, while Sava smacked the deer on the rump.

The creature flinched, tossed his head, then dashed across the meadow.

Pavel screamed, his face as white as snow, then he shouted, "Yippee!" as they took to the sky.

Sava caressed Theo's deer while Pavel flew. "This is Shar. He was your mother's companion."

Theo's heart raced. "He said he wouldn't choose anyone again."

"Oftentimes, they won't."

"I thought he was helping only to save Diva."

"Possibly," Sava said, "but perhaps Shar sensed your connection to your mother."

"Why wouldn't he tell me that?"

"Ask him now." Sava drew Theo closer to the deer. "Speak to him with your mind."

*"Did you accept me only because of my mother?"* Theo asked.

*"No,"* Shar replied. *"I recognized her gentle nature in you. I wish for us to remain connected. I have a feeling you'll come back to Zmeykovo often."*

"Will you tell me—"

The ground shook when Whirl landed among the group.

"What a blast. That was so much fun," Pavel said.

"Now that that's all settled, let's get going." Mraz nodded toward his group, and he, Jega, and Ula set off on their mission.

"Follow me," Sava said. "We have one stop to make before we rescue my sister." She called her deer, mounted, and flew into the sky to join Zima.

Theo stroked Shar as he got back on. "Ready, Pavel?"

"Yes, sir. Ready to get this show on the road. Diva needs us."

With that said, Theo and Pavel took to the sky.


AFTER A SHORT FLIGHT, the deer landed with a *thud* in a grove, surrounded by a forest. A fenced-in area sat a bit farther back. All around them, a myriad of different-sized copper bells on the trees rang out chimes. Some of the deer nibbled leafy delicacies shooting up from a garden. Others ambled toward a small pool to drink.

Theo ran to push them away. "Stop! The water might be poisoned." That had been one of Lamia's undertakings when she had set about destroying Dragon Village. Perhaps Zlo had done the same.

Sava followed and pulled Theo away. "Don't worry. The water's as clean as a tear. The fish wouldn't be darting around if it was poisonous. The Znahar Tree is weakening, but parts of our land protected by magic are still strong. Let's hope we have time to stop this madness before Zlo destroys everything."

Theo investigated the depths. Dozens of multicolored fish played hide-and-seek among the reeds. The darting fish resembled an ever-changing picture on a kaleidoscope. As he leaned over, his head spun, and a coughing fit overtook him. He dropped to his knees and laid his forehead on the ground.

"Theo, are you okay?" Sava kneeled beside him and hummed while drawing circles on his back.

The pain receded. "I-I think so."

"Was the deer ride too much for you?" Pavel stepped closer.

Theo stood. "Maybe that's it."

"Why'd we stop here? Did the deer need a break? We weren't flying that long." Pavel paced and waved his arms. "We need to get going. We have to save Diva."

"We will. I'm as anxious as you are," Sava said. "Our best shot at defeating the Youdi lies with the person who lives here."

As the bells continued to chime, Pavel said, "I don't see anyone."

"You will in a moment," Sava told him.

"I'll wait over there." Pavel huffed and walked toward the fence. "Triple cat hairballs! What is that?" He ran back to be with the group. "That fence … is … is made of human skulls and bones. And … and … the skulls have glowing eyes."

"That's—" Theo started, but a terrible noise drowned out the rest.

Over the fence and into the grove hopped a cabin on chicken feet. It raced around until coming to a screeching halt. The house door slammed open and an ugly woman with scraggly gray hair stomped down the steps. A winged purple cat flew around the woman as she shook her broom at the intruders.

"What do you think you're doing?" she screeched. "Look at my herb garden. It ain't in need of fertilizing yet, so get those deer out of it."

"Your herb garden?" Sava stepped forward. "It's filled with poison and dark magic, so don't worry. There's nothing deer fertilizer will harm."

"Oh, it's you." The woman scowled, displaying sharp, iron teeth embedded in green gums. " 'Suppose you're here to collect on a debt."

"Who is that?" Pavel whispered to Theo in a shaky voice.

"Baba Yaga." He'd managed to survive his last encounter with the witch, and even played a trick on her, but she still sent quivers through his body. Those skulls belonged to her victims.

"Oh, right. I remember her now. She looks scarier than she did when we left her," Pavel squeaked.

"What have we got here?" The witch drew closer and sniffed Theo with her crooked nose.

The cat flew around Theo, yowled, and zipped back inside.

"Human boy, I see you've returned. You've put some meat on you." She licked her lips and pulled him in for a hug, pawing at his arms. "You looking for more favors, too, from your dear ole friend?"

"Get away." Theo pushed her aside, gagging from her foul breath. "No, I—"

"Something's strange about you." She poked her nose closer and sniffed all around. "You smell … different."

Pavel, his face white, said with a squeaking voice, "That's because he's not human. He's part dragon, part Samodiva."

"Pfftt. I know all that." The witch sniffed again. "My cat's afraid of you. I wonder why? Demons terrify her." She cackled. "Well, not me, but all the rest."

"Theo's not a demon." Pavel regained his voice. "He's a hero."

Baba Yaga hobbled over to Pavel. "What a nice *hero* he is. He brought me a present. How yummy."

"What? No way." Pavel backed away before she could grope him—or worse.

Even so, she sniffed the air where he had stood. "You smell familiar, too. And you're definitely all human. Much more to my taste than a strange-smelling dragon child."

Sava pulled Baba Yaga away. "Stop tormenting the boys, witch. You're right. We've come to redeem a favor from you."

"Well, get on with it. I ain't got all day. What'd'ya want?"

Theo stepped closer. "My father's gone. Kosara and the Firebird have disappeared. And the Youdi have Diva in their fortress."

"Yah, yah, I know all that." She ignored Theo and turned back to Sava. "So, what'd'ya want from me?"

"We want you to help us free my sister, devise some clever scheme to break into the fortress."

" 'Suppose I could do that." The witch scratched her chin. "Paying a debt or not, I'll still need something in return, a small token of our friendship."

Sava rolled her eyes. "And what would that be?"

"I could use a new vehicle." The witch pointed to her peeling, weather-beaten mortar, which stood by the bone fence. "My old Chutura has lost its springiness."

"Done," Sava said.

"Wait, wait. That's not all. Lemme think. Lemme think." She paced the yard, casting a glance or two at Pavel, then muttering, "No, not what I need quite yet."

Pavel scooted closer to Sava. "Stop looking at me, ugly hag."

"Ugly?" Her eyes brightened. "That's it. I need something that'll bring me true rebirth. The living water that one," she said as she pointed at Theo, "gave me last time didn't do what I expected. It only made my body younger. I'm still ugly."

Sava sighed. "So, what is it you think will make you beautiful?"

"A feather from the Firebird. It'll transform me into a young, wise maiden and make my hair shine like the sun again. I'll turn into a goddess." Baba Yaga entwined her hands in her tangled gray hair and hopped around like a chicken with her skinny legs covered in dirt.

"I don't think we can do that," Sava said, but Baba Yaga continued to dance and giggle.

Zima strode over. "Witch," he yelled.

Baba Yaga stopped mid-hop. She stared at Zima with an open mouth.

Zima gave a brief nod to Sava. "You may continue now." He stepped away to return to the deer.

Baba Yaga glared in his direction but directed her words to Sava. "Well?"

"If we can," Sava said, "we'll get you a feather, but no promises."

"My father has lots of gold and treasures," Theo said. "I'm sure he'd be willing to give you what you want if you help."

"Guess I'll have to settle for that," Baba Yaga grumbled.

"And the Youdi's fortress must be full of treasures, too," Sava said. "I'm sure you could … *convince* them to give you some."

"Gold … treasures. As much as I want." Baba Yaga's eyes sparkled with greed. "That'll do, but if you can get me a feather …"

"If the Firebird allows it, we'll get you one."

"Good, that's settled." Baba Yaga plucked a hair growing from her chin. "Yah, I'll help you get the feisty Samodiva back. I'm rather fond of her, and I'm getting tired of those spiteful witches. Always on a rampage. It's time someone punished them and locked them away."

Pavel crept closer. "How do we get Diva back?"

Baba Yaga poked his chest with her bony finger. "You still look tasty. I might want to add one more condition to find your friend."

Sava slapped the witch's hand. "Don't touch the boy. We'll never assist you again with your herbs. Help us find Diva, or you're likely to feel Zmey's wrath when he returns."

"And mine." Zima had crept back unaware.

Baba Yaga shuffled away. "Fine. Let me get my things for the trip. If I'm going to help you, you better make sure I get gold in my hand and some to adorn my hair."

Theo laughed, thinking about gold in that tangled mess. His laughter turned to coughing, and he doubled over again from a severe pain in his chest.

"Theo!" Pavel rushed over.

Baba Yaga pushed him aside. "Lemme have a look. I told you he smelled strange."

"No," Theo said between coughs. "I'm okay."

"Okay my crooked nose." The witch tugged at his sleeve. "Come inside, dragon boy."

Zima stood in her way. "No tricks."

She darted her eyes around. "No, no, of course not. No tricks."

"Theo, it's okay to go with her," Sava said. "She'll have something to help you."

Theo nodded and followed the witch. He didn't feel he had much choice. The pain was becoming more frequent, more unbearable.

Pavel started to follow, but Baba Yaga stopped him. "This one only."

She walked up the creaky steps of the chicken house and opened the door. Theo stumbled past her. Inside, Kotka emerged from the darkness like a bat and, hissing, flew over his head with her purple wings stretched out.

Theo wrapped his hands around his middle. He felt as if he was going to explode: his muscles ached, pain pierced his chest, and his head throbbed. "What's wrong with me? Help me, please."

"Sit here." The witch removed a ratty animal skin from a rotten wooden chair and motioned him over.

"I … can't … move." He choked out his words. His voice sounded foreign, as if someone was attempting to suffocate him.

Baba Yaga circled him and seemed to read his mind, or perhaps only his body's reactions to the pain. "Headache?"

He nodded.

"Anger? Chest pain? Body aches? Suffocating?"

"Yes, yes, yes, and yes," Theo shouted, but regretted it as the pain intensified. "Stop jabbering and help me, please."

"Don't snap at me, dragon boy. You'll make me angry. And when I get angry, I become hungry." She snarled at him, snapping her iron teeth.

Theo reined in his frustration and spoke softer, despite the pain gnawing at his insides. "Is my dragon nature starting to take over? Is there a way I can control this? You're a witch. Don't you have instructions on how to deal with body shifting?"

"Haven't you heard the stories that it isn't wise to ask me too many questions?" The witch crossed her eyes and sniffed.

"Yes, but—" Theo burst into another coughing fit. "Am I losing my human nature?"

"No, no, it's nothing like that. You've got a uroki, a bad spirit."

She hobbled to a wooden shelf filled with jars, the contents of which Theo didn't want to know. Tapping on the lids with her crooked sharp claws, Baba Yaga grabbed one, snatched a bug hidden underneath, and ate it with gusto. She burped and removed what looked like dried herbs from the jar and smooth, shiny seeds from another. Using a pestle, she ground them together in a clay cup, then mixed in a greenish liquid. She brought the concoction to Theo.

"Drink this. It contains anise, which drives away uroki. It's not permanent, but it'll help until we rescue the Samodiva girl."

Theo gulped it down. It had a bittersweet flavor. He shivered at the thought of having some evil spirit inside him. How had that happened? Could it have something to do with—

"Alrighty, let's get going." Baba Yaga collected items and added them to a satchel. At the door, she clutched her broom.

Theo hadn't moved. Too many questions battled in his mind.

"Come along, now, dragon boy."

"How do I get rid of this uroki permanently?"

"I know someone who can help. We'll visit her later."

Theo stood and held the door open. "Thank you. I feel better already. Why did you help me?"

"Well, I don't really like children, except the tasty ones." She licked her lips while Theo cringed. "But everyone seems to think you're special. Besides, Zunitza was always nice to me."

"And it doesn't hurt that I can ask my father to give you gold and jewels?"

"He he. That never crossed my mind." The witch did a little crooked dance before stepping outside.

"Yah, right." As Theo started to close the door, flapping wings and a muffled cry sounded in a darkened corner of the room. "Something's hurt back there."

"Come, come. It's just mice for Kotka." Baba Yaga scurried down the stairs.

*Mice indeed. Not unless they have wings like the cat.* Theo took a step toward the sound.

"Hurry." Baba Yaga grabbed his arm and pulled him out. "Let's go save your friend. I'm in the mood to outwit those Youdi."

The witch rode inside her wooden mortar, which chugged like a broken muffler, and the others followed. The witch's noisy transportation drowned out the tune of the bells. From time to time, a note escaped and sounded as if the forest was saying goodbye. Theo hoped it meant only for now and not forever.

# Chapter 6
# Friends to the Rescue

THE AIR WHIPPED at Theo's face as he flew on Shar. Pavel and Zima rode on either side of him, with Baba Yaga in the lead, and Sava taking up the rear. In a short time, they reached a meadow filled with blood-red poppies. Beyond that lay a village, with a gray, stone-walled fortress towering above everything else. A river flowed on the other side of the fortress.

Baba Yaga twisted her scrawny turkey-like neck to look back and hollered, "We'll stop in the meadow near the village and walk in."

Like airplanes waiting for the signal to land, the deer reduced their speed, circling the meadow. One by one, they gathered. Theo landed next to Baba Yaga and jumped from Shar onto a patch of soft grass. Devastation hadn't struck this area, likely because the Youdi aided Zlo.

Caressing Shar's neck, Theo said, "Thank you, my friend. We'll be back soon, I hope."

Sava and Zima joined them. Pavel's deer landed farther from the others, near leafy vegetation. Pavel left Whirl after wrapping his hands around the deer's neck and hurried toward the group.

"Time to rescue Diva," Pavel said, out of breath. "What's the plan?"

Baba Yaga's eyes gleamed. "You can't just walk into the Youdi's fortress. They'll be expecting you to come after your friend again. And they've got spies throughout the village. They ain't gonna expect me to help you, though. Besides, they shouldn't recognize me, as young and beauti— well, as young as I look now." Grinning, she caressed her smooth skin.

"How will we get in, then?" Theo asked.

"I'm getting there. First, we'll need a horse-drawn cart. The deer would give us away."

Zima snorted. "I don't see a horse or a cart in the vicinity. How do you plan to get them?"

Baba Yaga scowled at the Kuker. "Says the one who already failed getting inside. I'm a powerful witch, much cleverer than those Youdi who kept you out. Watch." She pulled out a jar of powder from her satchel.

She squinted and scrunched up her face as she walked around the meadow, looking at the flowers. Theo recalled how the ones they'd wandered into before had been poisoned. He opened his mouth to say something but stopped. The witch would know what she was doing.

"You're going to pick them a bouquet?" Pavel looked over the rim of his glasses. "That sounds like something Jega would do."

"No, no, no. You people have no imagination." Baba Yaga opened the jar and sprinkled powder onto two dragonflies hovering over a poppy. She waved her broom handle over the insects and chanted, "From fast and fragile to steady and strong. Seeing all to guided vision. Colors meld and essence grow."

With each rapid beat of the insects' wings, the transparent material dissolved, filling the air with glittering specs of orange, red, yellow, and black. The dragonfly bodies bloated, forming muscles. Spindly legs thickened and sprouted hooves. Their needle-like tails split into dozens of long strands of black hair. The floating specs swirled into a long spiral, attaching to the black horses' jaws in the form of multi-colored harnesses.

"Amazing," Pavel said. "You're like Cinderella's fairy godmother. Now all you need is a pumpkin."

Baba Yaga huffed. "I'm no fairy. Puny creatures. And this is not the season for pumpkins."

"Are we going to find a chariot in the village," Theo asked while admiring the sleek coats of the horses.

"Nope. This'll do the trick." Baba Yaga pulled a hazelnut from her bag and dropped it onto the ground. "You all might want to step back. This works mighty fast."

After everyone took a few steps away, the witch sprinkled more of the powder onto the nut and jumped back herself.

Waving her hand toward the nut, Baba Yaga chanted again, "Smooth brown skin, stretch and grow. A new kernel soon to hold."

The hazelnut began spinning. Sparks and cracking sounds came from it as its shape distorted and expanded like a lump of clay molded on a potter's wheel, an invisible hand creating a hollow in its center. As the nut swelled and turned, it tossed tufts of grass and pebbles into the air. The clumps crumpled and coated the whirling nut with a layer of rich black soil, while the pebbles shattered into a fine powder, expanding outward into circles. The nut, now as tall as an adult, stopped spinning. It cracked and sparked more as it changed again, squaring off into a black covered cart, with pale brown curtains flapping over the rear entrance. The spinning rock circles hardened and attached themselves to the bottom of the cart, two on each side, to form wheels.

"I've seen better tricks." Zima pulled aside the fabric, exposing the empty interior. "What's your great plan now? Stuff us in there? We won't all fit."

Baba Yaga looked at Sava. "Who invited that one? He might have muscles, but we can do without that snide mouth." She reached for the powder. "I think I'll turn him into a—"

"Enough of this." Sava stood between the witch and Kuker. "Will you tell us the details about how we're going to save my sister?"

Baba Yaga hitched the horses to the cart and started walking. "When we get there."

Inside the village, she halted behind a building not far from the crumbling fortress walls. Nine towers circled the enclosure, and the battlements around them had gaping holes, revealing the parapet behind them. Armored sentries walked along the edges, seeming to take more care not to fall through holes than they did looking for possible dangers to the fort.

"Enough dawdling, witch." Zima pointed his spear in her direction. "What's your mysterious plan?"

"This." She removed a ratty piece of cloth from her bag.

Zima sneered. "A rag? What are you going to do? Pose as a servant and clean their home?"

"Still such unbelief. You'll see." She tore the material into pieces, set them on the edge of the cart, and sprinkled her transforming powder onto them while she chanted, "Rags to riches. Silky replace coarse. Vanity sees finery to match its own conceit."

The fibers fizzled into black smoke. When the air cleared, bolts of colorful silk lined the cart.

Baba Yaga smirked. "The Youdi might be leery of strangers and keep the doors of their dark fortress locked, but they're much too vain. They love to buy silk fabrics for their dresses. Plus, some of my beautifying herbs."

"You could use that." Zima lowered his spear.

Sava held out her hand to the Kuker in a gesture to stop. "What do we do now? Even if we can get past the locked gate, the Youdi will recognize me, Theo, Pavel, and possibly even Zima—or at least know he's a Kuker."

Baba Yaga said nothing, but she scooped up dirt and rubbed it on Pavel's and Theo's faces.

"Hey!" They both jerked backward.

"That's to disguise you as my helpers if anyone sees you." Baba Yaga pulled the curtain aside. "Leave all your stuff here and get in and hide behind the fabric."

"Why do we have to leave it?" Pavel clutched his backpack.

"You have to fit inside the cart. If anyone discovers you, those bags and that magic bow will give you away."

"What about this?" Theo searched in his backpack for the lightning-bolt shaped knife.

Baba Yaga scrunched up her face. " 'Suppose so. It's small enough to hide. Might come in handy to have a weapon. Now get in. Once we're inside, you two can unlock the gate after everyone goes to sleep."

"Well, I can take a few small things, too." Pavel rummaged around in his backpack and withdrew his Pavel-o-paralyzer and another gadget.

"And how are Sava and I supposed to get past those red monsters in the moat," Zima growled, "so we can wait outside the gate."

"You're so smart, you figure it out." Baba Yaga grinned.

"Here, use this." Pavel held out his Pavel-o-paralyzer to Zima. "This will immobilize those red creatures, so you can swim past them after we're inside. We used it in Selo, and it stuns them for about twenty minutes."

Zima swatted it away. "I trust your inventions even less than I have faith in the witch."

"Thank you." Sava reached over and took the device. "You got yourself and Theo here, so I believe it'll work."

"C'mon, c'mon. Let's get going." Baba Yaga climbed onto the driver's bench and clicked to get the horses moving.

Theo and Pavel scrambled inside the moving cart.

Zima watched a bird flying over the fortress gates. "I wish I could turn into a bird and fly inside. I doubt this crazy scheme will work."

"Be careful what you wish for …" Baba Yaga snarled at him as she drove away.

Theo crawled toward the front of the cart and peeked out a knothole. At the edge of the moat, the witch yelled to the sentry on the other side, "Let down the drawbridge. I wanna come in."

"Who are you and what do you want?" the sentry asked.

"Just a peddler with beautiful silks for sale, high quality but low price." Baba Yaga spoke with a trembling voice. "Please let me in. I need to get a roof over my head before night falls."

"You should have stopped at another village. The Youdi aren't interested."

Baba Yaga wailed. "Please ask them. No one else would open their doors to me. I'm afraid of the evil creatures lurking in the dark."

The sentry spoke to someone on the other side of the gate. Silence ensued, then quiet murmuring. Something heavy grated against metal as it slid to open the gate.

A face peered out and laughed. "It's just an ugly woman. Not our Samodiva sisters."

"Let her in," a husky voice on the other side of the gate said. "I could use a new dress. The wild girl tore mine."

The gate creaked open, and the drawbridge lowered. A hand inside waved Baba Yaga forward. "Come on in. The silk better not be expensive."

"It's cheap for this quality." Baba Yaga cackled.

"You're fortunate," the husky-voiced woman said. "We were about to retire for the evening. You'll be the last person to come in tonight."

A crowd of Youdi gathered around the cart. The husky-voiced one threw aside the curtains and gasped. "Ohhh. So lovely." She pointed toward the fortress. "We'll go there first. Youda Stana always gets the first pick."

Baba Yaga drove up the incline, with the husky-voiced Youda escorting her. They stopped in front of the ruined building.

The Youda pounded on the door. "Stana, come see the beautiful silks this woman is selling."

Several more Youdi poured out the door and surrounded the cart, pulling at the bolts of material with shouts of "That's mine" or "I want that one."

Theo scooted lower beneath cloth in the back. If the women kept removing the material, he and Pavel would be exposed.

"Quiet, all of you." Stana snapped a whip in the air. "Put it all back, you thieving witches."

Like the parting of the Red Sea, the Youdi made a path for their leader. Those who had material threw the bolts back into the cart.

Stana pawed through material near the opening, selecting a deep-blue Turkish silk. "How much for this one?"

"It's yours free if you'll let me stay inside for the night." Baba Yaga trembled and looked around with wide eyes. "I'm exhausted from my travels and afraid Harpies might attack me in the dark."

Stana wrinkled her brow and pressed her lips flat. She glanced into the cart again. "There's too much for me to look through now, so I guess I'll let you stay, but only tonight."

"Many thanks to you." Baba Yaga bowed. "The fabric you chose complements your beautiful blue eyes."

Stana grinned. "What else do you have to offer?"

Baba Yaga pulled a colorful earthen jar from her bag. "Honey that rejuvenates and beautifies the skin."

"I certainly don't need that." Stana stuck her nose into the air and waved the jar away. "I doubt it works anyway; if it did, you'd use it yourself. You might be young, but you're an ugly old thing."

A pair of hands grabbed the jar and shoved a gold coin into Baba Yaga's palm. "Let me buy it then. Two Pendari should be enough for all that you have."

"Yes, of course, mistress." Baba Yaga pulled two more jars from her pocket and handed them to the waiting woman.

The Youda opened one jar, dipped her fingers into the sticky substance, and took a taste. "Mmmm. Heavenly. Sisters, you have to try this."

Murmurs of contentment filled the air, and soon all the jars were empty.

Stana pointed toward two of the Youdi. "If you gluttons have had enough, bring the wagon into the stables. I'll look at the rest of the material in the morning, then everyone else can grab, uh, pay for what you want."

The two women hastened to do as commanded.

Stana yelled after them, "And don't you *dare* touch any of the material until I've had a chance to look it over. I'll let Zlo use you for his experiments, and you know how cruel he can be."

The two Youdi trembled, and one said, "Yes, Stana. We won't even look."

As Stana was about to step inside the castle, Baba Yaga said in a meek voice, "You said I could stay the night."

Stana grumbled. "Yes, come along. You can sleep on the floor by the door, but I'll have to have someone guard you."

One of the two Youdi walked past the cart to lead the horses to the stables. Theo pulled away from the knothole he had gone back to looking out. When the animals stopped moving, Pavel opened his mouth to speak, but Theo put his finger to his lips.

The curtain on the cart moved, and Theo held his breath.

The other Youda screeched, "What are you doing? Get away from there!"

"I just wanted to see—"

"Stana will kill us both if you even *look* at the material."

The curtain fluttered closed, and the two Youdi argued as they left the stables. Theo and Pavel sat without moving until all was quiet.

"Do you think it's safe to leave now?" Pavel whispered. "My legs are tingly."

"Let's try." Theo moved a stack of fabric to the side and crept toward the curtains. He listened before he drew them aside a sliver.

"We're in a stall," he said over his shoulder. Theo slid to the floor and peered through the bars into the stables. "It doesn't look like anyone's here. Let's hurry."

Darkness covered the courtyard as they crept from one bush to another toward the deserted gate.

"Keep an eye out while I open the door," Theo said.

"Aw, man. I want to help, but I guess you're the boss."

Crouched down, Theo ran toward the door. He pushed the end of the heavy beam, but it didn't move away from the metal latch. His second attempt failed—and his third. He still wasn't strong enough.

Sighing, Theo gestured toward Pavel. "I can't do it alone. Come help."

Pavel ran over, and Theo pushed the beam while Pavel fiddled with the latch. This time the beam moved a fraction of an inch.

Theo wiped his brow. "Did you bring your Paveltron?" Pavel's invention housed a variety of tools that had gotten the two of them out of jams when Lamia had captured them the previous year.

"Nah, that's at home. I took it apart for an upgrade. I have this, though." Pavel revealed another gadget and fiddled with the device, finally holding up a thin tube with coils inside. "This would work better with the Kukeri one-two, heat-cool effect, except we have only one of the brothers here—the grouchy one."

"I heard that, and I'm getting impatient to get this over with, so stop talking," Zima said from the other side of the gate.

"Zima, glad you're there—" Pavel started.

"Where else would I be? Sava and I have been waiting forever for you to get here."

"Can you freeze the gate here." Pavel tapped on the wood. "I'm going to heat the latch, and we'll see what happens."

Icicles grew from the grooves between the wooden planks like mushrooms pushing up leaves. Pavel touched a button on his gadget and laid the tube on the latch. The metal buckled right before the tube shattered.

"Rat droppings!" Pavel said. "That took forever to make."

Theo pushed the beam away from the latch. "When we get back to Selo, I'll help you make another one."

The door creaked open, and Zima strode through, followed by Sava. The Samodiva handed Pavel back his laser-stunning device. "Worked great. Thank you."

"No problem." Pavel looked on the other side of the gate. "I don't see our backpacks or Theo's bow. Did you bring them?"

"No," Zima said. "We had our own weapons to carry."

Theo shook his head. "Glad I have the dagger then."

"Where should we start?" Pavel asked.

"It might be better to split up," Zima said.

"We're stronger as a team." Theo pointed to the tower nearest the gate. "This one seems a likely place to start."

At the top of the tower, Theo put his ear to the wooden door. A muffled sound, crying or moaning, came from inside. He grasped the handle and twisted it. To his surprise, it moved.

"It's not locked," he whispered.

Zima, who was directly behind him, spoke with a low voice. "That was too easy. It's probably a trap."

"We won't know unless we go in." Theo turned the handle all the way and pushed the door open into the small round room.

Dust motes floated in dim light penetrating the room from arrow-slit windows. A black canvas sheet fluttered over a larger opening. The room appeared empty except for a bundle of black rags along the wall. Where was Diva?

The rags moved, and a moan came from a figure huddled beneath them.

"Diva?" Theo moved closer, reached out, and touched the person.

The figure turned around to face him. "Who allowed you to enter our home uninvited?"

Youda Stana held a bound and gagged Diva captive.

"I told you." Zima pushed Theo aside and drew his spear. "Run!"

Theo looked down the stairs. Lights flickered at the bottom, revealing several Youdi restraining wolves on chains. Angry growls came from the creatures as they strained against their leashes.

Stana took a step closer. "Your friend with the material thought she could make my assistants sleep soundly for the night with drugged honey, but not all Youdi are so vain."

"What did you do with Baba Yaga?" Sava asked.

"That was her?" Stana laughed. "We … oh my. Still as ugly as the day she was born. She got away, but I won't forget her treachery."

"Theo, get Diva while we take care of the Youdi," Sava said while she and Zima faced the threat coming up the stairs. Her bow arched, the Samodiva took aim below.

"Don't think any of you scare us," Stana said. "We're stronger and more dangerous and—"

Pavel rushed into the room, saying, "Sorry, Diva," before he rammed his head into her stomach.

Diva groaned, and Stana fell backward, releasing her grip on her captive.

Theo pulled out his lightning knife and pointed it at Stana's throat. "Not so cocky now, are you?"

Stana spat on the floor. "As I was about to say, we have friends."

She tore the black canvas sheet off the window and waved toward the tree branches. Screeches erupted. Harpies, half-women, half-bird creatures, descended on Theo and his friends.

"*Shar, we need help*," Theo thought. "*Bring the other deer.*"

"Theo!" Pavel screamed.

Theo turned to look. A Harpy had cornered his friend. Grasping the knife, Theo plunged it into the creature, cutting a ragged gash in her back. The Harpy screeched, and spun around to face Theo. A thick, yellow liquid oozed down the creature's leg. She staggered toward him.

"Pavel, help Diva," Theo shouted as he jabbed at the hissing Harpy.

Pavel crept along the wall. He unbound Diva and removed her gag.

"Where'd Youda Stana go?" Pavel asked.

Screeches from the Harpy drowned out Diva's response. Outside, Sur and the herd struck the creatures with their antlers, and sent out rays of blinding light, repelling the Harpies into the darkness. The deer turned their attention to the Youdi and wolves as Sava continued to rain arrows down on their enemies. Some wolves escaped and thundered up the narrow steps. Zima jabbed at them with his spear, kicking the dead and wounded beasts over the edge of the tower. Bereft of their mascots, the Youdi changed into hawks and flocked among the deer, their claws like daggers piercing any deer they could reach.

Theo thrust his knife time after time toward the Harpy inside the tower. Using all his strength, he lunged forward, piercing her in the heart. She let out one final screech and dropped to the floor. A puddle of yellow slime seeped from her wounds, but the Harpy remained silent and still.

A flutter of wings sounded behind him.

"Watch out, Theo," Pavel yelled. "Stana's a hawk."

The bird slammed into Theo, and he staggered to remain upright. Again, the bird knocked him forward, and he fell.

Returning to a woman, Youda Stana grabbed Theo and hurled him toward the window.

Pavel dove for her legs, but Stana kicked him across the room. Diva pushed against the floor to rise but fell back in a heap.

Stana laughed. "You think you'll defeat us? I'm stronger than death. Like the Vodnik, I collect souls. It's a simple matter to steal a soul, and I'll soon have yours." She grabbed Theo by the edge of his T-shirt.

Exhausted from his fight with the Harpy, he threw weak punches at the Youda.

The witch scratched Theo's neck with the tip of her sharp claws that had remained hawk-like.

Drowsiness overtook him, and he slid to the floor.

"A potion is seeping into your blood. When you die, your soul will be set free, and I'll capture a piece of it."

Theo looked up at the witch. He lifted his hand, but it moved only a few inches. Barely able to speak because the poison was closing his throat, he asked, "Are you going to kill me now?"

Laughing, Stana said, "No. The poison has to course through all your blood first."

Theo sighed with relief.

Stana's eyes sparkled with malice as she lifted Theo and shoved him out of the window. "By the time you hit the bottom, the poison should have done its trick. Then your soul will be mine."

A whip cracked above Theo, followed by crazy laughter. Unable to scream as he fell toward the ground, he stared at the chariot pulled by black wolves with bloody eyes. Animal skulls lining the vehicle's edges held their jaws open in an eternal scream of agony.

Youda Stana zipped back and forth saying, "You'll be mine soon."

She cracked the whip again and sped away, leaving only a trace of black smoke.

*"Shar, I need help."* Theo thought to his deer companion.

*"Surrounded. Wounded. Trying."*

Who else could help him? *"Mom, can you hear me?"* His Samodiva mother had guided him once when he'd fallen from the castle, but he hadn't felt her presence since he'd come back.

*"Weak,"* came the reply. *"Remember ... before."*

His mother's voice faded. The Forest of Souls where her spirit rested must be withering away like the rest of Dragon Village. He couldn't let his mother and the other spirits disappear forever. He had to save them. Anger raced through him, but also love. These were his people. He wasn't going to let Stana or Zlo or any other monster destroy those he loved.

What had his mother wanted him to remember? He recalled his fall from the castle. She'd told him to remember his gift, the combined strength of a Samodiva and dragon.

*Yes, I can do this.*

His father was a majestic dragon: sharp claws, scorching fire, massive tail, and magnificent wings.

*I. Am. A. Dragon's. Son.*

Faster than he could blink, red wings shot out from beneath his arms. He moved them gracefully and soared upward. He looked around ready to fight, but the Harpies and Youdi were retreating. Amber and purple lights flashed near the base of the fortress.

*"Shar."*

*"I'm hurt but will heal,"* came the reply. *"We've won. The Youdi and wolves are dead or gone."*

*"What about Diva and Pavel? And Baba Yaga?"*

*"They're fine, but worried about you. At least your friends are. The witch is ... her normal uncaring self. Hurry down."*

Theo glided on the breeze. Lower and lower he flew until he landed where Diva and Pavel were sitting on the ground. Theo tucked his wings up, and they disappeared until only bumps remained.

"Magnificent … I knew you could do it." Pavel had his phone directed at Theo. "No one in Selo will ever believe this."

"No one will believe you even with that, pal," Theo said. "They'll think it's another one of your inventions."

"Can you turn into a full-blown dragon, too? That would be way cool."

Theo shrugged as he squeezed himself between his two friends and wrapped his arms around them. "I guess time will tell. Are you both okay?"

Diva placed her hand on his. "Yes. Sava gave me herbs to counteract what the Youdi made me drink. I'll be stronger than you again in no time. Thank you for coming for me."

"And I'm fine." Pavel rubbed his head. "Son of a rat's tail, Diva sure has a hard body."

Theo laughed and tightened his embrace. "I could use some of those herbs. Stana scratched me and said my poisoned blood would let her take my soul when I died."

"I don't have anything for that here," Sava said, "but—"

"Don't worry," Baba Yaga poked her nose toward Theo and sniffed. "My friend can fix this problem, also. Two-for-one solution."

"We've accomplished what we came to do," Zima said, "so I'm going back to help Mraz."

"Good riddance." Baba Yaga spat on the ground.

"I'll stay and help," Sava said.

"No, no. You go, too." Baba Yaga stomped her feet. "My friend won't help if she's overwhelmed with too many people."

"I'm not sure I—"

"It's okay, Sava," Diva said. "I'll make sure she doesn't play any tricks."

Sava nodded and gave a searing look at the witch, before following Zima.

"Diva, was Boo here with you? Or the Firebird?"

She shook her head. "Haven't seen either."

"I wonder where the magpie went?"

"C'mon, c'mon." Baba Yaga walked away, dragging her satchel, clinking and clanging and fuller than it had been when she'd arrived. "You want to get rid of that bad blood, don't you? Just let me stop at home and get my Kotka first."

# Chapter 7
# Something Is Brewing

THE TWO MOONS cast their uncanny glow over the night, making even Sur's fireball appear evil as red and blue danced with its amber. After the boys had retrieved their backpacks and Theo his bow and quiver, Theo had sent Shar to rest and recover from his injuries. Sur was strong enough to carry both Theo and Diva. Before they left the fortress, they found where the Youdi had hidden Diva's bow and arrows and her pouch of herbs, so they all had their weapons for whatever they might encounter next.

Now, they flew endlessly in circles, waiting for Baba Yaga. The witch had descended to her chicken cabin, to get her cat, she said. She claimed she didn't want to leave her pet alone overnight. "The rest of you remain here," she'd said. "Quick as a wink, and I'll be back."

And so, they waited, and waited, flying above her cabin. Every so often, glowing lights lit up the yard below, as if the skull eyes on the fence acted as motion detectors. What was taking the witch so long? What was she up to now? Theo would have left and sought out the Kukeri if the coughing and burning pain hadn't returned. He had to rely on the crafty witch, even if he didn't trust her.

"I think we should go down and see what the witch is doing," Diva said as if reading his thoughts.

"I agree. Maybe her Chutura finally got out of breath."

As they began their descent, Baba Yaga hobbled outside holding Kotka. She placed the cat into her mortar, hopped in beside the feline, and flew up to the sky, leaving a trace of white smoke.

"That's settled, so off we go," she said when she reached them.

Without giving Theo or Diva a chance to respond, Baba Yaga departed into the night, flying a little south of the direction of Vida Fortress.

Where was the old witch taking them?

Theo didn't have long to wait. They flew to the edge of the Forest of Whispering Bells, the tinkling of the copper bells becoming faint. Without warning, the witch veered her mortar headlong toward a marshy area. Sur and Whirl followed her path. After circling a few times, the deer landed on a solid patch of ground.

The odor of rotten leaves and something strange permeated the area. Theo looked around to try to pinpoint the source, but a dense fog covered the ground. He was sure this was the Cold Marsh. He and Diva had passed through it before when looking for Jabalaka. Surely the witch wasn't bringing them to see him. No, she'd mentioned a female friend. Who else lived in this smelly swamp?

Baba Yaga straightened a colorful scarf that covered her tousled gray hair before she jumped from the mortar. She bent over her transportation, pulling a snarling cat from within, and clutched Kotka under her arm. The cat hissed at Theo as he approached. Scratching and spitting, Kotka tried to squirm away, but the witch held on tight.

"If we're lucky, we'll find my dear old friend without getting lost." Baba Yaga stroked the cat with her free hand as she scoured the edge of the swamp. "According to my memory, the path should be nearby." She sniffed the air and walked away.

As she neared Pavel, she licked her lips. "Don't stray from the path. You never know what might grab you."

Pavel scowled and waved his hand in front of his face. "You need a bath and a toothbrush," he muttered.

"What'd you say, boy?" She poked him in his ribs. "Mmmm, I wonder …"

"Nothing, nooo." Pavel backed away, bumping into Theo.

"Can you please stop? Both of you." Theo pressed his arms over his chest and coughed. "We need to find Baba Yaga's friend soon."

"Theo's right," Diva said as she patted Sur. "We'll have to leave the deer here. They can't fly through the swamp; it's too thick. And we can't have them walk beside us. Their hooves would get stuck in the slime."

Pavel gave Whirl a hug. "Be back soon, I hope."

"Yes, yes. Leave them here," Baba Yaga said. "They can guard my mortar. You don't need to fly. You all have legs."

"Can we go now?" Theo gritted his teeth against the pain.

"I've been waiting." Baba Yaga dug in her mortar and thrust a torch made from a skull at Theo. "Here, you'll need this. Don't lose it. That was a special child."

Theo cringed, but held on tight. "How do I light it?"

"The eye sockets will glow by themselves when you enter the swamp." Supported by a crooked stick and clutching Kotka, Baba Yaga plunged into the fog.

"Wait." Theo ran after her, followed by Diva and Pavel.

Baba Yaga had disappeared, but she hadn't lied. The skull eyes lit up, glowing red in the fog. Theo followed the path, hoping the witch wasn't too far ahead. Each squishy step he took released noxious gases from the moss. From time to time, he slipped on rotten leaves and stumbled into branches. Bubbling and belching from the fetid water increased in volume the farther into the marsh he walked. Another sound, light scratching, chirping, he thought, seemed to follow them.

He turned around. "Diva, Pavel, you okay?"

"Yes." Diva's breath tickled his ear.

"So far so good," Pavel said. "Oomph, something poked me. Wait a minute. I'm stuck on something scratchy."

Theo took a few steps back toward Pavel.

"Hey, don't leave me," Pavel shouted.

"I'm not. I'm coming back."

Pavel groaned and scrambled backward. "Help! It's pulling me into the swamp."

Theo and Diva rushed back as fast as they could on the squelching path. The glowing torch eyes cast shadows around Pavel, making it look as if spirit creatures were pulling him away.

"Hang on," Theo shouted, his voice echoing around the swamp.

Diva nocked an arrow, ready for defense.

"Theo, help!" Kicking and screaming, Pavel tumbled off the path into the water.

"Pavel!" Theo yelled.

Diva pointed the arrow around, like a soldier ready to attack an unknown enemy.

A slimy hand reached up to the path, and Pavel pulled himself free of the muck. "Stinky swamp grass. What was that? A Harpy? It scratched like the dickens."

"No, Harpies don't like swamps," Diva said. "And I didn't hear any beating wings."

"Why are you all screaming?" Baba Yaga, still clutching Kotka, tore down the path, waving her crooked stick at Theo. "You don't want to disturb the peace of the creatures living out here."

"Someone dragged Pavel into the swamp," Theo said.

"Which direction?" The witch sniffed the air.

"Here … there … here … oh, maybe there?" Theo pointed everywhere with uncertainty.

"Hmmm, that doesn't help me." The witch cackled. "I did warn him not to step off the path."

"I didn't *step* off the path," Pavel said through gritted teeth. "I was *pulled* off."

"And where were you?" Diva asked. "You left us here, trying to find our way."

Pavel wiped off some of the grime. "It was probably her trying to scare me."

A soft chirp and scratching came from nearby, followed by light footsteps scampering away.

"Or maybe not." Pavel gulped and looked from the witch to where the sound receded.

"Hmph. Told you. Now, everyone, stay close this time, or I'll change my mind about helping. Understand?"

One by one, they each nodded.

"And you, dragon boy, stay at the back." Baba Yaga pointed at Theo. "You're terrifying my cat."

Theo handed Diva the torch so she could lead them, glad to be rid of the ghastly light. Pavel stayed in the middle, with Theo following. Diva replaced the arrow in her quiver and, walking with the stealth of a cat, kept pace with Baba Yaga. It was her land; she knew how to traverse it. Pavel, on the other hand, ran to keep up, slipping like on a water slide. Theo's shoes and clothing were soaking wet from the backwash and from his own frantic pace not to lose the others in the thick fog.

The witch stopped abruptly and turned to face them. "For the rest of the way, don't speak. Remain absolutely silent. Whatever you see or hear, keep quiet. One sound, and you're lost."

Theo shuddered and closed the distance between him and Pavel, while Pavel crept closer to Diva.

All around them, glowing eyes blinked in the marsh like fireflies in the darkness, appearing close one moment, then at a distance the next. All the while, the chirping and croaking of frogs built to a crescendo. For a moment, all went silent, like the prelude to a terrifying event in a horror movie. Theo's heart thumped loudly.

Waiting, waiting, waiting.

A rush of wind swept past him, and he covered his mouth to stifle a scream. A mouse squealed, and an owl swept past Theo again with its prey. It wasn't him the creature had sought. Screams of other wounded animals sounded like a lament. Another splash nearby made Theo scoot closer to his friends.

Soon, a large amber glow appeared ahead. Theo breathed a sigh of relief as they got closer. It was a hut covered with moss and leaves. A flickering light inside revealed the outline of a window. That must be the witch's friend's house. A curtain moved, then fell back into place before Theo could glimpse the person inside.

"I'll enter first," Baba Yaga said. "Wait until I tell you it's okay to come in. Do you understand?"

Theo nodded, still not sure if it was okay for the rest of them to speak. He looked around the marsh, wondering what was out there, ready to seize them the way it had tried to capture Pavel.

"Do we have a choice?" Pavel whispered.

"Don't be smart with me." The witch snapped her teeth.

Theo, Pavel, and Diva huddled near the house, avoiding the swaying reeds and anything else that could conceal a foe.

Baba Yaga turned away, grumbling as she tapped her stick on the narrow door, "Kotka, children are only good for eating."

What sounded like the clattering of pots, pans, and plates came from inside, followed by the scraping of a chair across a wooden floor and the clucking of chickens. The door squeaked open a crack, and two squawking black hens pushed their way out and raced into the darkness. Kotka yowled and squirmed in Baba Yaga's tight grip as the cat stared in the direction the hens had disappeared.

A bony, clawed hand reached around the door, and pieces of rotten wood fell off the frame. The hand opened the door a little more. "Wow! Ho, ho. Look who's here," a soft voice chirped. "What a surprise. Come in, my old friend."

The witch entered, and the bony hand shut the door with a click.

Theo whispered to Diva, "Do you know who lives here?"

"No. Maybe one of the Vodni."

Theo had met some of the Vodni on his previous trip through the Cold Marsh. The creatures were child-sized but looked like little old men. They had green hair and beards, webbed claws, and sharp, pointed teeth in a broad mouth. Worse of all, they had a nasty habit of trying to steal shiny possessions and drown people. Perhaps a Vodnik had grabbed Pavel earlier. But what was that other noise? Unless—

The door creaked open, and more hens rushed outside past Theo.

"Children." Baba Yaga grabbed her cat as Kotka tried to sneak out. The witch stood in the open doorway and motioned to them with her crooked finger. "You can come in now. But first, listen. Don't ask questions. And leave that torch outside."

Diva drove the glowing skull torch into the ground before entering the house. Pavel followed close on her heels, and Theo hurried after them.

The smell of rot and fermenting brew overpowered the tiny room. In a small fireplace, a brown, foamy liquid bubbled inside a vat over an open flame. Chickens pecked at crushed grain scattered on the floor. Dirty dishes, a mallet, and more grain lay in disarray on a small table. Baba Yaga's friend was brewing beer?

A bird-like voice tittered, "Oh, he is a handsome young boy. Won't you introduce me?"

Theo looked for the speaker, but whoever had been standing next to Baba Yaga had vanished, as if dissolving in the air. A claw from behind him lightly traced a line down his arm. He spun around to face a strange creature looking up at him with bright, bulging eyes.

A bit hunchbacked, the scrawny creature barely reached the middle of Theo's chest. Her nose jutted out from her forehead, forming a long beak, curved up at the end like a pug nose. Two goat-like horns stood straight up from her head.

In the fashion of married village women, she wore a headscarf. It was so worn and faded it barely covered her disheveled hair. Her clothing was likewise tattered, covered with patches of moss and grass, and what once must have been an intricate embroidered design was now nothing more than loose red strings.

Her clawed hand rested again on his arm, and she shuffled her chicken-like feet on the dusty floor. Theo couldn't tell if she was old or young, but her face, although strange to him, held a gentle innocence. She fluttered her eyelids at him and chirped. Since she was a friend of the witch, he wasn't sure if the sentiment was sincere or feigned.

He looked over at Baba Yaga for introductions, but the witch remained silent. So, he said, "I'm Theo, and these are my friends, Pavel and Diva."

"So pleased to meet you, Theo." She ignored the others and held out her claw as if she wanted him to kiss it in the fashion of knights of old. "I'm Kikimora, but friends call me Kiki."

He shuddered and shook her claw instead.

The corners of her mouth turned down for a moment, but then she put her claw over his chest. "Baba tells me you have a problem. Indeed, I feel something strange in you. Tell me how you feel, dear."

"I keep getting angry, and I have terrible pain all over, sometimes so bad I can't move. And it feels like someone's suffocating me. Maybe it's normal because I'm a mixture of Samodiva and dragon?"

"No, no, no." She shook her head. "That should give you strength. There's something else. Something quite bad."

"Can you help?" Theo begged her with his eyes.

"Yes, yes, yes." She chirped. "But I can't work in this mess. Too distracting. I can't abide living in an untidy house."

She scurried around, hopping from foot to foot. In her effort to tidy the room, she gathered a pile of dirty pans and dumped them onto a shelf, dropping bones and rotting vegetables from them, making more clutter than was there before.

"Ejko Bejko," she repeated over and again as she looked under furniture. "Where are you?"

"Who's that? A kitten?" Pavel asked.

"No, no. My dish towel." Kiki scurried around more, knocking items onto the floor. She sighed and gathered a rag and a bucket of water, which she handed to Diva. "Girl, I hate lazy people. Look my sink is full of dishes, a good job for you. This cloth will have to suffice since I can't find my Ejko Bejko."

Diva set the offered items aside and sat on a chair in the corner. Theo was surprised she hadn't responded. He expected a snarky remark from her, but she'd been quiet since they'd rescued her. The herbs her sister had given her must not have completely cleansed Diva's system of the Youdi potion.

"And you, boy." Kiki grabbed Pavel by the arm and dragged him over to an old spinning wheel wrapped in yarn. "Just look at this disaster. Every night I try to spin. I can't sleep, so I spin, and spin, and spin. It drove my husband, Lesnik, crazy, so he finally left. I can't help myself. But, look. It gets all tangled. You can unwind it for me."

Pavel sat on the stool, an impossible task in front of him. He looked at Theo, but Theo just shrugged. Baba Yaga smirked and drank a beer Kiki must have given her earlier. Kotka was nowhere to be seen. Theo guessed the cat was stalking an unsuspecting chicken somewhere else in the house.

"There, that's settled. Now for you, dear." Kiki returned to Theo and guided him to where an object was covered with a purple velvet cloth. Come look in my special mirror." She pulled back the material.

Theo looked into the mirror and fell to the ground, convulsing. His spirit seemed to detach from his body, and he helplessly observed everything going on around him without being able to communicate to the others.

Diva was at his side in a moment. "What did you do to him?" She shoved everything out of his way to keep him from hurting himself. "Theo, Theo?"

Pavel tried to get up but was tangled in the mess of yarn. Chickens scattered, flapping their wings and squawking as Kiki ran around the room. Startled by the commotion, Kotka came out of hiding and scratched her way up a wooden beam to hide near the ceiling.

"Oh dear, oh dear. My poor Theo." Kiki stopped in front of the table where Baba Yaga sat smirking. "You were right, old friend, and didn't just come here for a beer. This is urgent. I haven't seen a uroki this bad in ages. I'll try to drive the demon away, but I need help."

"Don't forget about the Youdi poison, too." The witch gulped her beer, then burped. "It's strong, making the uroki even more powerful. He has two battles going on inside him."

"Oh dear. You, boy, help me." Kiki pointed at Pavel. "Oh no, look at the mess you've made. I'll do it myself."

Pavel found a pair of scissors and cut the tangled yarn away. He joined Diva at Theo's side. "Theo, help's coming."

Kiki went to the back of the hut and returned with a bowl of water, salt crystals, a ball of string, and a spindle.

"How can *water* help him?" Pavel asked. "He's convulsing."

Kiki opened her big eyes even wider. "Water is powerful, eternal. It can wash the evil out."

"You tell 'em, Kiki." The witch belched. "She's been doing this for ages. Trust her. I prefer beer myself." Cackling, Baba Yaga gulped down the rest of her brew and poured another.

"Girl, I need more hands," Kiki said. "Hold dear Theo up so I can wrap him with the string."

Diva picked Theo's feet up, while Kiki twisted string around them. She kept dropping the ball. "Oh dear, oh dear. You, boy, hold this." Kikimora tossed the ball to Pavel.

"Phew, it stinks. What is this?"

"Rat hair, bats, and spider web." Kiki continued to twist the string around Theo as Diva held him aloft. "The strongest material found anywhere in Zmeykovo."

"Disgusting." Pavel scrunched up his face as he unwound the ball.

In a few minutes, Theo looked like an Egyptian mummy all the way up to his neck. Only his face remained uncovered.

"Give me your hand," Kiki told Diva.

"My hand?"

Without waiting, Kikimora grabbed Diva's hand and pricked a finger with a sharp metal spindle and squeezed out three drops of blood into the bowl of water. The blood turned purple and dissolved.

Diva sucked on her finger and glared at Kiki, who didn't pay any attention. Kiki arranged four crystals around Theo and began to mutter as she stared into the bowl of water.

Theo's spirit watched from above as his body shook more and more. Sweat coated his face that had turned almost translucent.

Kiki hopped and jumped around his body and sprinkled the blood-tainted water on him. The drops turned into small purple crystals. Theo's face changed from translucent to a greenish purple color, with black veins running through it. The string binding him crackled, and one of his arms shot free of the cocoon as he struggled.

A foul black mist snaked out of his mouth. It took the shape of a dragon and spiraled and whistled in the air as it twirled faster and faster. Theo felt his own spirit lunge back into his body. He jerked awake and opened his eyes.

Swift as an arrow, the swirling black mass shot toward the ceiling. Kotka hissed and clawed at it, but the blackness entered the cat's mouth. The flying cat snarled and contorted, swatting at itself. She flew around the room like a frenzied fly, bumping into walls, until she found an open window and escaped into the darkness.

Everyone stared blankly.

"Kotkaaa!" Baba Yaga rushed after her pet.

Theo wiped the sweat from his face and unwound the threads from his body. He felt sore, but the pain eating away at him was gone.

"How can I thank you, Kiki?" he asked.

Kikimora looked at the pile of dirty pans and plates and chirped.

Theo laughed. "Okay, I'll clean the house." He lightly tapped Pavel's shoulder. "And my friend will help, too."

She fluttered her eyelids at him again. "I don't have guests often, and it's been lonely since Lesnik left. Let me cook you a meal." She looked at a black hen pecking at spilled grain.

"And make more dirty dishes," Pavel said under his breath.

"Here." Theo found a broom and shoved it into Pavel's hands. "You can sweep, and I'll wash."

"What about Diva?" Pavel looked, and somehow she'd managed to untangle Kiki's spinning that Pavel hadn't cut. "How? Okay, okay, I'll sweep the floor."

While Theo washed the dishes, he asked, "Kiki, do you know anything about Zlo, Lamia's master?"

Her skinny hands shook, and she dropped the chicken. It hopped away. She darted her eyes around the room as if someone was watching her. "I don't know much. No one has seen him, but I've heard he can shape-shift into anything. He's unstoppable. Stay away from him. He's pure evil." She hurried away to chase after the escaped chicken, returning later with it ready to be roasted.

While the bird cooked, the door opened, and Baba Yaga returned alone, a sour look on her face. She plopped down at the table and poured another beer, which she drained. "Oh, kitty, kitty."

"Dear friend." Kiki hopped over to her. "Let me get you a glass of my special summer recipe to cheer you. Kotka will come back." She went to a back room and returned moments later with a jug.

"Dear beer for me and you." Baba Yaga took the jug and filled her mug with the amber liquid. She drank it in one gulp and burped. "I should visit you more often. A great beer needs a good appetizer." She winked at Pavel and licked her lips.

This time, he only rolled his eyes and finished cleaning while Baba Yaga and Kikimora sat on a small wooden table, trying new beers. Baba Yaga talked about her beloved Kotka, and they both told stories from the past.

Later, after they all finished eating, Kikimora went to spin.

"What a day," Pavel said. "I'm exhausted." I claim that pillow in the corner. He pointed to a rolled-up bundle lying on a pile of hay and moss. He stretched out and laid his head down. "Ouch, it's a little prickly. Maybe this will work." He rolled up his jacket and placed it over the pillow.

"I'm too tired to care if my head's on the floor." Theo plopped down beside his friend and closed his eyes. It wasn't a bed, but he was glad they didn't have to sleep outside in the dark, foggy marsh.

# Chapter 8
# Threats in the Marsh

**JUNE 19** 

A BLANKET OF FOG covered the ground so thick Theo couldn't see his feet, but he felt the softness of the grass beneath them. His legs seemed to move forward on their own accord until he reached a forest. Blackened, skeleton-like trees held out their branches toward him like grasping arms. Instead of leaves, the branches cradled glass spheres that pulsed with a dim amber glow.

The Forest of Souls? How had he arrived here?

This place brought him warm memories. It was here, for the first time, he had heard the voice and had beheld the image of his birth mother, Zunitza. He searched for his mother's sphere so he could gaze at her beautiful, gracious smile again. Where was it? It had glowed the brightest before. Now they all seemed faded, as if their energy had been drained.

The air became immensely cold, and the spheres turned from amber to blue-gray.

Something was terribly wrong.

A red light like a lighthouse beacon flickered deeper within the forest. Theo took cautious steps toward it, his heart pounding.

"Mom." He reached for her sphere.

The light within the globe turned into a spiral of purple and red rays swirling like a typhoon. Then a shadowy face appeared inside the sphere. Theo stepped closer.

*No, it can't be!*

Lamia's sinister, sneering visage stared at him.

"Surprised to see me, dear nephew? My time will never end; my strength grows every day. Nobody, absolutely nobody can stop me, even my stupid brother."

Sweat poured down Theo's face and into his eyes. He wiped it away. *What happened to my mother?*

Lamia continued her taunt. "I offered you a chance at greatness, an opportunity to share the throne with me, but you turned me down. We could have been friends. We needed each other. We were both lonely, forgotten children. I would have taught you how to use your powers. But now, I'll destroy you and your father forever."

"That'll never happen."

"Never say never. Who else can you rely on?" Her face morphed between her human and dragon forms as scales appeared and disappeared. "Your mother is a spirit, and your father with his good heart and stupid head will be a slave forever, locked deep in the bowels of the earth. My useless brother."

"Don't talk like that about my father." Theo stuck his face close to the globe. "He's stronger than you. Sooner or later, good wins."

Lamia laughed. "Don't be so sure. Even in the human realm, corrupt people rule and mold the world to their whims. Evil is powerful, intoxicating. Life isn't meant for romantic dreamers like you and your father."

Theo stepped back, but his legs failed him. Something pulled him to the ground. Spiders, thousands of spiders, crawled up his arms and legs, covering his entire body. He batted at them under Lamia's insidious gaze, but they multiplied, biting, pinching him.

The dragon-woman laughed like an insane person. Louder and louder the noise grew. The sphere expanded, growing darker and murkier. With a *bang*, it exploded.

"Help!" Theo covered his head and face with his arms, but shards of glass embedded into him, his face stinging.

Pavel shook Theo and slapped his face. "Stop that. Why are you poking me like that? Ow, that hurts."

Theo shot up, staring around the room with wide eyes. "Where is she?"

"Who?"

"The dragon Lamia. My aunt."

"You were dreaming. We're still at Kikimora's in the swamp. You scared me with your shouting." Pavel wiped his glasses on his T-shirt.

Theo looked around the room. "Have you seen Diva? Or even Baba Yaga or Kikimora?"

"I haven't seen anyone. You just woke me up." Pavel stretched and yawned. "Man, I miss my soft bed. And I'm starving. I wonder if Kikimora left us anything for breakfast. I'm dying for bacon and eggs."

Theo sniffed the air. "I think the chicken goddess is making something, but it's not bacon and eggs. Smells more like she's brewing more beer." He got up and peeked through a door at the back of the hut that was open a crack. Kiki was alone, stirring a bubbling pot.

The door creaked, and she turned. "Oh, hello, dear. Did you sleep well?"

"Yes, thank you." He didn't want to bother her with his nightmare. She'd already done so much for him. "Pavel and I are leaving. I wanted to thank you again for driving out that demon."

"My pleasure. My pleasure." A smile crossed her face, and she chirped. "Come visit any time. I have something for you before you leave." She poked around on a shelf, knocking items onto the floor. "No, not here. Let me look inside."

Theo followed her back into the main room, where Kiki shuffled through items, making the tidy room a mess again. "Here it is." She handed him a metal spindle. "This might come in handy in your endeavors."

"Uh, thank you. I don't plan to do any spinning."

"No, not spinning." Kiki closed her eyes. "I saw you needing it in a vision. Scraping … not sure what or where." She opened her eyes. "I'm certain you'll figure it out when the time comes."

"Thank you." He stepped closer and hugged the petite creature. She felt as thin as his mother in Selo had become when Theo had returned from Dragon Village last year. He imagined his mother's warm hands embracing him. What was she doing now? He hoped everything was okay at home. He was sure Nia would take care of their mom. Kiki was kind and thoughtful like his mother, and he was glad he'd met her. "You've been so good to me."

"Glad to help." Kiki scanned the room, knocking more items off shelves. "Oh, where is my Ejko Bejko? Have you seen him? I'll be lonely when you leave."

Pavel whispered to Theo. "Didn't she say that was her dish towel? How can that keep her company?"

Theo shrugged. "Anything's possible here. Maybe it talks."

Pavel's stomach grumbled. "Kiki, do you have anything to eat?"

"Oh, look." Kiki came over and picked a slug off the back of Pavel's shirt. "I can use this for—"

"Not hungry anymore." Pavel covered his mouth, grabbed his backpack, retrieved his jacket from the pillow he'd slept on, and ran out the door.

Pavel's pillow uncurled and made a sniffling noise.

"Oh, there you are, Ejko Bejko." Kiki picked up the pillow-turned-hedgehog and brought it to the sink. She washed a dish and ran the animal's bristles down it to dry the plate. She placed the animal into the cluttered sink, and it curled back into a ball. "There, that's done. Oh, what a mess this room is. Where is that girl?"

Theo bit back the laughter. "I'll go look for her."

He retrieved his bow, quiver, and backpack. He opened the creaking door, waved goodbye to Kiki, and went outside. Yellowed grass swayed in the dim light. He shivered and removed a jacket from his backpack.

Something was watching him. He scanned the withered trees as he put on his jacket. A raven sat on a branch. It reminded him of the magpie Boo. The bird hadn't been with Diva, so where could he be? Could he be protecting Kosara and the Firebird? Theo hoped Boo wasn't in trouble, too.

"We should look for Diva," Pavel said.

"Where?" Theo spread his arms around in a circle. "We could get lost out here. Let's go back to the deer and wait for her. She probably wandered off to help an injured animal. I'm sure she'll return there soon enough if she doesn't find us here."

"You're right." Pavel looked around. "I don't want to stick around here where Whirl can't protect me."

The raven took flight, cawing and circling overhead, before it flew away.

In silence, Theo and Pavel hurried back to where they'd left the deer. As they approached the end of the marsh, a gentle melody floated in the air. It wasn't the ringing of the copper bells. Singing accompanied the tune. The boys ran the rest of the way to see who was creating the lovely music.

Theo rubbed his eyes, not sure he was actually seeing what was in front of him. Diva sat under a tree with Sur lying beside her. She strummed a harp's golden strings. Theo blinked and looked again. Diva wasn't holding the harp; it lay between Sur's horns where his amber fireball normally glowed.

"Diva's song is as beautiful as she is." Pavel repeated the word "beautiful" under his breath until Theo nudged him with his elbow.

Diva stopped singing and smiled at them. "Good morning. I hope you both slept well."

"Don't stop." Pavel's eyes glazed over, and he stared at Diva like an adoring puppy. "That's so enchanting, melodic, lovely, beautiful, beautiful, beauti—"

Theo elbowed him again.

"Oh, sorry," Pavel said. "Do you think Whirl can create one of those?"

"It depends." Diva stood, wiped grass from her clothing, and caressed Sur. "You need to get to know your deer better, connect with him, care for him. It takes time. Sur and I have been together for a long time, but we're still learning about each other."

Pavel crept closer and reached out to touch the strings, but they dissolved. In their place the fireball reappeared. It sparked with red, green, and violet lights. Sur rose, huffed, and lowered his horns toward Pavel.

"Sur's sensitive this morning, so you better not tease him, Pavel."

Pavel took a step back. "Maybe he's angry I interrupted your serenade. He's probably jealous of us."

Sur snorted, sounding like laughter. With lights flickering in his eyes, the deer stared at Pavel, as if Sur were saying, "Boy, you don't know anything about me."

Theo rolled his eyes. "What's really bothering him, Diva?"

"The witch." She paced. "She left last night when she thought we were all sleeping. I followed her back here."

"Maybe she was worried about her cat and wanted to find her," Theo said.

"Partly, but she was trying to poison the deer." Diva's eyes turned cold. "I found this." She held up a vial of yellow liquid, which she poured onto the ground. It scorched the grass.

"Whirl!" Pavel ran to his deer, who was grazing a few feet away.

"Your deer's unharmed," Diva said. "Sur kicked the witch before she succeeded, and she escaped in her mortar."

"Why would she do that?" Theo asked.

"Who knows with her?" Diva shrugged. "She's traitorous, always looking to see who'll give her the best deal. Someone must have offered her something better than Zmey's gold."

While Theo thought about what Baba Yaga might be up to, he absent-mindedly reached over and removed a leaf from Diva's hair.

"Spider?" she asked.

He shivered, remembering the insects crawling over him in his nightmare.

"What's the matter?"

Theo told her about seeing Lamia while he slept. "Do you think the dream means anything?"

"I hope not."

"You may think it's crazy. I know I killed her, but she haunts me every day." Theo clenched and unclenched his hands, the memory of that day replaying in his mind. The silver arrow piercing Lamia's third eye. Her ungodly shriek. The dragon heads disintegrating. And … "I never told anyone, but when she died, a black mist flowed out of her and into me. I think the demon Kiki expelled from me was Lamia."

"That's bad." Diva ran her hand along Sur's flank as if it soothed her. "Could Baba Yaga have brought you here to drive the demon out of you and into her cat? But why?"

Pavel came back, leading Whirl. "What's our plan now? Are we going to join up with Mraz and his team to see if they've found where Kosara and the Firebird are?"

"No," Theo said. "I think we have to find Jabalaka. Mraz said he went back into hiding. Perhaps he's at his house in the Cold Marsh. We have to find clues in *Lamia's Bible* about what's going on."

"I agree," Diva said. "Sur and Whirl, thank you for your help. My friends and I have to continue from here alone. Return to the herd. If we need your help again, we'll call you." She stroked the deer's head.

Sur snorted and pawed at the ground.

"I know it's a risk, but we have to take it," she told him.

Pavel's stomach grumbled. "I think maybe I should have tried that slug."

Theo laughed, despite his unease.

Pavel hugged Whirl. "Bye again. I'll miss you."

As the two deer flew away, Theo and Pavel followed Diva, trampling their feet in the soaked grass, until she veered off and followed a path into the marsh.

"Do you remember how to get to Jabalaka's house, Diva," Theo asked.

None of this looked familiar. One path resembled the next. Smelly water. Rotten trees. Mushy, mossy walkways. And the endless slurping, croaking, and twitters of the creatures living there.

"Not exactly, but I know it was on the other side of the marsh." She continued making her way forward without looking back.

No one spoke when the path they followed entered a tunnel of intertwined trees with moss dangling from the branches. This was definitely not the way they had come before. Walking became even more difficult and slow as their feet sank deeper into the swampy path. The tunnel narrowed and darkened from the thick branches surrounding it. After some time, the column of trees ended, and they found themselves facing a fetid pool. The path, if it continued at all, was submerged in the water.

"Now what?" Theo sighed. "Do we turn back and look for another way across?"

"Why don't we try this raft." Behind swamp grass, Pavel uncovered a pile of boards tied to a dilapidated wooden pier.

"That's not a raft." Diva shook her head. "It's a pile of rotten boards that will break at any moment."

"I agree," Theo said. "Do you have another idea, Pavel? Maybe something in your backpack to carry us to the other side?"

"I'm sure it'll work. I'll try it." Pavel took a tentative step onto the raft.

"I wouldn't—" Diva started.

The boards cracked, and Pavel slipped, falling into the murky green water with a shout. Theo and Diva waited for him to resurface, but a moment or two passed without any sign of Pavel.

Theo kneeled by the edge of the water, thrusting his hands through the grime. "Pavel? Pavel? Where are you?"

He didn't feel anything solid.

"Here, try this." Diva handed him a long piece of the broken board.

Theo swirled the piece of board through the water where Pavel had disappeared. A green hand with long claws grabbed the board and tried to pull it away.

"What the …?" Gripping the board, Theo leaned away from the water.

Diva grabbed him around the waist and yanked him from the edge. "Theo, let go of the board. Let it go."

Stunned, he released the board, and he and Diva fell onto their backs on the path.

The water stirred, and a monster covered in green algae surfaced, holding the board. It crept onto the raft and spluttered.

In silence, Theo and Diva shimmied backward toward the tunnel. What had the creature done with Pavel?

The creature shook itself, and green algae fell away. It wiped an arm across its face to remove the slime.

Theo cried out with frantic joy, "Pavel!" and rushed over to the raft to hug his friend. "I thought we lost you when you didn't come up right away."

Pavel looked as terrified as Theo had been the day on the beach when Pavel had pretended to be a sea monster chasing Nia. If Theo hadn't been so scared for his friend's safety, he would have laughed at the karmic payback.

"What happened?" Diva added as she joined the group hug.

"A large … green … ugly creature. I didn't get a close look. Too murky down there." Pavel coughed and spat out greenish water. "I'm glad I was wearing my Rusalka belt."

"When did you put that on?" Theo asked.

"At Kikimora's house, after something tried to pull me under the first time." Pavel crawled farther from the edge of the marsh. "Do you think whatever it was has been following me?"

Diva shook her head. "More likely, it's one of the Vodni. They like shiny things. Do you have something we can use to attract him?"

"Attract him?" Pavel squealed. "I don't want to see it … him again. He wanted to drown me."

"I was thinking he might be able to help us find Jabalaka."

"All right. Let me see." Pavel searched through his backpack and pulled out a couple of flat metal cans. "Hey, I forgot I packed these."

"Canned fish?" Theo wrinkled his nose.

"Well, I'm part of the hiking club," Pavel said. "We have to be prepared whenever we travel. These are on my regular checklist, so I included them."

"You put fish inside metal?" Diva stared at the can as Pavel pulled the tab to open it. "Oh, that smells bad. No offense, but the Vodni eat fresh fish."

"This is for me, not him. I'm still starving." Pavel gobbled the tiny fish. "He can have the can."

"I'm not sure that's the kind of shiny thing he's looking for," Theo said. "Last time, he wanted Diva's barrette. What else do you have in there?"

"Let's see." Pavel moved items around. "How about an emergency road flare? The bright lights are sure to capture his attention."

"A flare." Theo grabbed Pavel's arm. "No way. You'll set the marsh on fire."

"Don't worry. It's an LED one." He shook off Theo's hand and removed a small orange disk and pushed a button on top. The flare lit up like a small alien saucer. Flashing bright lights swirled in a circle, lighting up the darkness.

The water stirred like a whirlpool. From the turmoil came a loud splash, followed by a frenzied shriek. Pavel jumped back, almost dropping the LED flare. A large moss-covered log floated over to the rotten pier. It rose into the air. It wasn't a log. It was a creature with a huge frog-like head covered with algae. The creature appeared mesmerized by the flashing light.

"Lord Vodnik." Diva gave a slight bow with her head. "I should have guessed. I thought maybe it was one of your offspring."

*A Vodnik? He doesn't look anything like the ones we met before.*

Whereas the other Vodni looked like little old men, Lord Vodnik had an amphibian appearance. Swamp slime covered his glowing, bulging eyes and protruding nose and dripped from his long, green catfish-like beard. His bloated face matched his extended belly. Theo could imagine both body parts expanding and contracting like a bullfrog's when the creature belched out croaks.

Lord Vodnik pulled himself up onto the pier with his huge, webbed hands. The curved claws on each paw were a foot long. "Diva Samodiva, it's been too long since I've seen one of your kind."

"Perhaps if you'd been kinder to the Rusalki, they would have let you stay. Then you'd have seen more of my sisters when they visited the water kingdom."

"I hear their current reigning queen isn't much better."

Theo had met the queen of the Rusalki, and he had no wish to ever return there. The monstrous creature had terrified him.

"What brings you—and these strangers—to this part of the Cold Marsh?" Lord Vodnik asked.

"We're looking for Jabalaka," Diva said.

"He's not—"

"No, he'll see us." Theo raised his hand to stop the creature from saying Jabalaka wouldn't see anyone.

When they'd sought him last year, the Vodni had said Jabalaka didn't want any visitors, but he and Diva had bribed one of the creatures to bring them to the man anyway.

"As you wish." Lord Vodnik appeared to shrug. "And what is that marvelous light?" He returned his gaze to the flashing beams.

"That's a warning light." Pavel picked it up, and the light flashed across his face.

"You're the one who escaped my clutches. Most drown." The frog creature's eyes swiveled back and forth as it watched the beams. "Impressive. I must have that in exchange for your life."

Diva stepped in front of Pavel, blocking most of the light.

Lord Vodnik turned his gaze upward to look into her stern eyes.

"Perhaps Pavel will give it to you in exchange for your help." She stepped out of the way and looked at Pavel.

He nodded and held the flair toward Lord Vodnik with trembling fingers. "A gift if you help us find Jabalaka's house."

"Of course." The creature's eyes glowed brighter, and he extended his webbed paws.

"No tricks?" Diva said.

"No tricks." He grabbed the glowing disk. "And do you have other propitiations for me? Some *rakiya*, perhaps? Most people bring me alcohol when they want my protection."

Theo looked again at the creature's bloated belly and believed the Vodnik.

"We're not most people," Diva said. "One special gift is enough."

Lord Vodnik belched. "I tried." Then he disappeared into the dark water.

"Do you think he'll return?" Theo asked.

Diva didn't have time to reply because Lord Vodnik swam back, dragging a familiar face with him. "Here, my youngest son will lead you to Jabalaka's place."

"Sly," Diva said. "You're going to help us find Jabalaka?"

The son looked nothing like the father. Although green like Lord Vodnik, Sly resembled a child-sized little old man with sad, green googly eyes. Theo and Diva had met him before when he and another Vodnik had fought over who would get a barrette for helping them. The other Vodnik had won. Now, it appeared Sly would have the opportunity to help, but again without winning the offered prize.

Sly nodded. He tugged at a wet hemp rope and pulled a small fishing boat with oars to the shore. "Come. Sit here. Me bring you to Master's home."

The three of them settled in the vessel with all their gear. Sly pulled the boat away and swam across the pool of water.

"Good luck. Say hello to Jabalaka from me." Lord Vodnik laughed before he disappeared beneath the water.

# Chapter 9
# River of Memories

THE MOONS, ALREADY MERGED to each other's midpoint, formed two paths of blue and red lights as Theo and his friends traveled deeper into the marsh. Hundreds of glowing eyes followed on either side of the boat as Sly swam with barely a sound. Theo kept such a tight grip on his bow that his fingers tingled. To him, the heads popping in and out of the water felt like spies, ready to report back to Lamia. He had to keep reminding himself he had killed her. Even if it had been her spirit inside him, and he wasn't certain that it was, what damage could she do? Especially now that she was inside a cat.

Whispers grew louder the farther they proceeded into the marsh, unnerving him. And a smell like charcoal wafted on the breeze. Theo clenched and unclenched his fists, wishing he could get out of the boat to stretch his legs—and to stop thinking about the beastly dragon. The ride hadn't been that long, but Sly had meandered so many ways that Theo would never be able to find his way out unaided.

Finally, Sly crept out of the water and tugged the boat snug between tree roots. "We here."

Theo jumped off behind Diva, who was out the moment they touched solid ground. Pavel stayed inside, peering around.

This couldn't be Jabalaka's hideaway. Where was the tree the frog-man had lived in? Only scorched, toppled trees lay scattered in the area.

"Oh no." Diva held a singed fragment of parchment.

Theo surveyed the scene more closely. Devastation ruled the area. A massive tree lay on its side, like a giant overthrown in battle. Its gnarled roots had been burned, and they twisted in the air in a grotesque fashion like creatures trying to escape the jaws of the underworld. What had once been a hidden door in the tree, now lay askew, allowing papers to flutter from inside with each passing breeze, only to settle on the surface of the water like lily pads.

"We're too late." Diva clutched the parchment to her chest.

Theo picked up a piece of paper from the water by the tree. "What are these? Books?"

Diva rushed around, collecting the torn, burned pages scattered on the water. Tears filled her eyes. "Who kills books? Who did this blasphemy? Books hold the memory of our land."

"Where's Jabalaka? Do you think whoever did this got him?" Theo asked. "Jabalaka? Jabalaka?"

The frog-man didn't appear or respond, but the whispering and scrambling within the trees stilled. Glowing eyes circled the area, staying just out of reach.

"Vodni, don't hide. We're friends." Diva spun in a circle, holding out her hands. "We need to find Jabalaka."

"We're not here to harm him," Theo said. "Can you help us?"

Sly tugged on Diva's clothing. "They scared. Me ask. See what they know." He dove into the water.

"I don't blame them. Look at this place. Everything is destroyed." Theo couldn't see where Sly went, but murmurs spread around the area.

Soon Sly popped out of a hole in the giant tree, dragging with him a trembling Vodnik, who was covered in ashes.

"Tell her," Sly said, pointing to Diva. "She help."

Diva crouched to the Vodnik's level and looked him in the eyes. "Do you know what happened here and where Jabalaka is?"

"Take Master, burn house, chop tree. Burn books. Big fire. Hot, so hot. All gone. All gone." The creature shivered. "Scared. Run and hide."

Diva covered her head with her hands. "His entire library is gone, hundreds of books. The history of the village. Our memories."

"Who did that?" Theo asked as he squeezed Diva's shoulder. "Can you tell us, Vodnik?"

"Black … black monsters. Iron scales. Iron helmets have snakes. Carry torches. Water bulls pull carts. Hold iron cells. Eyes glow like coals. Red burning coals." The Vodnik hid his face in his clawed hands as if trying to blot out the memory. "Take Master and friends. Some still here. Escape." He pointed to swamp creatures who had gathered around the massive tree.

"Do you know where they went?" Diva grabbed hold of him. "Do you know why they took him?"

The creature squirmed to get out of her grasp, and she released him. He stared at her with his eyes bulging. "Monsters want book. Look for secret."

"*Lamia's Bible?*" Theo asked.

"Yes, yes. That book." The Vodnik clapped his hands. "Secret in book."

"What secret?" Diva asked.

The creature looked around and backed away, as if ready to hide. He whispered, "*All* secrets."

Flapping wings came from above, and a raven swooped down toward the Vodnik. He shrieked and darted back into the uprooted tree. "Hide. He kill us."

"Wait. Come back. Did they get *Lamia's Bible*, too?" Diva ran to the tree and peered inside. "It's too dark to see anything in there. We have to find him."

Pavel jumped out of the boat and carried a flashlight to Diva. "Try this."

She swayed the light around the interior. "I don't see anyone."

Theo absent-mindedly pulled out his medallion from around his neck and rubbed it. What were they going to do now? They had to find Jabalaka. They had to know what *Lamia's Bible* said.

Sly poked his hand at Theo. "Show me?" He pointed toward the medallion.

"This?" Theo opened his palm to show the Vodnik the seven-pointed star that bore the words "Unborn Hero" on them. He kept a firm grasp on it in case Sly thought it was a "shiny" and grabbed it.

"It okay." Sly smiled and came up to Diva. "Me know. Me can help."

"What do you know?" she asked.

"Where book is."

"How do you know?"

"Master ask me to help. He worried when Firebird and our king gone." Sly tugged on his green hair. "He say, 'They come for me next. You help me hide book, yes?' Me say me help. Only me and him know where book is. Master say, 'When boy with star come, give him book.' He boy with star." Sly pointed at Theo.

"You'll bring us to the book now?" Theo asked.

"Yes, me lead you there." He hopped over to the boat.

The creatures of the swamp scrambled into the trees, all eyes following them as Sly pulled the boat through the water. At last, they left the Cold Marsh and entered a river headed north, toward Cherna Mountain.

"Me ride now. It long way." Sly crawled into the boat, squeezing himself between Theo and Pavel.

"You were part of the rowing club, weren't you, Pavel?" Theo said as he scooted around to face the Vodnik. "So you can take the oars first."

"Gee, thanks, friend." Pavel flexed what little muscle he had.

Theo imagined his friend was trying to impress Diva, but she wasn't paying attention. Still clutching the fragments of books she'd gathered, she stared at the landscape. He ached for her, knowing how he'd feel if every trace of his heritage had been obliterated.

Devastated. Lost. Angry.

Theo looked at her sitting at the back of the boat, her eyes glazed. He started to speak, but stopped. What could he even say besides asking her if she was okay? He knew she wasn't. Telling someone you were sorry about their pain did little to ease it. Later, when she'd had time to process the disaster, he'd be there for her.

He shook his head, wanting to stay focused on their mission. If all of Dragon Village died, then lost books would no longer matter. *Lamia's Bible* must hold the key. They had to find the book.

Time passed with the only sound being the oars sloshing through the water as Pavel rowed. Occasionally, his friend grunted. A sporadic sigh escaped from Diva as well. Sly seemed unaffected by the turmoil going on in the others. The Vodnik trailed his claws in the water, snatching up a bug from time to time and popping it into his mouth. The crunching made Theo's stomach churn. He needed a distraction.

"Sly," Theo said.

The Vodnik glanced up, a startled look on his face as if he'd forgotten where he was. "Yes?"

"Tell me about yourself."

Sly scratched his chin. "What you want to know?"

"What's it like living in a marsh?"

"It wet."

Theo laughed. He was going to have to be more specific. "What do you do when you're not swimming or bringing people to visit Jabalaka?"

"Me take care of cattle. My father, Lord Vodnik, has many black cattle, horses, sheep, pigs."

"They live underwater?"

"No, no," Sly said. "In stone courtyards outside swamp."

"And you feed and groom them?"

The Vodnik nodded. "Graze them in fields at night. Me like them. They kind to me."

"It must get lonely there all by yourself."

"Not lonely. Me read."

"Read?" Theo felt ashamed of himself. He'd thought, from Sly's speech habits, that the Vodnik didn't have any kind of education. But maybe Sly understood a lot more than Theo gave him credit for.

"Yes. Love books. Master teach Sly words. And Sly teach friends." The Vodnik wiggled in his tight spot. "Hide books in tree hollow near field."

Diva sat up straight. "You have books?"

"Yes, yes. Many. Master let me read. Then me return."

A sparkle grew in Diva's eyes. She dropped the crumpled papers onto the bottom of the boat. "Did Jabalaka hide books, too? Besides *Lamia's Bible*?"

Sly's shoulders slumped. "Not know. Sorry."

"That's okay, Sly," Theo said. "But this is good news. Once we restore Dragon Village, we can begin to rebuild the library."

"And me help Master?"

Theo nodded. "Yes, I'm sure Jabalaka would let you assist in the library."

"That's a great idea, Theo," Diva said. "Sly's so helpful, I think he would be good in that position."

Sly jumped around in the boat, rocking it from side to side. He squeezed Theo's hand and reached his webbed paw across Pavel to grasp Diva's hand.

"Hey, keep it down," Pavel said as he leaned to the side. "You'll capsize us all."

"Sorry, sorry." Sly sat back in his spot between Theo and Pavel.

"I like to read, too," Theo said. "My mom told us stories about Dragon Village, but they were nothing like the real place. Did your mother read to you?"

"No, she sing. Beautiful voice. Like croaking frogs and buzzing flies." Sly got a far-away look and hummed a soothing tune as if his mother was singing to him.

Theo smiled at the different notion of what was beautiful, but glad the melody wasn't as harsh sounding as Sly had described it. "Tell me about her, your mother."

"She beautiful." Sly sighed. "Long black hair. Many tangles me can caress and poke claws through. Her hair float like lilies. Cold, cold hands like flowing water. She rub my back until me numb and fall asleep."

Theo found himself humming Sly's tune as he thought about his own mother. He'd been gone for two days. Was she frantic? He hoped Nia had been able to convince their mother that Theo would be okay, even if he was unsure how things would turn out himself.

Sly had stopped speaking. The Vodnik's eyes were wet. "Me miss my mother."

"Me, too. You can go home as soon as we get the book. I promise."

"No, she gone." Sly looked away, trailing his fingers through the water. "No more songs. No more rubs."

"I'm sorry," Theo said, finding himself mimicking the Vodnik's actions. "My mom's still around, but she hasn't been the same since last year when she thought she'd lost Nia and me. She's lost her smile."

"Yes, yes. Mine lose smile. Unhappy here. Lord Vodnik …" Sly looked around as if making sure no one else was listening, then said in a low voice, "He cruel. To family. To animals. Me see him ride horse hard. It foam and fall. Sometimes die. He leave it to rot in reeds."

"Did he hurt your mother? Was she a Rusalka?" Diva had said Lord Vodnik wasn't kind to them.

"No, not mine. Mine Vodianikha, like me." Sly's eyes went wide, and he shivered. "He cruel to human wife." Theo wasn't sure he wanted to know more, but he eventually asked, "And … what did he do to his human wife?"

"Oh, so cruel, so cruel." Sly hid his face in his claws. "She visit mother, and not want to return. He kill their child and leave dead baby on doorstep. When wife come out, he kill her, too, and keep soul in jar."

"I … I'm sorry."

Theo had heard stories about how a Vodnik would float red flowers on the water to attract a human girl. Sometimes, the creature would tie colorful ribbons in willow trees. When the girl came closer, the Vodnik would jump out of the tree and drag her to the water and drown her. Then he'd let her bruised and bloated body drift back to shore. In olden days, the poor girl was left there, without a burial, because people believed the Vodnik was jealous and laid claim even to the dead body.

Theo hadn't realized until his last visit that an even crueler fate awaited some of the Vodnik's victims. One of Sly's friends had tried to drown Theo. If the creature had succeeded, he would have kept Theo's soul in captivity, to be forever a servant. Theo imagined that Lord Vodnik must have jars and jars full of the souls of those he'd drowned. These possessions showed other Vodni how powerful and wealthy he was and earned him their respect. Or at least their fear.

Pavel piped in and asked, "What do you do for fun with friends?"

"Like the one Diva gave the barrette to," Theo added.

"He no friend. He bully." Sly looked as if he was pouting. "Shiny mine. He thief."

"I'm sorry," Theo said. "Bullies have tormented me, too."

Sly gasped. "But you unborn hero. You son of Zmey."

"Where I come from, people don't know that, only my family and Pavel."

Pavel added, "A boy named Stefan in our village thinks he's so smart and cool. He acts like he knows everything. He always picks on the littler kids. He leaves me alone because I have an older brother."

"But I don't," Theo said, "and I didn't have a father to protect me from bullies either. Stefan always makes fun of me because I'm different."

Sly curled into himself. "No one protect me."

"We will. We're your friends." Pavel patted Sly on the shoulder.

"Yes," Theo added. "We'll do what we can to protect you, once we make Dragon Village safe again. Sometimes just acting brave is enough to stop a bully."

"Yah," Pavel added. "Just wait until everyone in Selo knows who Theo really is. Even Stefan will be afraid to bother him."

"Thanks, for always believing in me, Pavel." Theo smiled. "I hope you're right."

"You good friends." Sly's eyes lit up. "Me have friends, too. Swim to mill and ride around wheels. Round, round, round. We jump off. Splash into water."

Theo smiled as the Vodnik moved his hands in a circular motion.

"We swing on willow branches. They touch water and we climb," Sly continued. "And we play like frogs in reeds. Swim in and out. In and out. When tired, like to sleep under wheel in mud. Soft. Cool. Like mother's hug."

"That does sound like fun. Pavel and I live near water, too." Theo thought about the mill where he had met up with Pavel on their first trip to Dragon Village. Was that the one Sly was talking about? It was rather run-down. "Is there a mill near the Cold Marsh?"

"No more. Lord Vodnik destroyed." Sly fell silent again.

From the back of the boat, Diva's said, "Lord Vodnik tore the other one down because he doesn't like anyone to stop water from flowing. He also didn't want any other Vodnik vying for his empire. Each mill has one water master. Lord Vodnik chased the other one away and took control of his servants, wives, and children."

"Was Sly ..."

Diva nodded. So Sly had belonged to the other kingdom. He'd lost his own father and had to do service to his new master, even though he called him father. No wonder he was bullied. Not much different from Theo's own world. Those in power abused the ones they were supposed to protect.

Zmey had been a kind ruler before Lamia stole his kingdom, and he'd put the kingdom back in order again. Theo himself would make things right in Dragon Village if he ever became the ruler people said he would be. The bullying would stop.

"Hold on tight," Pavel yelled.

The boat scraped past a boulder in the middle of the river and spun in circles. Theo clutched the sides. When had the river become so rough? He had been so intent on finding out about Sly's life that he hadn't even helped Pavel with the rowing.

Were his friends okay?

Sly appeared calm, enjoying the rough ride. Of course, he was a water creature. He liked jumping off of the mill wheel. This would be fun for the Vodnik. Diva had braced her feet onto the sides of the boat. While looking alert, she, too, didn't look worried. Pavel clenched the oars so tight his knuckles were white. His arms moved this way and that as he maneuvered the boat to shore.

Water erupted on all sides and splashed over the edge. Theo had trouble holding onto the slippery wood. He slid into Sly, who tumbled toward Pavel. Pavel lost his grip, and the boat plunged toward another boulder. Theo's heart raced. Pavel grabbed the oars again and strained against the current. The boat crunched as it slid past the obstacle. Pavel grunted and swung the tip of the vessel toward shore. With a *thud*, he jammed the boat between the branches of a fallen tree.

"Whew. Glad that's over." Pavel wiped his sleeve across his face.

Sly jumped out. "We here."

# Chapter 10
# Walled-in Bride

WHERE EXACTLY WAS *HERE*? A stone bridge spanned a river so wide that it required three arches. On the other side of the river, the bridge abutted the sheer cliffs of Cherna Mountain, which rose high into the sky. Zmey's castle had been built at the top but wasn't visible from this far down.

Had Jabalaka hidden *Lamia's Bible* in the castle? Time was running out. They had to find the book soon. The two moons were merging so fast.

Sly bounced on his feet as he peered across the raging river and at the stone bridge. "This Kadin Bridge. We need be on other side."

"Let's cross the bridge then," Theo said as he retrieved his gear and scrambled out of the boat.

"Can we rest a little first? My arms ache from rowing, and my legs are tingly." Pavel rubbed his arms.

Diva nodded, and Theo said, "Sounds good to me."

Pavel left the boat, climbed the incline, with Theo, Diva, and Sly following, and plunged like a sack onto the ground by the bridge. He cleared away ivy overgrowing the column, placed his backpack behind his head, and leaned against the wall. Theo and Diva sat on either side of Pavel.

Sly scurried around in a circle. "No like it here. We hurry. Danger."

"Exhausted. We can leave soon." Pavel yawned and mumbled, "I don't see anything. Whatever it is, it can't be worse than Lord Vodnik."

"No, no." Sly stuck his face close to Pavel's. "It bad, real bad. We go."

"We. Go. Soon." Pavel closed his eyes. "Mmmm, Diva. That massage feels good."

She nudged him with her shoulder. "I wasn't touching you. Are you dreaming and talking in your sleep?"

"Uh, Pavel, open your eyes," Theo said, his voice shaky.

Pavel did and screamed. Transparent fingers were gently running through his hair and caressing his cheeks. "Help! Help!" He pulled himself out of the arms and crawled away from the wall.

A shiver ran up Theo's spine, and goosebumps emerged all over his body. A ghostly woman clothed in a white wedding dress and veil, with a wreath of flowers in her hair, emerged from the wall like an enchanting fog. She removed her veil and stared at Pavel with eye sockets like a black void. Her long, albino hair framed her unsmiling face. She stretched out her ghostly hands toward Pavel, her pulsing, marbled veins deprived of light and sustenance.

Theo dug in his backpack for his lightning-bolt knife, ready to defend his friend. The moons shone on the metal, casting a brilliant glow toward the ghost. She backed away from Pavel, covered her face with the veil, and approached Theo.

Heat like a microwave overwhelmed him. The air thickened and bristled with electric, menacing power. It stunned his body, and he barely had the energy to remain standing. He forced himself to move and scurried in front of Pavel like a shield.

"Who are you? What do you want?" Theo asked.

A beam of light lit up the ghost from within, and with a sigh, she said, "I'm Struma, the walled-in bride."

"What do you mean 'walled-in'?" Theo asked, keeping his distance.

She tilted her head slightly to the side, glancing from the boys to the stone columns. "Walled in alive into the bridge, of course."

"What?" Theo and Pavel both shouted.

Diva looked up from her seat by the wall, but her eyes held a distant stare.

The ghostly woman spoke louder. "Built into the bridge."

Theo shook his head. "Sorry, I … we heard you the first time. I … You were literally built into the wall?"

"Yes," she said. "Is this something you no longer do?"

"Of course not. I've never heard about such a barbaric ritual," Pavel said.

Theo asked, "Who did that to you, and why?"

Her ghostly face appeared to pale even more. "My husband, Manol. The master builder. To keep the bridge strong, he sacrificed me."

Pavel added, "Your husband? Why on earth did he do that? I don't understand."

"They had no choice." Struma sighed. "Night after night, these turbulent waters destroyed the progress my husband and his builders achieved on the bridge. They agreed that a human sacrifice was required."

She glided toward the bridge and caressed the stones. "Each morning, we wives brought the men their breakfast. One day, they decided to immure the first wife to arrive the next morning. I left my infant son, my little angel, at home and arrived at the site early, to make sure Manol and his builders were fed and strong to be able to work. But my fate was decided that day forever. I never saw my son again."

"But how does building you into the wall protect the bridge?" Theo asked.

"According to our ancient ritual, my shadow does. When I died, my shadow, my spirit, remained to guard the bridge and keep it strong."

"Some of the older residents of my village sacrifice a rooster when building a house," Theo said. "They claim it protects the site and chases away evil spirits when it crows at dawn. But … but to do this to a *human* is so cruel."

"It was our way," she said. "Nothing else worked. They needed the bridge."

Pavel stepped closer. "Is there something we can do to release you, Struma?"

She uncovered her veil, this time revealing vivid green eyes, not the black void. They brightened with unshed tears as she looked at Pavel.

"No one can help me. I only wish …" She reached out her skeletal hand toward him.

"Yes? Go on," Theo said.

"I've lost a loved one." Phosphorus tears pierced her pale cheeks, dropping like pearls onto the ground. "I'll never see my child, my little boy, and never will have a family and feel the love and warmth of my own home again. No one can help me, no one."

"Maybe we can visit you." Pavel reached for her outstretched hand, but it was only mist.

Diva called out from her seat by the wall. "We'll make sure people, especially children, come here, but right now we're on a mission to save Zmeykovo. We've rested enough and Sly says we need to get to the other side of the bridge."

"Yes, yes, danger here." Shaking, Sly huddled close to Diva.

Pavel narrowed his eyes and crossed his arms. "Struma's not a danger. The poor woman has lost her family and has to guard the bridge for eternity."

"No, no, no. Not her." Sly peeked around Diva, surveying the bridge. "Horseman come. Bad, so bad. Ghost protect bridge. Horseman not let anyone cross."

Struma nodded. "Yes, a Karakonjul guards this bridge. He leaves at the first roosters. To pass, you'll need to go after the second roosters or even the third to be safe."

At the mention of the beast's name, Sly trembled and covered his face.

Theo looked around. "Do you know where he is?"

"No, I haven't seen him for quite some time." Struma floated toward the wall. "He hides until someone steps onto the bridge. Let me look around to see if I can discover his niche." The walled-in bride glided to the river and dissolved into the water like a white fog.

"Do you know what a Karakonjul is, Diva?" Pavel asked.

"He's a shape-shifter, so he could be any animal around us," Diva said. "He's dangerous and lures victims close so he can ride on their backs. He whips them with a stick and digs his nails into their flesh until daybreak. Even worse, he'll throw people from cliffs and trees into deep water or tear them apart between mill wheels."

"What creature isn't dangerous here?" Pavel rubbed his neck. "Even Kikimora has a dark side. I'm sure she's the one who tried to grab me off the path."

"You're probably right, but I don't see or sense anything evil here. I don't think we have to worry about the Karakonjul now." Diva strode toward the bridge entrance and peered inside.

"No, no." Sly scrambled over to her and pulled her back. "No go there. He here. He hide. Me seen him."

Diva shrugged. "Must be Zlo's doing then. I guess we'll have to listen to Struma's advice. To make sure we avoid meeting him, we must wait until the second roosters."

"How do we know when that is? I don't see or hear any roosters here?" Theo scanned the mountain and the fields surrounding them.

"A rooster's crow measures time, like a natural clock, similar to the sun." Pavel smirked as he removed and cleaned his glasses on his shirt. "The time after midnight is divided into first roosters, second roosters, and third roosters. The first rooster crow is soon after midnight, the second at two a.m., and the third just before dawn."

"Okay, got it, but that's a long time to have to wait here, especially when we don't see the creature," Theo said.

Time was running out. They had to find the book, locate and interpret the passage, and rescue everyone before the two moons became one. They'd already used up too much time healing him of his demon and Youdi poison. Now they had to wait again. He stared at the river. Maybe …

"Sly, you said we have to get to the other side of the bridge, right?"

"Yes, book over there." The Vodnik pointed to the far end of the bridge.

"It's on the bridge? And not up the mountain?" That made it a little easier, Theo hoped.

"Yes, yes, hidden in bridge wall. Other side." Sly bounced on his webbed feet. "But we no get it now. Too dangerous."

"Pavel, are you sure we can't use the boat to get to the other side?" Theo asked. "Or maybe we can find a shallower place downstream and wade across."

Pavel walked around the riverbed and studied the water, then shook his head. "The current's too strong, and I don't have ropes to tie us together to keep everyone safe, even if we did find a good spot to cross. The river's probably no safer than meeting the Karakonjul."

"Could we summon the deer?" Theo said hopefully.

This time Diva shook her head. "No, that will get the beast's attention. It's already getting too late to try to make it out of here. It's better to wait until the morning, when the creature's gone. I'm sure we could all use some sleep."

"I'm so nervous I don't know how I can sleep," Theo said.

"I have herbs that can help you rest in minutes." Diva dug through her pouch and handed him a small glass bottle.

Theo recalled the mixture she'd used before to make another being sleep. "No, thank you. I know you have a cure for everything, but I'd rather stay alert."

"Okay." Diva turned on her heels, removed the bow from her shoulder, and lay on the mossy grass near the wall, with Sly huddled close to her.

Pavel sorted through his backpack and pulled out a jacket, which he wrapped around his shoulders. He curled up next to the masonry wall. The misty hands of the walled-in bride once again patted his hair and cheeks, but this time he didn't scream.

Theo paced a while. A baby's muffled cry came from within the bridge. He shook his head. That had to be his imagination after the story Struma had told them. He examined the strong stone walls of the bridge, thinking about the young builder Manol and how he had sacrificed his wife. Would Theo have done that? Or would he have tried to find another way to save those he loved?

Dragon Village wasn't the magical, fantastic place he had once imagined from the stories his mother told him. Even before Lamia, and now Zlo, had wrought their terror here, injustice existed the same as in the human world. Sly and other Vodni were bullied. Kikimora's husband had abandoned her. The walled-in bride was murdered for a belief in an ancient ritual.

How did Zmey manage to run his kingdom so that his people adored him? At least the ones who weren't evil. What other secrets and terrors did the lives of those in Dragon Village hold? What else had so many people had to sacrifice for safety?

*Lamia's Bible* held all these secrets. Would having that knowledge give Theo the opportunity to right wrongs? Or would the power of it corrupt him? Perhaps this was where Lamia had gone wrong. Theo was certain she couldn't have always been evil. When he'd seen her lying, dead, on the castle floor, she had reverted to a beautiful young woman with golden hair, not even half-dragon. Her countenance was peaceful, as if she'd never had a care to mar her appearance. What had happened that she became so filled with hate and anger? Theo's father could tell him, but Zmey was locked away somewhere.

Theo walked along the river's edge, turning right and left, until the cool evening air relaxed him. He entangled his fingers in weeping willow branches that swayed along the bank. The night was so peaceful. After a while, he returned to the bridge and lay close to his friends. Tomorrow would be soon enough to worry again. He closed his eyes and fell into a deep sleep.

# Chapter 11
## A Bridge to Cross

*TAP, TAP, TAP.*

Theo opened his eyes to Diva standing over him, poking him with the tip of her bow. She did the same to Pavel.

"Get up. Eat. It's already five o'clock." She walked briskly to the riverbank to wash her face.

Pavel stretched and yawned. He ran his fingers through his hair and then put on his glasses. "I dreamed I was at home and Mom made a whole bunch of warm pancakes."

"Lucky you. Too bad it was only a dream." Theo handed him nuts and berries lying on top of Diva's pouch. "For now, you'll be satisfied with what Diva left us. Or eat your canned food, unless you want to catch fresh fish."

Pavel refused the offered food. "Let me see …" He opened his backpack and pulled out a packet of chocolate cookies.

"You're full of surprises, aren't you?" Theo's stomach grumbled. "Can I have one, please?"

"I guess. I don't have many." Pavel handed over the box with reluctance.

"What's that?" Diva asked as she strolled up from the river.

"Cookies." Pavel twisted around to hold the box out to her. "Do you want one? They're good and give you energy."

She lifted one from its slot, sniffed it like a dog, and crinkled her nose. "That smells … odd. Nothing from Zmeykovo has that odor. Not as bad as your canned fish, but still strange. And it looks like fossilized animal feces." She raised her arm to throw it.

"Wait," Pavel shouted. "It's good. You have to taste it. It's sweet and chewy and … and … Well, just a little taste, please?"

"Oh, all right." She licked the edge of the cookie with the tip of her tongue. Frowning, she turned the cookie all around, then threw it into the river. "I'll stick with fruit if I want something sweet."

Pavel opened his mouth, but Theo shook his head at his friend. Pavel bit his lip and looked toward the river.

Theo stood and stretched his legs. "How do you know the third roosters have passed. It's been mostly dark since we got here."

"It's my land. I just know." Diva glanced around. "It'll stay overcast until we find the Firebird and bring him back to the holy tree. Are you ready? Where's Sly?"

"Here." The Vodnik appeared, huddled behind Theo's backpack.

"We're ready to find *Lamia's Bible*." Diva strode toward the bridge entrance.

The rest of them followed her up the path. Theo's sneakers slid on the cobblestones, worn by water and weather. At the top, Pavel waved to the walled-in bride, who waved back sadly, like a mother sending a son on a long, dangerous journey.

Theo looked inside the bridge. Along both sides ran two rough stone railings, no higher than three feet, covered with green moss and grass. The floorboards looked worn by time, but had no gaping holes.

"You ready to lead the way, Sly?" he asked.

The Vodnik's eyes opened wider than normal. "Scared."

Diva gave him a gentle nudge. "We have to cross the bridge. The Karakonjul is only one, and we're a group. We'll be okay."

Sly took a small step forward, placing one webbed foot onto the bridge.

"Wait." Theo put his hand on Sly to hold him back. "I think I hear a galloping horse."

Pavel scanned the area. "I don't see or hear anything. Do you, Diva?"

"Shh …I think Theo's right." She kneeled and put her ear on the stones.

A clatter of hooves in the distance made them all turn to look. A rider galloped toward them along the path. Sly scrambled away, quivering as he half-hid behind Diva.

"It's a man on a horse," Pavel said.

Moments later, as the rider approached at a swift pace, Theo said, "I don't think that's a man on a horse. He's … a horse-man."

"I thought he wasn't supposed to appear after the third roosters." Pavel ducked behind Theo. "What are we going to do?"

"Let's try to talk with him first." Diva prepared her bow and arrow for a fight. "But be ready to defend yourselves."

The Karakonjul came to an abrupt stop in front of the group and pointed a wooden spear toward them. The smell of dung clung to him. The lower part of his body was a gray horse, while the upper resembled a hairy man. The creature had a large head from which four bull horns sprouted. The horse's tail was covered with sharp silver dragon scales, its tip an arrow-shaped blade. Tousled hair covered his head, and in the middle of his face sat a single red eye, mesmerizing them with its angry expression. It was obvious he hadn't come for sweet talk and dating.

"I'm Bor Stobor. This bridge and the land around it are my territory." His thunderous voice shook even the bridge. "Who are you, and why are you here?"

Diva made a slight bow, while still clutching the bow. "I'm Diva Samodiva. These are my friends, Theo, Pavel, and Sly. We come with good intentions and in peace. We need to cross the bridge to help save Zmeykovo and our king, Zmey. We won't linger or do mischief."

"A Samodiva?" He circled her, swishing his tail. "I haven't seen one of your kind for a long time. I have debts to repay them."

Diva smiled and held out her hand. "Really? I'm glad our destinies crossed paths."

"So am I." He grabbed her hand with his big hairy paw, pulling her close, growling. "Because of them, I lost everything. They ruined my life, so you'll pay for everyone."

Diva's smile disappeared, and she struggled to pull away, but Bor Stobor held her tight. He pulled her up onto his horse's back and sped toward the forest. Diva's bow clattered to the ground.

"Stop. Come back," Pavel shouted and ran after the creature.

A burning sensation gripped Theo's chest, and he doubled over. His pulse raced, and his heart pounded. He had to stop Bor Stobor, but the creature had almost disappeared into the forest.

*Concentrate. You can do this*, he told himself.

His muscles quivered, his bones cracked, and his breaths came out hot. Pain radiated through his entire body. The bumps under his arms swelled so quickly he barely saw his red wings unfolding. The pain receded and power surged through him. He spread his wings and raced after the Karakonjul. As soon as he lifted a foot from the ground, the wind sped him toward the clouds. The air embraced him. Below him, the earth receded until Pavel and Sly looked like toys.

With a few flaps of his wings, Theo rose higher. Bor Stobor galloped beneath him. The Karakonjul had passed through the forest and was headed toward a lake. Theo had to stop him before the creature drowned Diva.

*What do I do now to go down?*

Flapping his wings only made Theo go higher. He pulled his arms and legs into his body and plunged through the clouds. The wind tickled his ears and made his eyes water. The speed of his descent increased, and he soon caught up with Diva and the monster. Theo spread his wings and flew parallel to Bor Stobor. The creature galloped faster, trying to outrace Theo.

*"Diva,"* Theo shouted, although the words seemed to come from his mind. *"Are you okay?"*

"Yes." She pummeled the beast with her free hand. "Fire. He's afraid of fire."

How could he start a fire without matches? Even if he managed, the wind would blow them out as soon as he lit them.

Bor Stobor thrust his spear at Theo, interrupting his thoughts. The weapon struck Theo on his wing and he roared. Flames shot out of his mouth.

*Fire. I can breathe fire?*

Stunned at the new development, Theo slowed his flight, and the Karakonjul raced ahead.

"Theo!" Diva's shout became faint.

Bor Stobor had almost reached the lake. Theo had to hurry and get the Karakonjul away from the water. He put all his energy into reaching Diva in time. Flying as fast as his wings enabled him, Theo soared into the sky over the lake, before reversing direction and plummeting toward Bor Stobor.

Fire. She'd said the creature feared fire. Theo's insides burned with rage.

"*Let. Her. Go!*" He took a deep breath and exhaled with all his might.

The lake water steamed and fizzled in front of the creature. Bor Stobor jumped to the side.

Diva took advantage of his loss of concentration and wrenched her arm loose. Free of his restraint, she pulled an arrow from her quiver and plunged it into his side. It broke on his tough skin, and the enraged beast galloped faster, roaring like a raging bull.

"*I'm coming, Diva.*" Theo flew after the creature and snatched Diva from Bor Stobor's back.

The beast twisted his human body backward and jabbed at Diva with his spear, but Theo struck the Karakonjul with his powerful serpent's tail.

*Tail? I grew a tail this time?*

Momentarily stunned again, he lost track of where Bor Stobor had gone. Theo flapped his wings and flew like a hawk to the heights.

*"Diva, are you okay?"*

He wasn't sure if it was her body or his that was shaking when she nodded. He pulled her closer to him, hugging her tight to his chest as he carried her to where Pavel stared upward, his face pale, his mouth wide open, and his eyes bulging.

Theo landed and set Diva down. She wobbled a bit on unsteady legs. Her pale face had flushed, and her curls were in a disarray. Even so, she smiled at him. "Thank you so much for saving me."

Theo's body turned warm and made cracking noises. His wings shrank until all that remained were the bumps beneath his arms.

Sly jumped out of a bush he'd been hiding in and bowed to Theo. "My King, my King."

Theo examined his shaking body, touching his warm face, his arms, his legs. He poked a finger into his mouth and felt only his tongue. Everything was normal. He had regained his human appearance. It had all happened so fast, it felt like watching a movie. "Was I dreaming? Did I really …?"

"Yes, you one hundred percent just became a dragon." Pavel walked around Theo, touching his arms, his face. "You were so cool, magnificent. How did you do that? Show me again? Can you give me a ride? I want to fly with my dragon friend."

"Stop. You're giving me a headache." Theo clutched his head in his hands. "I can't … I don't know. It just happened. I guess I wanted to help Diva. I felt great danger and anger and the transformation began."

"Can you burn this tree?" Pavel pointed to one near the bridge. "I want to see you breathe fire again."

"I can't," Theo shouted.

"C'mon, try." Pavel begged. "Just open your mouth and blow."

"I'll try, just for you, if you stop pestering me."

Theo wanted to know himself if he still had that ability while in human form. It was exciting and terrifying, but if he didn't try again now, he might not have the nerve later. Or worse, he could breathe fire unintentionally and hurt someone.

"I will. I will. Please." Pavel put his hands together as if praying and stared at Theo with wide eyes.

Theo inhaled through his nose. He held it for a few moments, then opened his mouth and exhaled as hard as he could.

No fire.

Disappointment and relief filled Theo. "Sorry, Pavel. You'll have to start our campfire with sticks and flint."

"Horse pucky. Why can't things like that happen to me?" Pavel waved his hands as if trying to fly. "I have to always rely on science, not magic."

"It'll take time to learn to control yourself and your abilities." Diva squeezed Theo's shoulder. "I still have problems sometimes when I change. The gift is given to do good, and today you used it to save me. Don't ask yourself how. You'll learn. Listen to your intuition. Everything has a purpose and time."

"I'll call you Dracosam or maybe Dracoville," Pavel said.

"I like that," Diva added. "Dracoville, the Red Dragon."

It all felt strange and unreal. Theo wished he had more control over his powers, wished his father was here to teach him. They had to continue their quest, so he could make that possible.

"Do you think it's safe to cross the bridge now?" he asked.

Diva nodded. "After what we did to Bor Stobor, I doubt we'll see him here again. Even if he seeks assistance from Zlo, by the time he gets help, we'll be gone. Let's hurry."

Theo turned to Sly. "Lead the way, please."

"Yes, my King, my King."

"I'm not a king."

"Yes, yes, you be king. You dragon king. Great red dragon." Sly bounced on his webbed feet around Theo. "Master say dragon will save our land."

Theo ignored him and walked with Pavel and Diva to the other end of the bridge. Sly stalked after him, continuing to mutter, "My King, my King."

"Where to now, Sly?" Theo asked. "Where's *Lamia's Bible* hidden? To the left or to the right of the bridge?"

"Left, left. Left, for sure." The Vodnik pointed to the right with his sharp green claw.

Theo groaned. "Great, it looks like our guide doesn't know the difference between right and left."

"Sorry, my King. Me confused." He bowed and scratched his chin, pulling at a few long hairs. "Book this way, in wall under bridge."

Theo followed the Vodnik to the outside of the bridge. Sly chattered to himself as he paced along the masonry wall. After half an hour, he stopped, rose on his webbed toes, and pointed to a stone block. "Here. Master put book here."

Theo examined the wall, feeling the stone with his fingers. In one spot, the lime was softer and whiter. He scratched at it with his fingers, but only managed to crack his nails.

"How am I going to get the stone out?"

"You hold me?" Sly asked. "Me have sharp claws."

Theo looked at Sly's claws. They curved to a point. "I think something straight would work better, to get deeper into the mortar."

He removed his backpack and checked what he had. He pulled out the metal spindle from Kikimora. "This might work." He scraped away the mortar. After a few minutes, he pulled out the stone, reached into the niche, and felt around with his fingers.

Pavel poked his head around the bridge. "Did you find the book?"

Theo felt a sharp pain. He cried out and pulled his hand from the hole. Droplets of blood pooled on his palm. As he wiped them away, a black snake crawled out of the niche, slithered down the wall, and curled itself on the rocks.

"No, it's empty, except for that snake." Theo shook his hand, keeping his eyes on the reptile. A coldness slid through his veins, and black lines spread out from the bite marks. "Ow, this really hurts." He waved his hand up and down and jumped from one foot to another.

Diva was at his side by the wall in no time. She removed a small green glass bottle from her leather pouch. "Quick, give me your hand. I have an antidote."

Diva grabbed his hand, not waiting for him to agree, and smeared the liquid into the wound. "Lie down to minimize movement to avoid having the poison spread faster into your bloodstream."

Theo did as he was told. Diva put his backpack next to him, and he rested his head on it.

Sweat ran down his back, his skin bristling. Veins and muscles under his arms pulsed. The ground beneath him felt as if it was sinking, and the sky became fuzzy. He couldn't move. He trusted Diva to heal him. She'd done it before. It was her gift.

"Good. Now keep your palm at your side. If you hold it higher, the venom will enter your body faster and farther."

Pavel pulled a container from his backpack. "Do you want me to get cold water from the river?"

"No, cold will intensify the pain." She wrapped a small cotton fabric as a bandage over the bite. "Rest now. The antidote will remove the poison from your body, and you'll be fine in an hour or two."

Pavel took a flashlight out of his backpack and shone it inside the niche. "It's empty, all right. Someone's playing games with us. They stole the book but left behind a snake."

Diva and Pavel turned their heads to Sly, who crept behind a bush.

# Chapter 12
# Witness

SIGHING, THEO RESTED his chin on both hands as he stared at the fire. The warmth felt good after the coldness of the poison that had slithered through his veins. His friends were away, Pavel collecting more firewood and Diva sitting by the river's edge. Only Sly remained, and the Vodnik sat mesmerized by the bright, flashing flames. Theo leaned closer to the fire until sparks danced near his fingertips. The flames attracted him like a magnet. He kept replaying in his mind what had happened after he had recovered from the snake's poison.

Pavel had thought it would be funny to ask Theo to light their campfire. "Try again. Breathe life into our fire." Pavel had laughed.

But Pavel wasn't laughing when he looked in his backpack for his matches, and they were gone. Only his flint remained. Later, they'd discovered that Sly had taken the matches when they caught the Vodnik striking them against the bridge stone wall. It was a "shiny" for him to enjoy. After Pavel had lit the fire, he told Sly he could have the shiny if he let Pavel use them when he needed to start another fire. It was easier than having to resort to the flint.

That episode wasn't what troubled Theo so much. It was being distraught over what had happened to *Lamia's Bible*. Poor Sly. The Vodnik had trembled, hiding in a bush, thinking they blamed him for playing a trick on them, for hiding the book. The shiny helped make him feel more at ease.

"Sly, are you sure you don't know who might have followed you when you went to hide the book?" Theo asked.

Sly took his eyes away from the flames and shook his head so hard his green whiskers swished like reeds disturbed by a swimming fish. "My King, me no see anyone. Only Master and me know plan. Me not share. Master silent like grave, too. Me sorry."

"It's okay. It's not your fault." Theo scuffed his sneakers in the dirt. "How will we learn Zlo's plan if we don't have the book? Who could have stolen it? We need a miracle to help us."

Pavel appeared with a handful of wood in his arms. He dropped it by the fire. "Instead of a miracle, how about a witness?"

"This place is deserted." Theo gestured in all directions. "Unless Bor Stobor wants to come back and tell us, but that's unlikely."

"You're forgetting someone."

"Who?" Theo asked.

Pavel rolled his arms in a theatrical way and bowed. "Will our mystery guest sign in, please."

Next to Pavel, the walled-in bride materialized. "I saw everything."

Theo jumped up from the ground. "You're the witness? What did you see?"

"The bridge is my home. I know who passes, when they come near, and what they do while here. I don't keep a diary of everything, of course, but I have a good memory." She looked at Sly. "I remember you and that fat man with the plaid coat coming here and leaving something, a book, I think, in the niche."

This wasn't what Theo wanted to know. "But did you see who took the book after that?"

"Yes," Struma said. "As soon as Sly and the fat man left, an old woman … well, she had young skin, but she appeared old in every other way … She came flying in an old flask—"

Theo shouted, "Traitor, thirsty for gold."

At the same time, Pavel grumbled, "Baba Yaga, that old hag."

"Grandma who?" Struma asked.

"Sorry," Pavel said, "That's the old witch."

Theo motioned to Struma. "Please continue your story."

"The old woman spun around, sniffed the stones with her ugly nose, and finally pulled out the correct one with her sharp claws."

Struma demonstrated each action, putting a smile on Theo's face. He understood how lonely the woman must be, and how little opportunity she had to entertain guests. Now that they knew who had stolen the book, they could make plans to get it back. They needed to hurry, but a few more moments being kind wouldn't hurt them.

"The thief put the book into a large tattered purple bag and shoved something else inside the niche." Struma cast mournful eyes at Theo. "I didn't see what it was, only that it was black. If I had, I could have warned you not to put your hand in there. I didn't realize you were looking for the book."

"You're not to blame," Theo said. "I should have looked inside before I put my hand in there."

Struma nodded in silent acknowledgment. "Then the grandmother replaced the stone, tucked her skeleton body into the old jug, and flew away with crazy laughter, waving her broom in the air."

"Thank you, Struma. You don't know how valuable this information is." Theo turned to Pavel. "Will you go get Diva and tell her what we've learned? We need to discuss what to do next."

"Sure thing." Pavel ran to the river and soon returned with Diva.

A spark had returned to her eyes. Theo recognized her desire to enforce justice. She had the same look of determination after she'd changed into a hawk and destroyed Lamia's third soul, a dove. There was no stopping Diva now from doing her part to end this latest threat. Baba Yaga's deceit, as terrible as it had been, had done the trick to bringing Diva out of her melancholy state.

"We won't let her get away with this." Diva clenched her bow as she walked in circles. "This is her home, too. Why would she do something that could cause permanent damage? She must know she can't trust Zlo. He's even more deceitful than she is."

"What are we going to do to her?" Pavel asked. "How will we get the book back?"

"I know what I'd like to do to her." Theo would lock her away for good, so she couldn't cause any more trouble. The castle cell Lamia had kept the Samodivi in would do nicely.

Diva stopped walking. "We'll have to surprise her, because the old woman is insidious and cunning. If we're lucky, the book will be in her hut."

"We have to do something fast." Theo pointed to the sky where the two moons were crescents, surrounding what looked like a black dragon eye. "Time's running out."

"Diva, can we summon Sur and our deer to bring us to Baba Yaga's house?" Pavel asked.

"That's a good idea …" Diva fell silent and put a finger to her lips. She kneeled close to the fire and pressed her ear to the ground. "I hear a horse."

Sly shrieked. "Bor Stobor come back?"

"No, it's not him," Diva replied. "I hear the clatter of two or three horses."

Theo had heard the sound, too, moments before Diva had shushed them. He rubbed his temple. Had the poison—or even the antidote—done something to his inner ear, making him hear faraway sounds? He'd worry about that later. For now, they had to be cautious.

"Do you think it's someone else looking for the book?"

Diva shrugged. "Possibly."

Pavel wrung his hands and glanced around. "We better hide until we make sure, but where is it safe?"

Diva kicked dirt over the flames. "Pavel, quickly, get branches so we can scatter and cover the ashes." She picked up loose kindling and handed them to Theo. "Scatter these away from the area. And, Sly, can you hide the boat?"

The Vodnik nodded and scampered away. When everyone had performed their tasks, the area looked as it had when they'd arrived.

"Now, where can we hide?" Pavel asked.

The walled-in bride appeared, holding a lit torch. "I know a safe place, the carpenters' room." She pointed toward a triangular ledge jutting out from the closest column. Above it gaped an arched opening. Ivy-covered rocks surrounded the column. At the base was a barely visible metal door.

Theo led the group to the column and tugged on the metal latch. The door creaked open. The walled-in bride placed the torch in a sconce by the door.

The musty room was slightly larger than the bed that occupied it. By the back wall, a metal ladder led to the opening at the top of the column. A stream of light crept through the gap. Theo climbed to an even smaller upper room. He sneezed from the disturbed dust.

"Theo, what do you see?" Pavel asked from below.

"Nothing yet."

"I'm coming up," Diva said.

"There's not enough room for two."

The clomping of horses came closer. Now, it was easier to tell it wasn't Bor Stobor, because the clatter of wheels traveling over the stone path joined the mix. Instead of crossing the bridge, the horses must have stopped at its entrance, still out of Theo's view. Loud female voices screeched as if arguing, then the horses trotted away from the bridge closer to where Theo hid.

Two horses pulled what looked like a pioneer's wagon from the Wild West era. The tattered brown hide covering the top flapped with the motion, and the wooden-spoked wheels wobbled as if ready to fall off. The horses pulled the wagon to the riverbank and stopped downstream from where the fire had blazed.

Two women stepped out. The first one was dressed in a dark purple cloak with a hood shielding her face. She hobbled away, leaning on a snakelike black cane. Next, a brunette emerged. She had the beauty of the Samodivi, but her sour expression marred her looks.

Theo pressed his lips into a tight line and mumbled, "Oh, no. Not them again."

"What's happening? Who is it?" Diva whispered, peering into the room from the top of the ladder.

"It's the Youdi." Theo climbed down after Diva and joined Pavel and Sly. "They're sniffing around the river like dogs. I'm glad we covered up traces of the fire."

"They find us here?" Sly hid under the bed.

Struma kneeled beside it and peered at the Vodnik. "You're safe here, little one. I've locked the door, and they can't damage the thick walls. Remember, I protect the bridge and everything within it. No one can enter or get out unless I desire it."

Sly crept out from beneath the bed but sat on its edge with his back against the wall.

Struma addressed the others. "I can also tell you what they're doing. I see through the stones." She disappeared into the wall.

"I'll keep an eye on them from upstairs." Theo climbed into the small room again.

"I'm coming, too." Diva scrambled up the rungs after him.

"Fine. I'll stay here and keep Sly company," Pavel muttered from below.

Theo and Diva lay squashed close to each other on the stone floor. Hidden in the darkness of the room, they rested their chins on their elbows and peeked out the opening at the two squabbling

Youdi. Theo wondered what had happened to the third one, the blonde, usually traveling with them. And why were they riding in a run-down wagon instead of their wolf-driven bone carriage?

The brunette said to the other Youda, "Stana, where did you put the horse food?"

"Where else?" The older woman snarled and waved her cane. She briefly moved aside the hood of her cloak, revealing her gnarled face. "Do I look as if I have deep pockets? The grain sack is inside the wagon, of course."

The younger Youda huffed and walked toward the wagon.

"Unharness them first," Stana yelled as she sat on a rock. "You should feed me before the animals, but the horses are tired to death, and we won't make it to the fortress without them. Oh, also make sure you bring the horses—nasty animals that they are— down to the river to drink. And toss in a morsel to our guest in the cage. Be careful not to let it escape. Baba Yaga did give it to us for free, after all, and I might miss the little creature." The old Youda cackled. "After that, start a fire and make me my dinner and drink."

Grumbling, "Old witch makes me do everything," the younger Youda stalked to the wagon and went inside.

Theo looked back at Stana, expecting the "old witch" to lash out at the comment, but she remained seated on a rock as if she hadn't heard.

Inside the wagon, pans clanged, and a creature let out a muffled screech, as if being restrained. Soon, the brunette returned, muttering and cursing, carrying a large purple velvet bag on her shoulder.

Stana shouted, "What are you doing, stupid?"

The younger Youda jumped and tightened her grip on the bag. "Going to feed the horses as you told me."

"Not with what's in *that* bag. Does that feel like grain to you?" With a groan, Stana pushed herself up from the rock, marched over, and slapped the brunette's face. "That's not the one I told you to take. As you become older, you get more stupid. Feel the bag."

The younger Youda hesitated.

"Go on," Stana yelled. "Do it."

The brunette lifted her free hand and felt the bag. Her eyes opened wide, and her mouth fell slack. "Is this …?"

"Yes, the book for Lord Zlo." Stana slapped her companion on both cheeks this time. "We paid so much gold and jewels for this book. You have to protect it with your life. If we mess up again, Lord Zlo will burn us both alive or torture us the way he did our sister."

The Youda trembled but remained silent. Theo shivered, too. That explained why the blonde was absent and why they traveled in a rickety wagon. The blonde Youda had been the one who commanded the wolves. Without her, Theo doubted the animals would obey the other Youdi, even Stana.

"Move! Move!" Stana yelled. "Don't look at me like that. We must hurry to get the book to Lord Zlo before the ceremony at midnight tomorrow. He has the Firebird and that stupid cat. Now his soldiers are all over the village, hunting to capture Zmey's son. The final ingredient."

*Ingredient? What does she mean?* To Theo, it sounded like a potion. Perhaps it was. They had to find a way to get the book away from the Youdi. Did Zlo have Kosara, too? Why hadn't the Youdi mentioned her?

The younger Youda staggered and returned the velvet bag to the wagon and soon showed up with a burlap one that she dropped by the horses.

Inside their hiding place, Diva scowled. "So, the nasty witches have *Lamia's Bible*."

"I heard, but how do we take it from them?" Theo whispered.

"I have an idea." Diva went down the ladder to the room below where Pavel was pacing.

"What did you learn?" he asked.

"We have good and bad news," Diva said.

"Better just say we have only bad news," Theo corrected when he jumped to the floor next to Diva. Dust and smoke from the torch made him cough. "The Youdi have *Lamia's Bible*. Baba Yaga must have sold it to them."

"Yes, that's the bad news, but the good news is I have a plan to get it back." Diva picked up her pouch and pulled a rose-colored glass vial from it.

"Is that magic powder to change them into rats?" Pavel asked.

"No, it's a sleeping herb. We'll steal back *Lamia's Bible* after I drug them."

Theo recalled how they'd tricked another monster into drinking a sleeping potion by putting the mixture inside a piece of fruit, but he doubted that would work with the Youdi.

"From what I can see, they'll sleep here tonight," Diva continued. "After they eat, they love to drink mead, a mixture of wine and honey. I'll put the herb in their drinks and voila."

"And how will we get it into their drinks?" Pavel shook his head. "The witches will see us if we approach their campsite."

"We need some sort of distraction," Theo said.

"I can do it." The walled-in bride appeared from the stones. "Over the years, I've developed many surprises for late-night guests. I'll give them a light show." She smiled and lowered a colorful veil over her face. "When you're ready, give me a signal. They've already put a cauldron of red wine and honey over the fire."

"I'm ready now."

Diva spun three times, and a multicolored waterfall of light covered her before she transformed into a hawk holding the vial in her beak. She flew into the upper room, with Theo following, hoping everything went as planned. Diva glided through the opening and landed on the triangular rock jutting from the column.

Below them, the walled-in bride separated from the bridge. Her body became a plethora of lights. The vision approached the Youdi and danced in a circle, golden, red, and violet rays rising like a fountain toward the black sky.

Youda Stana jumped and shouted, "What is that?"

"I don't know, but it's beautiful," the brunette said. "It's not Lord Zlo, is it?"

"Don't be stupid." Stana slapped her for the third time. "Why would he change into a woman dancer to entertain us?"

While the Youdi gawked at the walled-in bride, Diva flew from the alcove and dumped the sleeping potion herb into the mead cauldron, and then hurried back to where Theo waited.

The walled-in bride danced a while longer before she let her lights fade. In the darkness, the glow from the fire outlined the two Youdi, who sat motionless.

Finally, Stana grabbed her cane and waved it toward her companion. "Pour me some mead. Actually, give me a double dose tonight, too many surprises."

The younger Youda jumped up and returned with two cups. She reached into the cauldron with a ladle and poured the thick liquid into the vessels. After no more than half an hour, the two Youdi were snoring, lying on the grass by the fire.

"I'm going to get *Lamia's Bible*."

"Maybe I should go," Diva said.

"No, this is something I have to do," Theo insisted, and Diva shrugged, but nodded.

If somehow saving Dragon Village yet again rested with him, Theo wanted to do something brave. Who knew what other trouble they'd run into later? He could do this. He *would* do this.

Theo climbed down from the upper room, unlocked the door, and left the hidden chamber. He crept toward the wagon to look for the bag with *Lamia's Bible*. While rummaging through the Youdi's belongings, he bumped into a covered cage. A muffled "Waak" came from within.

"That can't be …" Theo slid off the cage covering. "Boo, it *is* you."

The magpie flapped his wings and knocked his beak against the cage bars, trying to dislodge the band that bound him from making noise.

Theo released his little friend and removed the binding. "I'm so glad I found you."

Boo let out a loud, raucous "Waak" and hopped onto Theo's shoulder for a moment before flying off.

"Shh, for now, please. You don't want to give us away." Theo found the purple velvet bag and jumped off of the wagon. He ran back to the dim room where everyone waited.

"You found Boo." Pavel gave the bird a pat.

"Yes, the Youdi had him. I got the book, too." Theo held up the bag. "But let's hurry and get out of here."

"I agree. The herb works only for ten to twenty minutes," Diva said as she handed Theo his possessions. "We have to leave before the witches wake up."

"You can escape and reach the field quicker through a hidden tunnel." Struma went to a corner of the room and lifted a wooden cover from the floor. Boo fled down the tunnel in a black whirl.

"You know so many secrets about this place, Struma," Pavel said.

"How can I not know? This has been my home, my prison, for so long." Sadness darkened her face. "I wish you success in your mission." Struma retrieved the torch from the wall and handed it to Pavel. She then stretched out her ghostly hands and caressed his face one more time.

Pavel wiped away a tear that rolled down his cheek. "We'll come back when we can."

"Me stay here," Sly said. "Me return home when witches gone. Me say goodbye to my new dear friends."

"Thank you for your help," Theo shook the Vodnik's web paw. "I'm sure we'll meet again."

Theo, Diva, and Pavel said a final goodbye to Sly and Struma and dove into the darkness of the tunnel.

# Chapter 13
# Puppy Love

THEO HUNCHED HIS SHOULDERS and crouched as he entered the narrow tunnel, which was no higher than five feet. He initially thought it was a naturally occurring cave, but as he passed wooden columns supporting the walls, he decided the builders must have carved it out of solid white rock.

*It must have taken them ages to create this.* Tunnels like this in the human world were used as escape routes. It made him wonder what type of invasion those living in Dragon Village may have experienced in the past. Or maybe they had used it as a mine for material to build the bridge. That made more sense. This one reminded him of a mine near Selo that he visited with his history class. It had a timber roof support but was much wider and more open.

An engraving on one of the columns caught his attention. "Hey, Pavel, can you bring the torch closer?"

Pavel crept backward to where Theo was and held the torch close to the column. The flickering light displayed a heart with

"M" and "S" initials carved inside. Theo reached his hand toward the letters.

"Don't touch the walls," Diva shouted from behind them. "Spiders and other surprises hide in the cracks." When she reached them, she looked where Theo pointed. "I guess it's for Manol and Struma."

"He must have loved her a lot," Theo said. "It makes no sense why he sacrificed his bride to make the bridge stronger. I don't think I could do that to a person I loved."

Diva shrugged. "Sometimes people have to make hard decisions, allow terrible things to happen. It might be out of their control. Maybe this was one of those times. We don't know the entire story."

"Can we get going now?" Pavel asked. "I'd like to make it out of here so we can stand up straight again."

"Lead on," Theo said.

*I wonder where Boo is?* Theo scanned the dark passage, but couldn't see beyond the flicker of the torch Pavel carried.

The bird must have flown ahead, perhaps enjoying his freedom now that he wasn't caged.

Theo continued forward, walking bent over and clutching to his chest the purple bag that held *Lamia's Bible*. Sweat flooded his face from the weight of the book. Or did he still suffer effects from the snake poison? His head spun, and the odors in the tunnel nauseated him. The place smelled of death and decay.

*Doesn't the rancidness bother Pavel and Diva?*

He glanced at Pavel. His friend's hands trembled holding the torch, but he didn't appear to have trouble breathing. Theo twisted his crouched body around to see how Diva was doing. The brave, strong Samodiva ambled forward as if she had no worries. Then again, Diva hadn't reacted negatively on their adventure last year when the two of them had been stuck inside a barrel, previously filled with rotting food.

What was in the tunnel that smelled so foul? So far, all they'd encountered were spider webs, tree roots, and mice the torch light had awoken.

"Bat guano," Pavel shouted from up ahead.

*Bat guano?* That's not smelly. Theo shook his head. No, Pavel hadn't read Theo's mind. That was just another of his friend's exclamations. What had he discovered?

Diva had already squeezed past Theo by the time the fog in his mind had cleared. He scrambled forward to meet them, his breathing rapid and his heart pounding. He covered his mouth, ready to gag. This was where the smell came from. But how? All that lay scattered on the ground was …

Bones.

The skeletons of two people.

Whatever smell would have occurred with their decaying carcasses would have long ago dissipated.

*So, why does the odor overwhelm me?* The pain in Theo's head intensified.

Pavel clutched his stomach. "Who do you think they are? And why are they here?"

"I can tell you that." The ghostly form of the walled-in bride emerged from the tunnel ceiling.

Her posture stiff, she lowered her nose to look at the bones. She seemed to smirk at their fate.

*What did these people do that makes Struma behave this way?* She'd been so sweet and protective of them, especially of Pavel, that the sudden change in behavior stunned Theo.

"These are my dear brothers-in-law." An ugly laughter erupted from Struma's lips.

"What?" Pavel sputtered as he stepped away from the walled-in bride.

"Don't hate me." She turned toward him, and her expression softened. In a low voice, she said, "There's more to my story that I didn't reveal earlier."

"Tell us," Diva said, a grim look on her face.

"They deceived my husband, their youngest brother." Struma sighed. "They were the other builders helping Manol construct the bridge. After the three of them had decided they needed to sacrifice one of their wives to make the bridge strong, these two," she said as she jabbed a finger toward the bones, "sent word back to their wives not to come to the construction site the next morning. Manol was too honorable to do such a thing."

"But how did they end up down here?" Theo asked.

"That was my doing." Struma wiped away tears that streamed from her eyes. "I was so angry that my child would grow up without a parent that I made sure theirs would suffer the same fate."

Theo barely heard her reply. The stench of death filled the air as if the bodies were newly deceased. He covered his nose and mouth, but the odor seeped through, making his queasy stomach lurch. He saw the scene play out in front of him. Struma leading the men into the tunnel, telling them Manol was trapped down there.

Once they were far from the entrance, she extinguished their torches with her ghostly breath. The men fell victim to traps she'd placed throughout the tunnel. One fell and cracked his head against the wall; the other broke his legs. She taunted the conscious man, telling him how rats were coming to consume him, how she had called them to do her bidding.

Theo screamed as he experienced the man's pain of being eaten alive. He dropped the bag containing the book onto the ground, now blood-stained and rodent-infested. He fell to his knees and leaned his throbbing head against the damp floor. The last thing he heard before he lost consciousness was Diva shouting his name.

When the darkness faded, so did the pain. He rose from the ground only to discover he was alone in a misty forest. Not ordinary woods. The gnarled trees appeared petrified, their branches devoid of leaves. A steady hum emanated from their roots and pulsed to the tips of their branches, which held glowing orbs. He'd been here before. The Forest of Souls.

*I must be dreaming.*

A figure began to emerge from the fog.

*Is the walled-in bride part of my dream? Or has Lamia's spirit come to torment me again?*

The apparition took on form. First, long red strands of hair glimmered around an ethereal visage. Sparkling eyes shone from a face he'd glimpsed once before—in his mother's globe. He looked at the tree, but the golden globe that had held his mother's spirit wasn't there. Could it be her? He held his breath. Little by little, the presence appeared before him—in the flesh.

"Mom!" Not caring it was a dream, he ran forward and wrapped his arms around her. "It's you. It's really you."

"I can't stay long, my sweet child," she said as she kissed the top of his head. "I have something important to tell you before your friends wake you."

"No, let me continue dreaming." Theo squeezed her tighter. "I want to stay with you."

"You're not dreaming. I'm with you. Always."

Theo loosened his grip and looked into his mother's pale-blue eyes, so much like his own. "This isn't a dream? How is that possible?"

"Your powers are growing, my darling." She caressed his cheek with her fingers. "Your senses are becoming stronger. By now, your hearing, vision, and smell should be heightened. Am I correct?"

He nodded, not wanting the sound of his own voice to drown out his mother's melodic words.

"And your emotions are intensifying," she continued.

Again, he nodded.

"Use your emotions to help you when you shift. Love is the most powerful and will ease your transformation, but justifiable anger, rather than hatred, is formidable, too."

"How will I know the difference?"

"You become angry at what someone else *does*. Justifiable anger is when you focus that anger at righting a wrong." Zunitza sighed. "To understand hatred, think of Lamia. Her envy of the love Zmey and I shared turned into hatred for me, because hatred focuses on who another person *is*. I think she still harbored a belief that if she got rid of me that Zmey would love her again."

"She said it wasn't love she wanted, but the power to rule."

"Those may have been her words, but deep down she craved her brother's love. Her feelings consumed her entire being." Zunitza's image flickered, and her voice faded.

"Don't leave me. Please stay." Theo grasped air. "How do I help my father? How do I save Dragon Village?"

"Your friends are calling you." Her soft words scattered in the air. "I have faith in you. You'll succeed and discover the way. The key lies with you …"

And then she was gone.

"Theo, Theo." Someone shook him and tapped his face.

"Mom," he mumbled and reached out.

Theo opened his wet eyes to discover, not his mother's caresses, but Diva's curls tickling his cheeks. Pavel sat at her side, fear in his eyes, but the walled-in bride had left. The overpowering smell of death had disappeared, and only the dankness of the tunnel remained. But it was so cold and dark. His friends' voices kept asking him questions, but he felt so alone.

He sat up and wiped away his tears. His mother was gone once more. A part of him had been ripped away, leaving a gaping wound where his heart should be. Tiredness weighed him down. How was he going to be able to continue his quest to save his father and Dragon Village? He just wanted to be a boy who didn't have such responsibilities. Let someone else be a hero. He wanted his mother's arms to comfort him.

Diva shook him. "Theo, look at me. Are you okay? You scared us. What happened?"

With a sigh, Theo explained about his sense of smell and empathy, and how he'd seen his mother while unconscious.

"Awe, man …" Pavel tapped Theo's shoulder.

Diva handed him his water bottle. "Here. Drink."

He gulped the liquid and felt better. "Let's get out of here."

Pavel stepped down the tunnel, while Diva helped Theo up.

"Quadruple bat guano." Pavel pointed with the torch to the side. "More bones."

Where Pavel shone the light, the tunnel split in two. The skeletons lay in a smaller passage, which was more like a rat hole, no higher than three feet.

"These must have been tunnel workers," Theo said. "I don't think Struma caused this. I hope that's not the way we need to go."

"I don't think so." Diva peered inside. "Struma said we needed to walk another thirty to forty minutes before we reached the exit, but she didn't say that we had to take a different tunnel."

"I agree." Pavel took off his glasses and cleared dust from them. "I think since this one's so narrow, it's more of a sound tunnel. In the past, many fortresses had what they called hearing tunnels, which people used to listen for their enemy. At a distance of about fifty yards, they could detect other tunneling activities."

Theo took another sip of water. "Since we don't need to spy on anyone, let's continue down the main corridor."

Diva steadied Theo from behind as he crept down the tunnel. Her strong grip kept him from falling. His back and entire body ached with each step, and his hand still throbbed. After they turned around another bend, Boo squawked at their arrival and pecked at a rotten wooden door. Sparkles of light penetrated it from outside. Theo breathed a sigh of relief.

"I see light," Pavel screamed and rushed toward the exit, making Boo take flight. Pavel slid on the damp soil and slammed his shoulder against the door, which burst into pieces. The magpie flew out behind him.

By the time Theo exited the tunnel, Pavel was lying on the green grass with the torch stuck upright into the soil near him. Swarms of fireflies lit up the night, and Boo was chasing them.

"How are you doing?" Diva stepped out from behind Theo. "I was really worried when you just stared into space after coming to."

Theo shrugged. "I'll survive."

"You know you can talk with me about anything, right?" Diva lifted his chin so he was looking at her. "We've been through so much together. I feel as if we've been friends forever."

"Yah, I know. It's just … it hurts so much to keep losing my mom." Theo choked back a sob. "I don't have her or my father. I feel so alone. Empty."

Diva hugged him. "I know. When my sister Neva died, I didn't think I could go on. I literally was alone. But I knew I had responsibilities. I had to care for the animals. I was the only Samodiva Lamia hadn't captured."

Theo squeezed Diva back. "Thank you. I'll be okay. I know I can't let Zlo win."

Pavel made a strange sound as he rolled on the ground. Theo wasn't sure if it was a moan or a laugh.

Diva looked from Theo to Pavel.

"It's okay. I can walk on my own now. The fresh air helps. Go see what's wrong with Pavel." Theo sniffed his shirt. "I still smell death on my clothes."

Diva took a few steps forward but looked back and smirked. "Nah, it's just your normal boy stink."

Theo laughed. Diva had a way of making everything right again.

Diva kneeled beside Pavel, and he began to giggle and roll around even more. A firefly landed on Diva's forehead and shone like a star, making her laugh.

"What's the matter with you, Pavel?" Theo asked as he inched closer. "Did you bump your head?"

"No, I'm fine." Pavel snorted back his laughter. "I'm taking a bath in the grass and enjoying watching the fireflies. It reminds me of my backyard in Selo."

"I could use a bath myself, but the fun's over," Theo shouted above the noise. "We don't have a lot of time left before the moons merge. We should get going."

"You're right." Pavel got up from the grass and dusted himself off.

His jaw gaped open when he looked at Diva. Hundreds of fireflies had congregated in her hair, creating an aura of light.

"You look like a goddess. The goddess of light."

Diva rolled her eyes but smiled as well. "I'm going to call the deer. That should make you even happier, Pavel."

"Shh, for a moment." Theo held out his hand. "I heard a noise. I think something's hurt."

They all quieted, and soon a whimper came from a basket at the edge of the torch's light. Theo hadn't noticed it when he'd left the tunnel. Boo squawked, flew over, and started pecking at the basket. The noise inside intensified.

"Stop that, Boo," Pavel said as he hurried toward the basket.

"Be careful. It could be a trap." Diva followed in his footsteps, with Theo trailing.

Boo hopped around and tried to peck inside, with Pavel nudging him away. Kneeling by the careworn basket, Pavel peeled off layers of ivy wrapped around it.

"Don't do that." Diva grabbed Pavel's hands. "There might be a poisonous snake inside. I don't have enough antidote left after giving some to Theo."

The whimpering inside the basket intensified.

Pavel tugged his hands out of Diva's grasp. "Does that sound like a snake?"

Boo said, "Waak," and pecked at Pavel's hands.

"Go away! What's the matter with you? Theo, take your bird." Pavel waited until Theo picked up the hopping magpie. Then Pavel tore off the final piece of ivy and opened the lid.

The white snout of a puppy poked out.

"What a surprise. I asked for a puppy for Christmas." Pavel picked up the tiny animal and hugged him. "Hello, Balkan. You do like that name, don't you?"

The puppy yipped and licked Pavel's nose.

"You're forgetting it's summer, not Christmas," Theo said above Boo's incessant squawking.

"Well, maybe it's an early Christmas gift." Pavel laughed as the puppy continued to slobber him with kisses.

"You've had your fun, rolling in the grass and playing with a puppy," Diva said. "Now put him back, and let's get going. Otherwise, we won't be able to hear ourselves over Boo's tantrum."

The puppy started shaking and whimpering.

"No." Pavel cuddled the trembling animal closer. "I'm taking him with me."

"You can't keep him," Theo said. "He's probably lost, and his owner is looking for him."

"More likely," Diva added, "it's a trick. Look around you. There's nobody nearby. Why would a puppy be out here by himself, never mind trapped in a basket? Someone intentionally left the animal here."

"I disagree," Pavel said. "You yourself just said there's nobody around, so who would have left him here to trick us?"

Theo added, "Either way, I don't think it's a good idea to bring him with us. We can't worry about a puppy now."

"I'll take care of him." Pavel looked at the two of them with his own puppy-dog eyes. "He'll be invisible to you, I promise."

The puppy wiggled and yipped in Pavel's arms, slobbering wet kisses on his face.

"That's not the only reason," Theo added. "Boo obviously doesn't like him, and we have too much to do."

"You have your pet. I want one, too," Pavel insisted.

"Boo's not a pet, but fine." Theo shrugged. "We're wasting time arguing about it."

Pavel hugged the puppy tighter. "I'm keeping Balkan."

"Boys. Human boys," Diva muttered. "They have no common sense."

She took a whistle from her belt and played a few notes that flew to the stars.

A short while later, three bright glows appeared overhead. Whistling and what sounded like copper bells filled the night. As the glows grew larger, the six-winged deer looked like fire-breathing dragons approaching. Theo shuddered. He recalled the terrifying storm that brought fire and hail when Lamia came to

Selo and captured Nia. The dragon's hot, rancid breath had burned his face, and her sharp claws had dug into his flesh as he tried to hold onto his sister. He rubbed his forearm, which still had a tiny scar from the encounter. Never again would he let something bad like that happen to those he loved. He'd do whatever it took to save them.

As the animals approached, Theo's terrifying memory receded. The deer now resembled majestic flying horses. The glow from their orbs silhouetted their wings, each pair beating in perfect rhythm. Sur, Shar, and Whirl glided toward the meadow. They folded two pairs of wings onto their bodies, while the third, largest ones continued to thrash against the air. The deer's hoofs were prancing as they came in for their landing. The deer would help them get to the Kukeri and Samodivi in time to save Dragon Village.

Diva approached her deer and rubbed the white star on his forehead and caressed his powerful wings. "Sur, we need to find Mraz. Can you take us to him? I also need to talk with my sisters."

The orb between Sur's antlers turned amber. Diva whispered in his ear. Sur butted her ear in return.

"Theo, Pavel, we're lucky," she said. "The Kukeri and the Samodivi are together. They've settled at a hut in the Forest of Whispering Bells."

"Great. We can visit the old witch while we're there," Theo said. "She has questions to answer."

Diva climbed onto Sur. Pavel and Theo mounted their deer and prepared to leave.

"Theo, hold on tight to the bag," Diva said as Sur took a running leap into the air.

Pavel tucked the puppy inside his jacket and zipped it up. He climbed onto Whirl, and then followed Diva into the sky.

Boo, now quiet that the puppy was gone, flew off on his own after Diva. Theo slung the bag with the book in it over his shoulder, along with his bow and backpack. He was glad they were flying, so he wouldn't have to carry so many items.

"Ready, Shar?" he asked his deer.

Shar snorted and took off after the others. Theo hugged the deer with both hands, the warmth of the animal's body relaxing him. The palm where the snake had bitten him pulsed a little, but he felt much better as Diva had predicted.

# Chapter 14
# Devil Plot

EVEN IF IT WASN'T his first attempt at riding the magnificent six-winged deer, flying in the darkness at this height was a new experience. The only lights visible were the fireballs between each deer's antlers—and, of course, the threatening glow of the two moons, getting blacker by the moment as they continued to cross paths. His body tense and his throat dry and scratchy, Theo wrapped his arms around Shar's neck, taking what little comfort he could from the animal's warmth.

*What if I fail, and Zlo takes over the world? Will I be able to protect Mom, Nia, everyone in Selo? If I die and no one can rescue Zmey, I'll have failed Sly, Struma, Diva, and all the others who live in Dragon Village.*

The deer must have sensed his insecurity and fear and thought-talked to Theo, "*Don't worry. I know a way to make you forget about what's going on for a short while.*"

"*How?*" Theo thought back to his companion.

*"A race."*

*"A race? Like fishermen sometimes do with their boats?"*

*"Yes, like that."*

*"But we don't have any boats here."*

*"I'm your boat, and Whirl is Pavel's,"* Shar responded. *"I've already spoken to Whirl, and he agrees. We'll head up to the clouds, then race to the ground."*

*"I don't know."*

Theo wanted so badly to say yes, to be a boy for a while longer, and not a hero. If Zlo succeeded in his demonic plan, Theo might not survive. A race sounded fun, a diversion. But should he think about having fun when so much was at stake?

Green and purple specks flickered inside Shar's amber fireball. *"You don't think I'll lose, do you?"*

*"No."* Theo stroked the deer's neck. *"Let's do it. We'll show my friend Pavel what we can accomplish together."*

The fireball between Shar's horns spun and sparkled with the colors of the rainbow. Muscles beneath the deer's powerful wings swelled as he brought them back before scooping up the chilly night air. The motion stirred up the scent of wildflowers mixed with smoke, and the smell drifted around Theo. He instinctively squeezed his knees around Shar and closed his eyes.

*"Trust me, Theo. I won't let you fall. Relax and enjoy the flight."* The deer rose higher and higher, its body splitting the air with ease and finesse.

Theo opened his eyes and looked for Pavel. His friend was almost at Theo's height. A contented smile covered Pavel's face as he sat upright on his chocolate-colored deer.

*I can try to be like Pavel and learn to have more fun. Worrying doesn't fix anything. We still have time to plan how to defeat this new monster. After all, we've survived so many other threats. Together.*

"Let's get this competition going," Pavel shouted, forming a funnel with his hands to make himself heard better. "My deer is definitely a champion."

Pavel spurred on his deer, not waiting for Theo to reply. Without warning, Whirl shot straight up, and Pavel screamed.

Ready to take on the challenge, Theo nudged Shar. *"Let's show them what we can do."*

The deer thrashed its wings, sending surges of wind around Theo. He clung on with all his might as Shar rose without effort like a mighty eagle, soon passing Pavel.

"Ahh, you caught up with us, my friend," Pavel shouted. "I see that you are … m … h …"

The wind chopped up Pavel's final words and they were lost in the air, scattered like atoms.

Theo blinked, and Pavel disappeared as Shar raced upward. At a higher altitude, the deer spread his wings, his muscles relaxed, and glided over the misty cloud pillows. Theo looked down toward Dragon Village and became still, not from the height but because he could see the land. His dragon vision had begun to equal his ability to hear faraway sounds. From this height, the mystical land appeared idyllic, with its green patches, hills, and rivers. He marveled at its beauty, a small land dotted with mountains, lakes, forests, and other natural resources. It could be an ordinary place if you didn't know about the anger and revenge covering the terrain. He must do everything possible to save this land from Zlo, to thwart his plan. But for now, the idea of racing was meant to make him forget about Zlo. He stroked the deer's back.

*I'm Icarus, soaring toward the sun.* Except there wasn't a sun.

Even though he'd flown since his return to Dragon Village, this experience exhilarated him. Feeling the freedom of gliding through the sky had been his dream, literally, since he could remember, before he knew he was the son of a dragon and Samodiva. He closed his eyes and imagined he was in full dragon form, soaring over his home, protecting it the way his father had done before Zmey had been imprisoned. In Theo's mind, his own mighty wings battled against the storms Lamia had once brought to destroy farmers' crops, and he fought the malevolent Zlo, who sought to destroy Theo's home. Fire erupted from his maw, destroying the evil creatures. His red scales sparkled like wine made from local grapes. He—

A sudden rush of air forced him to tense his body and open his eyes, returning to the reality of flying on Shar. The deer had folded his wings and was diving. He and Whirl must have decided to start the race to the ground.

*"Where is Pavel anyway?"* Theo asked Shar, having momentarily forgotten why they were flying so high. There his friend was, far below. *"They're going to win."*

*"Nothing to worry about."* Shar shook his antlers and increased his descent. *"I gave Whirl a head start."*

In moments, they caught up to Pavel and Whirl. "Heeeey, did you give up on winning?" Theo teased his friend as he and Shar flew past.

The fireball between Shar's antlers shot off sparks as they continued their furious descent. Theo looked back. Trailing by a small amount, Pavel was bent like a jockey who skillfully guides his winner across the finish line.

"No way," Pavel yelled as he flew past and raised his fists like a victor. "Let's see who'll win this new flying-deer competition. Pavel and his magnificent champion."

Theo hugged Shar. *Let's show him who's the best.* He normally wasn't competitive, but his new dragon senses made him want to win.

*I am mighty. I am fearless. I am—*

Shar dropped like a roller coaster.

Theo screamed. *Well, maybe I'm not fearless.*

Shar thought to Theo, *"As I said before, there's nothing to worry about. We'll win."*

Theo clung on for his life, but a smile spread across his face. The green carpet of land took shape in seconds. Trees appeared. The melody of chimes filtered upward. That meant they were near the Forest of Whispering Bells, their destination.

Within minutes, Shar touched ground at a gallop, but soon slowed his pace and came to a stop. Theo looked around. They'd beaten Pavel. His grin grew wider. He searched the sky. Pavel and his deer still circled, looking for a place to land. Theo slid off Shar and wrapped his arms around the deer's neck. *"Thank you. That was just what I needed."*

Instead of replying, Shar snorted and ambled toward Whirl, who had landed. The two deer butted antlers the way sports players shook hands after a game. The deer flapped their wings three times, creating a gentle breeze.

Pavel slid off Whirl. "Good race. For a while, we lost touch with the Landing Tower."

Theo laughed. It felt ages since he'd been so happy. "I'm sure the deer will let us do that again sometime. We'll have many more chances for you to seize the victory. Friends?"

"Friends forever." Pavel gave a high-five to Theo, and they bumped shoulders. "That was some crazy descent. I'm surprised the puppy remained calm during all of it."

"Crazy boys." Diva laughed as she approached. "Glad you finally decided to come down. Now, let's hurry to meet up with the others." She strode into the forest where a light flickered.

Momentary sadness filled Theo. He'd have to continue his quest now. He could do this. If this was his destiny, he wouldn't fail the others. It was time to put Zlo in his place … the dungeon.

"Have you seen Boo?" Theo asked as he ran to catch up.

"He's in the hut. I waited here for you two *racers*."

Theo was glad the magpie had made it safely. He walked with his friends in silence the rest of the way, along a path until they came upon a dilapidated hut. Dim light peered out the canvas-covered windows. Diva opened the door, and a shout came from within.

"Diva, Theo, Pavel." The Kukeri and Samodivi swarmed around them. Boo greeted Theo with his loud "Waak." And the same to Diva. When the magpie turned toward Pavel, he flapped his wings and headed straight for the puppy. He darted around the now-yowling animal and started pecking it.

Pavel pushed his new pet deeper into his jacket and shouted, "Theo, make him stop."

"Boo, what's wrong with you?" Theo grabbed the magpie. "Leave the puppy alone."

Boo continued with his "Waak, waak" for several minutes, until he finally stopped trying to escape Theo's grasp.

"I'll let you go if you promise to stop bothering the puppy. Do you agree?"

Boo waved his beak up and down as if responding yes.

After calming down, everyone sat around a crooked, creaking table. Mraz, the eldest of the Kukeri brothers, said, "Diva's told us about your adventures. You've had a bit of excitement."

"No more than normal." Theo laughed, although his insides were tight and queasy.

"Sava, I didn't get to ask one thing earlier," Diva said. "While we were at Kadin Bridge, Bor Stobor attacked us. He said the Samodivi ruined his life. Why does the Karakonjul hate us so much? What did our people do to him?"

Sava sighed. "He's been trying to conquer the forests for years. When he and his kind encroached on the forests near our homes, and started tormenting the creatures living there, we fought back. We didn't use weapons, but we fumigated the forests with incense. That made some of them ill. Others may have died. We never knew. I'm sorry to hear he lost his family, but we did warn him and others what we were going to do before we took action."

"Serves him right," Ula added. "You should have seen all the dead animals he and the others left behind. Not just dead, but cruelly abused before the Karakonjul tribes killed them."

"Baba Yaga is another problem we need to deal with severely," Theo said. "We plan to visit the old witch and have words with her."

"Ula and I have already been there," Sava said, "but her chicken hut was empty. It was strange because her wooden mortar was there, and she doesn't travel any distance without it."

Ula added, "It's almost like it's part of her body."

"Maybe she's planning on upgrading the mortar to a private jet with the money she got for selling *Lamia's Bible* to the Youdi." Pavel laughed.

"I've been to your world," Sava said. "I don't think the witch would want one of those noisy things."

"Besides that," Ula added, "where would she put such a large item?"

"Um, I was joking," Pavel said and looked at Theo.

Theo shrugged and went back to the topic of the witch. "I guess we can skip her place then. Maybe she's with Zlo. The Youdi said he has Kotka as well as the Firebird. So, it seems he needs either her cat or Lamia's spirit for whatever he's planning for his ceremony tomorrow at midnight."

"I don't like the sound of that." Mraz held out his hand to Theo for the bag holding *Lamia's Bible*. "It's time we look at the book and see if we can figure out Zlo's plan, so we can stop him."

Theo hesitated. "Will you be able to touch the book?"

Retrieving the book had sounded like a good idea, but that was when he thought Jabalaka would interpret it for them. Now, he wasn't so certain. Jabalaka had told him *Lamia's Bible* would cause catastrophe or illness to anyone who touched it. The frog-man was the keeper of secrets, so it didn't affect him. But now Mraz was preparing to open the book. What would happen when he held it?

"I think I'll be fine," Mraz said. "If you remember, I'm next in line to become the guardian of *Lamia's Bible*. I don't think I'll suffer any ill effects from the book."

"If you're sure." Theo pushed the velvet bag toward the man.

All eyes stared at the eldest Kuker as he pulled out the book. Waiting. Waiting. Waiting.

Nothing happened to Mraz, but Theo was drawn to a dragon's eye in the center of the cover. Straight lines bordered each side of the orb. He hadn't seen the etching before when Jabalaka had read from the book. The frog-man must have had it covered with his webbed paws when he'd retrieved it from his bookcase. Now, that eye seemed directed at Theo, even though it was only etched into the black dragon scales that made up the cover. Bile rose in Theo's throat as he remembered Jabalaka telling him how Lamia had made the cover from her own mother's dragon hide.

Mraz cleared his throat, and Theo returned his gaze to the Kuker.

"Here lies the past, present, and future." Mraz's hand hovered over the cover as he made eye contact with everyone. "We must keep this book safe at the cost of our lives. With it, Zlo will cause chaos—not only in Dragon Village, but also in the human world."

*Like those red creatures swarming Selo and other villages along the Black Sea.* Theo hoped they hadn't multiplied during the time he and Pavel had been gone. He crossed his fingers on both hands. They *had* to find the answer in *Lamia's Bible.*

Mraz brought his fingers to the edge of the cover and …

Nothing happened. The book wouldn't open.

Groans and rumblings sounded around the room.

Mraz held his head in his hands. "It's been so long since I've seen the book, back when I was a child. "Maybe I can't open it because I'm not its current guardian."

"Perhaps it needs a key," Sava said.

Theo hadn't recalled Jabalaka using a key, but he clung to that hope as Mraz turned the book to look at it from all sides. With a sigh, Mraz set the book on the table and shook his head.

"Now what do we do?" he asked.

"Maybe Zima and Jega can try their one-two punch, fire and ice, to break it open," Pavel suggested.

Mraz shook his head. "Too risky. We might damage the book."

"Theo," Sava said, "didn't your mother mention you had a key?"

"A key?" Theo thought back. "She didn't have time to go into detail. I thought she meant I was the key to solving the problems. I don't have any key."

"Can you tell us again her exact words?" Sava persisted.

"I think she said, 'The key lies with you.' But she didn't get a chance to finish what she was saying, because I came to at that moment. Besides, how would she know I had a key … unless …?"

"Unless she gave it to you," Ula shouted and danced around the room, a big smile on her face.

"The only thing I have from my mother is my medallion." Theo pulled out the seven-sided star from around his neck and handed it to Mraz. "You can try it if you want."

Mraz placed the amulet over the eye on the book. Everyone froze, staring, waiting. After a few minutes, a fly buzzing around a candle broke the silence.

The book remained closed.

"I was so sure," Sava said.

"Key … What else could be the key?" Mraz asked.

Theo took the spindle Kikimora had given him from his backpack and handed it to Mraz. "Maybe this will work. Kiki is

Baba Yaga's friend, and the witch once told me a cryptic message when she gave me a pin, that we ended up using like a key. Maybe Kikimora knew this would work some magic."

Mraz tried to open the book with it, but *Lamia's Bible* remained closed. "Anyone else have an idea?"

"I think the only thing that really makes sense is the medallion." Diva picked up the object and examined it carefully under the candlelight. "Theo, look. The back has a small hole, almost invisible. Dirt's filled it in."

Theo cleared the dirt from the hole. He was certain he'd never seen holes in the medallion before, and he had looked at every inch of the object long before he knew it was a gift from his mother. Back then, he thought it came from his human father who had drowned the night Theo and Nia were born. But he had felt a bump on the back when he and Pavel had gone to the Stone Forest. Was it possible his dragon abilities had detected it?

He picked up the metal spindle and inserted the end into the hole. It clicked, and a round cover opened. He removed the cover. On its back side, an eyelet secured a metal key no larger than a quarter. Not ordinary looking, the key was shaped like the letter "Y," although Theo thought it resembled a chicken's leg. He removed the key and looked closely at the dragon's eye on the cover. Three tiny holes in the eye appeared to match those on the key.

"I think this will work." Theo held the key out to Mraz.

"Where do I put it?" the Kuker asked.

"In the holes, here, here, and here." Theo pointed to the dots.

Mraz stuck his nose close to the cover. "Sorry, I don't see them. I'm an old man."

*He can't see them?* Theo looked again. The holes were small, but visible. *I wonder if it's my new dragon powers that let me see them.*

Mraz laughed and gave Theo back the key. "You should do the honors."

Theo inserted the top points of the Y into the corners of the dragon's eye, and the point at the stem fit into the bottom. The iris flashed in the candlelight. Theo jumped away, and everyone else backed off from the table. Twice more the iris flashed, each time lighting one of the straight lines to the side of the eye. Then the flashes dimmed to a steady glow. The cover clicked, and a radiance emitted from the edges of the pages of the still-closed book.

Mraz was the first to return to the table. "Well, look at that."

"What?" Everyone's eager eyes beheld the book.

"Our ancient symbol of the sun, which our deity Tangra personifies." He pointed to the IYI that now glowed on the cover.

"Does he live at the temple along with Bendis?" Theo asked.

Mraz shook his head. "No. He's a pure spirit of the entire universe, not a corporal being like our goddess Bendis. This symbol," he said as he indicated the IYI again, "stands for strength in unity and power over everything. I never truly understood the significance of the book until now."

"What do you mean significance?" Sava asked. "Wasn't this treacherous book Lamia's means to spy on everyone?"

"Yes, but it goes so much deeper than that." Mraz opened the book and flipped through one yellowed page after another. "Let me see if I can find the passage about the two moons that are supposed to bring destruction. I'm hoping that will explain the enormity of what the book means—especially in the wrong hands."

While Mraz looked, Jega poked his head between Mraz and Theo. "Need I remind you what our ancient poem said? 'Two moons in the sky, Portend all will die—' "

Mraz gave Jega a scalding look before Zima had a chance to shut up their youngest brother. "It's even more serious than that."

He scanned more pages until he found an image of the two moons: red and blue. Mraz started reading:

" 'When the sun disappears from Zmeykovo, the sky will give birth to two mighty moons. One as red as fire, the other as blue as water. Fire and water, eternal elements at constant battle with each other, both capable of causing devastation or bringing purification and regeneration.

" 'After twenty-one days, at midnight, the two forces will merge into one. Evil and justice battle to create chaos or to restore order.

" 'Evil strives to triumph. At the fated hour, innocent blood, silent water, and three golden tear pearls will give life to monstrous malevolence.

" 'Justice also strives to triumph. Sword of father. Sword of victory. The unborn hero wields its might. A bloody rose it must pierce.' "

Theo paced. "What does all of that mean?"

Mraz stopped reading, his chin trembling. "I'm not sure. Some I can explain, but first there's more. It's what I feared."

He read the final line. " 'The winner gains control of fire and water and rules the world.' "

# Chapter 15
# My Father's Sword

MRAZ'S WORDS CHILLED THEO. The situation was worse than polluting the Black Sea in Selo with those hideous red creatures. If Zlo secured control of both water and fire, everyone would be his puppets. Theo couldn't let the evil lord succeed. But how could a boy protect the entire world? The joy and exhilaration of his deer ride faded, and the heavy weight of his responsibility pressed down on him.

Theo desperately wanted answers. He looked around the room at everyone. They all needed answers. His long-time best friend Pavel played with the puppy on the floor, but Theo could tell he was listening to every word spoken. Diva had removed herself from the table and sat with her back against a wall. She held a faraway, mournful look in her eyes, but knowing her, Theo was sure her every sense was on alert, absorbing each detail. Ula paced the floor. She was the emotional one of Diva's sisters. The Samodiva was high energy and often exhausted

Theo merely by her presence. Sava remained seated at the table. The more logical of the two Samodivi, she'd become a grounding force for Theo. He trusted her advice to be wise. The two other Kukeri brothers had moved to the back of the hut and appeared to be having their own discussion. Theo was sure they'd share what they were talking about if it related to the rescue mission. And Mraz, even though the revelation in *Lamia's Bible* had rattled him, still was a formidable presence. Theo wouldn't want to be on the receiving end of the Kuker's anger.

Right now, Theo needed the man's wisdom.

"Mraz, will you explain the prophecy? The part that talks about the unborn hero. Me. Do you know what that means?"

"I do," Mraz said. "At least part of it. Your father's sword it mentions was made of pure silver. Our goddess Bendis personally purified the blade and put the power of the moon into the stone on the handle. The moonstone is said to guide heroes in their travels. The youngest of the Oristnizi gave Zmey the sword upon your birth to bring him strength and bravery."

"Who are the Oristnizi?" Theo asked.

"Let me explain," Sava said, and Mraz nodded his agreement.

She continued, "They are three sisters who determine a child's destiny soon after the infant's birth. As they circle the cradle, each one predicts the child's future. The eldest goes first and foretells the child's eventual death."

Theo couldn't breathe. Everyone died, but having someone bring up the certainty of it was unsettling. He hoped his death was a long time in coming. He finally exhaled and asked, "Is … is her prediction of how it happens certain?"

"Only the mother truly knows, as she's the one person who can be present during their predictions."

"So, my mother knows." Theo wasn't sure if that comforted him or made him unhappy for his mother to bear that burden. He was certain she would do her best to protect him whatever the sisters of fate had spoken.

"Yes, but a mother cannot speak about what she's heard," Sava said. "To be so daring would mean she'd lose her voice."

"Has anyone ever been able to change their fate?" Theo asked.

Sava and Ula looked at each other, then Ula spoke. "We've heard stories about those who have tried … and failed. However, I do recall one instance where a sister pretended to be her brother. The Oristnizi had predicted his death at his wedding. The girl wasn't supposed to have heard the predictions, but she had been hiding in the room. She loved her brother so much that she dressed up as the groom, and when death came, it took her."

Theo didn't want anyone to take his place. He didn't even know what kind of death the sisters had predicted for him. "What do the other sisters say will happen?"

Sava picked up where she had left off. "The second one foresees all the illness and misfortunes the child will endure during his lifetime." She looked at Theo to see if he had any questions, but he shook his head. "And the youngest, the one who gave your father the sword, predicts the child's good fortune. She tries to lessen the effects of her sisters' words, making the outcome of the child's life more positive."

Theo sighed with relief, grateful that he had hope to overcome whatever bad things the Oristnizi had predicted. "Do you think they would have wished for terrible things? My mother was their queen."

"I'm sure they did their best to keep it as positive as they could," Sava said. "But you must understand, this is who they are. It's their nature. They can't change it."

"And," Ula added, "they loved your mother. They did their best to protect her during her pregnancy. She was constantly in danger from your demonic aunt."

Sava smiled. "Besides that, your mother was generous with gifts for them at your birth. That makes them more merciful in their predictions. She gave them many pots of honey, bags of gold coins, and woolen garments made from the deer's hair."

A butterfly entered the room. It circled Theo before finally landing on Sava's forehead. The Samodiva's face beamed, and she laughed. "This is a clear sign. The butterfly whispered to me that the sword was meant for Theo. Zmey was its guardian until the time Theo would need it."

Theo's heart pounded. *The sword was meant for me? How can I ever compare to the great king of Dragon Village? I'm still a boy.*

Something in the back of his mind reassured him he was more than a boy. He had already defeated one monster, more than one. He had the power to win. That voice told him to remember love, remember righteous anger. Theo took several breaths to calm himself, certain the voice belonged to Zunitza. He would be brave for her and make her proud.

His mother's voice spoke to him. *"I'm already proud of you, my sweet boy. You'll never fail me."*

Theo returned his concentration to Mraz, whose lined face and eyes held sorrow. "I already know the answer to the next question I'd ask. You don't know what 'A bloody rose it must pierce' means, do you?"

Mraz slowly shook his head. "Sorry, I'm afraid I don't."

Theo let out an exasperated breath. Nothing about being a hero was easy. He'd hoped Mraz could give him the answer to *how* he was supposed to defeat Zlo. At least he knew *what* he could use.

Theo clutched his hands, steeling himself for more bad news, and leaned closer to Mraz. "Do you have the sword?"

"No, I don't know where it is."

Theo squeezed his eyes tight and let out a groan. *Of course not. Something more we have to find, and time's running out.*

"It's okay, Theo." Sava's gentle voice brought him back, and he opened his eyes, looking at her expectantly. "I know where his sword is hidden. Now that we know it's needed to defeat Zlo, I'll fly there to retrieve it."

With lightning speed, she turned into a hawk.

"Be careful, sister." Diva broke her silence. "You don't know if Zlo's guards are at the castle."

"Don't worry. I'm going with her." Ula hugged Diva. "Besides, Sava's not going to the castle. My friends have been guarding the sword in a safe place, to protect it from the Youdi and anyone else who might want to use it against Zmey."

Ula turned into an owl, and she and the hawk Sava spread their wings and flew out the hut door.

"I'm going outside to wait for their return," Diva said as she slipped out into the night.

Theo followed her and put his arm around her. "They'll be okay. I remember another Samodiva who got out of tight jams."

"You're right." Diva gave him a sad smile. "My sisters are more powerful than I am."

"I wouldn't bet on that." Theo nudged her with his hip. "You've done some pretty awesome things."

She sighed. "We're quite the pair, aren't we? Both learning more about what we can do."

"True. It would help if we could figure out the rest of the prophecy. If we knew what Zlo was planning, we might have a better chance of stopping him."

Diva rested her head on Theo's shoulder. "What else do you need to know? Maybe I can explain it."

"I was just wondering about the 'ingredients.' Youda Stana said Zlo had the cat and Firebird, but they needed me for the final ingredient." Theo paused, trying to recall the words. "The prophecy talks about 'innocent blood, silent water, and three golden tear pearls.' So what part of that is about me?"

Diva pulled herself away from Theo, looked into his eyes, and spoke softly. "I suppose it could be the 'innocent blood' part, although that could also refer to the Firebird, unless you can cry pearly golden tears."

Theo laughed. "Not unless that's one of my dragon powers. Do you know what they might be?"

"No." She shook her head. "Maybe something aquatic. The Rusalki probably could tell us, but they're not here."

"What about silent water?"

"That I can answer," Diva said. "It's magical and is a base for many cures. When I take care of the animals, I get it from our hidden sacred spring. When I'm ready to perform a healing ceremony, I dance to instill positive charges into the water, which strengthens it even more."

"Why do you call it 'silent'?"

"Because when I collect it, I have to do it in ritual silence," Diva replied. "Water has its own memory. We keep it pure by making certain it doesn't 'hear' charms until the ritual."

Theo rubbed his arms to chase away the chills, not from the night air, but from his nervousness. "I think we should go inside," he said. "Your sisters will be okay. We should see if Mraz knows where Zlo is." None of the ingredients or what Theo had to do would matter if they couldn't find the evil lord.


A PINCHED LOOK crossed Mraz's face, and he drummed his fingers on the table. "Every single Samodiva and Kuker has been searching throughout Zmeykovo and has spoken to each resident we could find." He ground his teeth. "Most people have said they haven't seen Zlo or know where his hideout is, but his guards are everywhere."

"Maybe people are afraid to speak," Theo said.

"That thought has crossed my mind. On the other hand, some people have said he's everywhere, which doesn't help us narrow our search." Mraz pounded the table. "He must have found an obscure place to carry out his infernal plan."

"He's not at the castle with his guards?" Theo asked. "I'd think it would be empty now that Zlo captured Zmey."

"No, we've already checked. The castle is half-destroyed and empty, except for a few soldiers," Mraz replied.

"I wonder ..." A thought spread through Theo's mind. "The Youdi were on their way to bring Zlo *Lamia's Bible*. When we were at Kadin Bridge, I overheard them arguing. They mentioned the word Kale ... Kalo ... I'm not sure with all their screeching."

"Maybe they were talking about the bridge?" Mraz replied.

"No, it was something like Kali …" Theo scratched his head. "They said it when they mentioned something about the best way to get to Zlo. The younger one wanted to go around the lake, but Youda Stana said it would take too long. She wanted to travel under the mountain."

"Under the mountain? Hmm." Mraz closed his eyes a moment before snapping his fingers. "I should have thought of that. It's the perfect place. It must be Kaleto, a place we call the Forgotten Land."

"The home of the Ispolini." Diva sighed. "I wish I'd been alive when they were around. I would have liked to know them."

"You mean they're all dead?" Theo asked.

"As far as we know," Mraz said. "No one has seen them for ages."

"What were they like?"

Mraz stroked his white beard, then scrolled through the pages of *Lamia's Bible*. "Hundreds of years ago, the Ispolini thrived in Kaleto. They were good-natured and didn't bother anyone. They cultivated their land, raised sheep, and their gardens were full of fruit and vegetables. Hala, Lamia's mother, wanted to conquer them. She made them suffer when they refused to send her tribute of food and gold. Soon, riots took place. The gentle giants had awoken. They did only what they had to so they could protect their homeland. Hala felt threatened by them and cursed them to turn into stone."

Theo recalled his first mission in Dragon Village. He, Pavel, and Diva had stumbled into a glen that had trees that looked like giants. Diva said they were indeed giants that Lamia's mother had turned into stone. Over the ages, trees had grown over them. Theo wondered how the Ispolini would react to him if they were alive, since they were the natural enemies of dragons. He hoped it had only been evil dragons like Lamia and her mother they hated. The giants must have adored his father, and Theo hoped they would have loved him, too.

Mraz stopped at a page and pointed to drawings of the Ispolini's battle with Hala's hoards. "No one has visited their land for hundreds of years. It makes sense Zlo would set up camp there. He'd be safe from discovery. It's a difficult place to access from any direction. Youda Stana's route under the mountain is the easiest way, if that's truly where they're going. I wish we had more time to make sure that's their destination."

"I can turn into a falcon and follow the Youdi," Diva said.

"I don't think that's a good idea." Theo laid his hands on hers. "They must know by now we stole the book back from them, since Zlo's spies are everywhere. I'm sure the Youdi are going crazy, knowing they failed their master. They'll do anything to please him, especially if it means harming one of us."

"I agree," Mraz added. "I'd like to keep you here to help us with our tactics if that's okay with you."

"Then who will go?" Diva asked.

From the floor where he still played with the puppy, Pavel said, "You can send Boo. He's smaller and won't attract as much attention." He shot the magpie a sour look and muttered, "That way he won't bother the puppy again."

"Will you do that for us, Boo?" Theo asked.

The magpie bobbed his head in agreement.

"Thank you." Theo ruffled the bird's feather. "I just found you. I don't want to lose you again, little friend. Be careful."

The bird spun around Theo and took off.

"Now it's time to do some planning." Mraz called to his brothers, who were still huddled together discussing something. "Zima, Jega, can you join us?"

The Kukeri gathered a paper and headed over.

"Mraz," Zima said, "Jega and I think we've discovered where Zlo must be. We have a map of the fortress at—"

"Kaleto?" Mraz said with a smile.

Zima threw his hands up. "How did you figure that out?"

Mraz told him about his discussion with Theo.

"So how do we get in there?" Zima unfolded a map. "This is the Ispolini fortress."

Theo examined it along with the others. Even though he couldn't read the words, he observed the many intersecting hallways in the building. What appeared to be a subterranean level displayed an even more complex interconnection of tunnels.

"How will we ever know how to get around in there or where to find Zlo?" he asked. "It's hard to follow."

"Careful planning, that's how. Our first task, though, is to decide how to get inside the fortress." Mraz peered at the map as he muttered what sounded like something he'd been taught to memorize in school or on the battlefield. "He who is in no hurry considers, judges, plans—and wins."

"If we climb the rocks here," Zima said as he pointed to a location at the eastern edge, "we'll avoid the central gate and can sneak into the fortress unnoticed through this entrance." He marked the second location on the map.

Pavel set the puppy down and joined the discussion. "To climb the rocks, we'll need strong ropes and metal wedges."

"We have plenty of them in the cart," Jega said.

"I suggest adding a net to trap the guards," Diva said. "The Samodivi have wolf nets and traps if you decide to use them."

"Good idea." Zima turned to Jega. "Will you come with me when we're done here to help collect them from the Samodivi?"

Jega winked. "Always glad to visit the lovely ladies."

"This is serious business." Zima scolded. "You can attempt your charming ways after Dragon Village is safe."

"How can we distract the guards enough to capture them?" Pavel asked.

Zima grunted. "I suggest throwing you in their path. I seriously doubt *you* or your strange gadgets figure into the *we* that's needed to succeed."

Mraz cleared his throat. "Zima, enough of the hostility. We all need to work together. That includes Pavel and his gadgets."

"I can become a fox to distract them. Or …" Diva said.

They all looked at her while she paused. Theo leaned forward, wondering what her plan would be.

Diva smiled. "Or maybe a chicken. I'm sure they're hungry and will gladly eat fresh meat."

Theo laughed along with everyone else. The joke even put a smile on Zima's face. Theo squeezed Diva's hand and grinned at her. The thought of her running around as a chicken with guards chasing her was an amusing scene, but her comment also meant she was coming out of her slump about the lost books on Dragon Village's history. His friend was ready to do battle, with no distractions.

Pavel stepped over to the eldest Kuker and spoke softly. "Mraz, I don't think Zima's plan's a good idea. What happens if there are too many guards where he suggests?" He glanced at Zima and backed away when Zima glared at him.

"It'll work." Zima bared his teeth as though he would snarl.

"Easy, brother." Mraz laid his hand on Zima's shoulder. "As a warrior, you know it's always good to have a backup plan or two. Another way to enter is to breach the fortress walls, but that could be more dangerous and time-consuming. We have no idea if they've set up booby traps anywhere along the perimeter."

Jega thumped the wall and waited until everyone looked at him. "I have an idea."

"I'd like to hear it." Mraz folded his hands at the table.

Jega bowed before continuing to outline his suggestion. "Our history tells us the Ispolini dug up all the blackberry vines and planted them along a certain section of the fortress walls, to keep them out of harm's way."

Theo recalled that the Ispolini that Lamia's mother had defeated had become entangled in blackberry thorns, and that made it easier for her to defeat them. It made sense that if the vines were a danger to them that they'd find some way not to encounter them. Along a wall would be a good location, so it wouldn't trip them.

"And what about those blackberry vines, brother." Zima acted bored, as if only his plan was worth mentioning. "Are we planning to have a snack while we wait?"

"Why not?" Jega laughed. "No, the vines are ancient and strong enough to support even the weight of a Kuker. One of us could hike up at an obscure part of the wall and go inside."

"What about the possible booby traps Mraz mentioned?" Theo asked.

Jega shrugged. "I doubt Zlo's soldiers would be keen on having hundreds of thorns digging into their flesh."

Zima snickered. "So, what's the plan once that one person is alone inside the fortress with who knows how many enemies?"

"Well … in the evening when the guards are less alert after they've eaten, or maybe even had a sleeping potion poured into their wine, that individual can open the fortress door for everyone else."

"I see." Zima rolled his eyes. "And that person is going to go searching through the fortress to discover where the wine is stored? That could take ages, and we don't have that much time."

"Maybe we could drug the wine beforehand and pretend to be their suppliers?" Jega's shoulders drooped as he appeared to be losing confidence in his plan. "We can stuff Theo and Pavel into a couple of empty barrels, and I'll dress as a peasant delivering the wine."

Theo wasn't keen on being squashed inside a barrel again, but he'd do it if that's what they decided. The last barrel he'd been in had moments before held rotten food. At least this one would be empty and clean.

Mraz stood and stretched. "We can bring a couple of barrels along in the cart in case we need to implement this plan. Any idea is good at this point. We'll decide what will work best when we arrive. So that's a couple possible ways to get inside. Anyone have any other thoughts?"

"I have one." A familiar voice came from the doorway.

Everyone turned to look. Sava entered the hut, with Ula following.

Diva ran over and hugged her sisters. "I'm so glad you made it back safely."

All Theo could concentrate on was the sword in Sava's hands. A fist-sized moonstone topped the handle, while it looked like hundreds of smaller ones decorated the scabbard, twisting around in a vine-like fashion. He itched to remove the sword from its sheath and examine his father's precious weapon. His desire must have shone on his face, because Sava grinned at him.

"First things first," she said as she strode over and handed Theo the sword. "Use it well, my friend."

"How long have you been standing by the doorway?" Mraz asked. "Have you heard all our discussion?"

Sava nodded.

"All right, then. Tell us about your plan," Mraz said.

Theo barely paid attention. Words filtered through: secret entrance, dungeon, egg-shaped stone, underground lake, hidden mechanism. Any other time, he would have loved to know what they were discussing. They continued to plan how they would locate Zlo once they entered the fortress.

Later, when everyone had finished speaking, Theo barely acknowledged the departure of Zima, Jega, Sava, and Ula to retrieve the wolf nets from the other Samodivi.

Even Mraz's request for the rest of them to get some rest, because they'd leave for Kaleto in the morning, was a blur.

He was completely engrossed in the silver sword. When he had unsheathed the weapon, he had expected it to be difficult to hold. However, it was amazingly light. He could wield it in one hand. He tapped it on the floor, and the sides tinged, leaving a small scar. It was not only lightweight, it was deadly sharp.

In the moonstone's glow, the face of a woman appeared. Theo blinked, and the image vanished. Maybe it was his imagination.

He examined the hilt. Sun rays circled another moonstone. The words "Discover your purpose" engraved in gold circled the sun. Theo sucked in a breath, amazed he had been able to understand the ancient words.

His blood tingled, and he felt his dragon abilities stir. In his hands, he held raw power.

# Chapter 16
# Message from Zlo

**JUNE 21** 

THEO COULDN'T SLEEP, spinning in the hay on the floor all night while Pavel snored contentedly with the puppy tucked under his arms. The Kukeri and Samodivi had returned sometime later in the evening, and they all lay peacefully on the floor. Boo had yet to arrive. The Youdi would likely leave to go meet Zlo soon. Boo would come back when the magpie was certain where the witches were going.

It must be almost morning. Theo sat up, brushed off straw from his clothes and hair, and searched through his backpack, removing a towel and shorts. He took a few steps forward, but then went back to retrieve his bow and arrows, leaving his father's sword behind. With so many dangers lurking, he didn't want to be caught unaware. He crept across the floor, hoping he didn't wake anyone. The hinge creaked as he opened the door, but no one stirred.

A burst of chilly air outside made him shiver. The sun remained shrouded in black clouds and offered little light or warmth. Worse yet, only a sliver of the two moons remained that hadn't merged. They would become one tonight at midnight.

The Forest of Whispering Bells was unusually quiet. Did that mean Baba Yaga hadn't returned? He looked closer at a branch. The sheen on the copper bells had dulled as if they were attempting to blend into the silver branches, trying to make themselves invisible. Did the bells react the way animals did when danger lurked—hide and remain silent? No, that was a crazy idea. It was probably their sleep mode, and he'd never noticed it before. He shook his head and walked along a path until he found a small pool of water.

*Good luck for once. Just what I was looking for.*

He wanted to wash away not only the grime, but also his fatigue and tension. A full bath would have to wait until he accomplished his mission. He set his bow and arrows and towel on a rock at the edge of the pool and kneeled to make sure none of the red creatures inhabited the water. He breathed a sigh of relief. The magic of the witch's forest must extend beyond her abode.

He removed his medallion and T-shirt and changed from pants into shorts. He stuck his big toe into the water and shivered. With both the water and air cold, what did it matter? He dove in. As the liquid hugged and cleansed him, he forgot about his troubles and worries.

Movement tickled one of his legs, and he scrambled out of the pool. Something red floated in the water. He backed away, expecting it to be one of the nasty creatures, maybe more.

A reddish tail splashed, and green hair surfaced.

"Ruslana?" His Rusalka friend.

"Theo, I was wondering who was so brave as to enter my waters."

"Your waters?"

"I like to come here to get away from all the drama at home. You know how tedious Dimana can get. And Zlo's red monsters are time-consuming to destroy. I needed a break."

Theo hadn't found the other Rusalka tedious. More like dangerous. She hated humans and had treated him with disdain. Ruslana had been the only one in the Rusalki world to befriend and willingly help him.

"Thank you for sending me the message through the shell. Those nasty creatures are in my world, too."

"We're glad you made it." Ruslana smiled.

Theo recalled what Diva had said about the Rusalki possibly knowing what the golden tear pearls were. "Can you tell me what—"

Screams and flaps of wings interrupted their conversation. A large black raven descended and grabbed Theo's medallion with its beak. Theo reached for his bow, nocked an arrow, and aimed at the escaping bird. The arrow missed the bird by seconds.

He gritted his teeth. *If only I could turn into a dragon now.*

He dropped his bow and arrows and waved his arms, concentrating as hard as he could. Nothing happened. He felt under his arms but touched only tense muscles.

The bird was already high in the sky. It was going to get away. What was Theo going to do? He had to shift. What had his mother told him? Love and righteous anger would work. Right now, he was angry and frustrated. He had to learn to control his emotions.

A second arrow whooshed through the air and pierced the raven's wing.

Diva stood by the hut with her bow, an arrow already nocked.

The bird screamed, letting loose the medallion. Theo raced after it, trying to keep an eye on where it might land.

As the raven rolled and tumbled downward, the bird kept pace with the medallion and reached out its claws to grab it. It missed and tried again.

Diva let loose a second arrow, piercing the bird's other wing.

The raven spun in a spiral, its feathers scattering, and formed a funnel of black smoke that grew into a whirlwind within seconds. Two fiery eyes from its midst stared at Theo.

"*Zlo waits for you,*" the bird-wind said.

Theo covered his face and shrank back. His body shook. Arms embraced him. Theo turned to find Diva by his side.

"Are you okay? This is yours." She handed him the medallion, its chain stained with drops of blood.

"What was that?"

"It must have been one of Zlo's servants. He seems to need your amulet to carry out his plan."

"Or me." Theo told her what the bird had spoken.

"Soon enough, he'll see you," Diva said. "But not in the way he expects. You'll be there to stop him."

Theo hoped she was right. "Thank you for saving my medallion. I was stupid to take it off and leave it on the rock."

"Carelessness pays dearly," she said as if quoting a proverb.

Theo nodded. "I won't be so stupid again. When the raven took it, I tried to use my dragon powers to defend myself, but I failed."

"You'll learn. Trust me. I didn't always succeed when I tried."

"I hope." He started walking back to the pool. "I was talking to Ruslana. I wanted to see if she could give us information about the prophecy."

They reached the pool, and Theo gazed into the water. "Ruslana?"

The Rusalka was gone.

"I'm sure she got scared," Diva said. "Everyone's awake. We should return so they don't worry and think we've been abducted."

Theo dried himself, put his T-shirt and pants back on, and retrieved his bow and arrow. As they walked back to the hut, a white blur sped past and rushed inside. Theo ran after it and found Pavel hugging a panting puppy.

"There you are," his friend said to the animal. "I was worried you'd run away."

Theo sighed with relief that it wasn't another of Zlo's spies.

"Has anyone seen Boo?" he asked.

"He hasn't returned yet," Mraz said. "If he's not back by the time we're ready to go, we'll have to make our way to Kaleto and hope that's where Zlo is."

It was a long way for the magpie to fly. Theo hoped he'd make it back in time. If they were wrong about Zlo's location, they'd fail.

LATER IN THE MORNING, Mraz sat in the cart, while Zima and Jega fed grain to the oxen. Next to Mraz were a coil of rope, a pile of spears and axes, vessels of water and food, the wolf nets from the Samodivi, and two empty barrels. Mraz clutched the purple velvet bag with *Lamia's Bible* to his chest.

The Kukeri were dressed for battle in shirts and leggings but lacked the belt of bells they used to scare away evil spirits. The evil they'd fight against tonight had a corporal, not spiritual, form, and so physical weapons were needed.

Theo was glad Jega hadn't insisted on wearing his bells. The Kuker had gotten them into trouble last year when his bells alerted soldiers of their presence. Now, Jega wore a necklace of sharp teeth, which he said brought him luck, and a belt holding other necessities for the journey.

All the Samodivi and Sur's herd waited in a column ready to take off. Theo hadn't seen the rest of the women since they'd been rescued from Lamia's dungeon last year. Back then, they had been a ragged band. Now, they all wore a fashionable metal belt buckle around their white robes. The large tear-shaped design of each differed. Some held gemstones, while engraved forest scenes embellished others. The belts reminded Theo of something Wonder Woman would wear.

Seeing the Samodivi on their deer was like attending a super-supermodel contest. Theo smiled as he thought about what Pavel would say if he told him that. His friend's words were sure to be, "But Diva's the prettiest of all." Although with Pavel's attachment to the puppy, Theo wondered if his friend would even notice.

*Where is he anyway?* Theo went into the hut.

Pavel sat on the floor, hugging the puppy. Theo was worried. Pavel hadn't left the animal for a moment since he'd found him.

"It's time to say goodbye to the puppy, Pavel. Someone in Dragon Village will make sure he makes it back to his owners. Get your stuff and be ready to leave as soon as Boo returns."

Pavel stood, keeping his arms around the animal. "I'm taking him with me. I'm bringing him back to Selo."

"You can't. Think of how dangerous this trip could be. If you care about the puppy, leave him here."

A low growl rumbled from the animal.

Theo reached to remove the puppy from Pavel's arms, but the animal bared his teeth and bristled.

"See, he wants to stay with me." Pavel held him closer. "He's smart and senses you're not human, and you can hurt him."

Theo had enough. Pavel wasn't thinking straight. He said over his shoulder as he left the hut, "Fine, keep your puppy. Don't blame me if something bad happens to him."

Pavel shouted back, "Don't worry. I'll protect him."

Outside, Theo stood near his possessions. He double-checked that he hadn't forgotten anything: backpack, bow, quiver, sword. A lot to carry. If Pavel came to his senses, he might let him use the bow and arrows. This mission, all Theo needed would be his father's sword. At least, that's what he hoped.

The door of the hut closed, and Pavel joined Theo. His friend had put the puppy inside his jacket, and only the animal's head poked out.

"Do you want me to carry the bow and arrows," Pavel asked.

Theo thought for a moment. He couldn't stay angry with Pavel. Even though Pavel had his gadgets, a weapon would be a better means of protection.

"Sure," he said. "I can manage the quiver for now, but if you'll take the bow, that would be great. Thank you."

One friend back where he belonged, now Theo paced waiting for his avian one. Mraz stirred in the cart. He wouldn't wait much longer.

*Boo, where are you? Are you okay?*

The leaves of the forest moved, and the bells chimed. Theo looked toward where the sound originated. A short time later, Boo descended like a small black ball and landed on Theo's shoulder. The magpie lightly pecked Theo's ear.

"Boo, buddy, you made it in time. We were going to have to leave soon."

The bird swayed left and right letting out a series of "Waak, waaks" as if speaking.

"I really wish I could understand you." He'd been able to a couple of times before, but that dragon ability escaped him for the moment. "Did you follow the Youdi all the way through the mountain tunnel?"

Boo swung his beak in agreement.

"Did you find where Zlo is hiding? Is it the fortress at Kaleto?"

Boo croaked out "Waak" and swung his beak up and down.

"As a reward, I have some of your favorite food." Theo reached into his pocket and tossed the contents of a packet of sunflower seeds onto the ground. While the bird pecked them fast as if someone else might take them, Theo made his way over to Mraz. "You were right. Zlo is in the fortress at Kaleto."

"Finally," Zima said as he gathered his weapons. "I thought the bird would never return."

"Boo," Mraz called to the magpie, and the bird flew over and perched on the cart. "I know you must be tired, but could you fly to the Kukeri sanctuary and inform the rest of my brothers about the location? It's okay for them to carry out a plan they devised."

"Waak, waak." Boo bobbed his beak up and down.

"Thank you, my friend." Mraz wrote a note on a piece of parchment and handed it to the bird, who grasped it in his claw. "Rest at the sanctuary once you've delivered the message."

Boo gave one final "Waak" before he flew away.

"We have just thirteen hours until midnight," Zima said as he approached the cart. "We should go now if we want to get there in time to defeat this monster."

"Let's go attack them. We're ready." Jega jumped around and waved a mace and spear in his hands.

Mraz got down from the cart and walked to where the Samodivi waited. "The fortress of Kaleto it is. Good luck with your plans. We can all meet back at the Kukeri sanctuary when this is over."

With that, the Samodivi took to the air. Each deer's fireball glowed purple.

Mraz returned to the cart and cracked a whip above the heads of the oxen. The beasts lumbered forward, heading toward the imminent battle.

Theo squeezed his medallion, hoping for success.

# Chapter 17
# Trouble on the Road to Kaleto

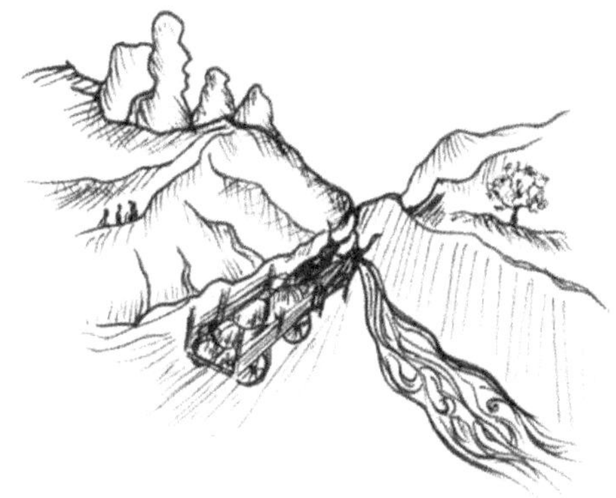

THEY LEFT THE CHIMING of the Forest of Whispering Bells far behind. Theo missed the sound, but the steady clomps of the oxen's feet as they trudged along the dry path were almost as soothing. The dust the animals kicked up wasn't, though. It clogged his throat and nose and made him cough and sneeze. He took a sip of water for what felt like the hundredth time. At this rate, he'd have to get a refill from the cart Mraz was driving before they'd even walked for an hour.

Pavel had been gulping down water at the same rate and gave some to the puppy tucked inside his jacket. Theo hoped the animal didn't have an accident. The Kukeri walked in front of the cart, and so they didn't seem affected by the dust. Besides that, they were so tall the particles had spread thin by the time the dust reached their faces. And Diva. How Theo admired her. The only thing he'd seen unsettle her was the destroyed books. Terrible smells and dust had little effect on the brave Samodiva.

As they traveled north in the direction of the Kukeri sanctuary, Zima and Jega strode along at a brisk pace, surveying each side of the path for dangers or traps. Zlo's spies and soldiers could be anywhere. They had all agreed they'd risk taking the flat, less arduous route for as long as they could.

Theo glanced at the trees lining the riverbed in the ravine below the path, wondering if the raven that had been following him, the one Diva had shot with her arrows, would reappear and try to steal his medallion again or even capture him this time. If it could transform into a whirlwind, Theo imagined Zlo's spy could become anything. He had sensed something watching him since they had left the hut but hadn't caught sight of the raven.

"Do you think the bird's out there?" he asked.

Diva squeezed his arm. "Don't worry. I doubt it'll be back." Her calm and confident voice relaxed Theo.

"Diva and I will both shoot it with arrows if it returns." Pavel stroked the black bow. "This is so awesome. I can't wait to use it."

"Okay, Robin Hood, but I hope you don't have to." The rhythmic beat of marching men reached Theo's ears. "Shh. They're coming."

"I don't hear anything," Pavel said.

Diva put her finger to her mouth and closed her eyes. "I can hear them, too."

A cloud of dust appeared far ahead.

"Soldiers," Zima shouted back.

"Time to head toward the ravine." Mraz turned the oxen down the steep slope.

"But the animals are trampling the path." Pavel wrapped his hands tight around the puppy. "They'll find us for sure."

"No, they won't." Zima arrived and began pushing them toward the path the oxen had made. "Jega and I will fix it. Just go."

"But they must have already seen our dust, the same as we've seen theirs," Pavel argued.

"GO!" Zima gave Pavel a hard shove.

Unlike Pavel, Theo didn't need to be told twice. He grabbed hold of Pavel to stabilize him and pulled his friend down the path as they scurried after Diva.

Stones clattered as they slid down the path the oxen had created. Theo skidded on the loose stones and banged into the back of the cart. Pavel and Diva fared no better. The heavy, lumbering beasts made the going slow, but the animals prevented them from tumbling all the way to the bottom of the ravine. More than once, Theo found himself pressed against the cart, steadying himself, with Pavel and Diva crushed on either side.

A boulder thundered past to one side, setting Theo's heart racing. Was the slope giving way? He chanced a glance up the path. The Kukeri brothers hadn't fixed the path the oxen had trodden. It still lay crushed all the way to the top.

Another boulder crashed down the slope farther away.

Zima and Jega appeared near where the sound had occurred. They each disappeared to the other side of the dusty path. Soon a third boulder thundered into view and rumbled down the slope, making an additional crushed path.

The Kukeri brothers were creating decoys. Zlo's soldiers wouldn't know which path was the real escape route.

Theo returned to his descent. Diva and Pavel hadn't made it much farther ahead while he'd been observing the Kukeri, so he easily caught up. If by easy, he was talking about timewise.

Nothing about scuttling down a path filled with loose debris and prickly thorns was easy. His arms and legs were scratched and scraped, dust filled his eyes, surely making them red, and the clay particles coated his clothing and body.

The thunder of more boulders crashing down the slope meant Zima and Jega continued to create fake paths. That alone wouldn't be enough to trick the soldiers. The cart and all of them were visible from the upper path. They needed somewhere to hide before the soldiers ventured closer.

As if Mraz had heard Theo's thoughts, the Kuker called out, "Cavern ahead."

The cart swerved to the side and disappeared into a dark hole. Theo, Pavel, and Diva followed, and moved to the back of the cavern. Pavel was near the cart, and Theo by the wall, with Diva between them.

The space wasn't much taller than Mraz, and with the oxen and cart, the cavern was barely wide enough to hold them with room to move. The cart took up half the area. Adding Zima and Jega would make for a tight fit. At least they had a place to hide.

The walls looked like someone long ago had carved vertical lines into the limestone, rather than being a natural effect of erosion. In places, age or the weather had made the surfaces uneven and smoky. Traces of ash littered the floor, among the overgrown weeds. Whoever had inhabited this place had long since abandoned it. As its new occupants trampled the undergrowth, the tight space filled with the aroma of lemongrass and freshly cut grass.

One of the oxen began licking the damp wall of the hiding place, and the puppy wiggled and whimpered in Pavel's grasp. The only other sound was heavy breathing.

The crashing of boulders continued a while longer. One rolled along the path they'd been traveling. Theo hoped that was to pack down the vegetation the same as the fake paths. The clacking of feet on stones followed soon after. That had to be Zima and Jega approaching. At least, Theo hoped it was the Kukeri brothers. He hadn't heard weapons clashing in battle, so the soldiers couldn't have arrived yet.

With barely a sound, the two brothers entered the cavern. Zima squeezed himself into the space in front of Theo, while Jega stood before Pavel. No sweat poured off either Zima or Jega, and their breathing was steady. How difficult was pushing several boulders for a Kuker, after all? Someday, Theo hoped he'd have their strength, along with his other developing abilities.

They all waited in silence until the steady beat of marching neared—and then stopped.

The soldiers had arrived.

Theo's heart pounded in his ears. *Please, keep going.*

The soldiers didn't listen.

The voice of the one who must have been their commander shouted orders for the men, if they were men and not some form of beast, to form pairs and search each newly made path.

Theo whispered to Mraz, "What do we do now?"

The Kuker put his finger to his lips.

*Thump. Thump. Thump.*

Heavy footsteps marched down the paths. These soldiers didn't slide on the scattered rocks. What kind of creatures were they?

Rocks skidded past the cavern opening. The pair assigned to their path were almost upon them.

*Thump. Thump. Thump.* Now the sound was Theo's heart.

The puppy barked, and the footsteps stopped.

"Did you hear that?" one of the soldiers asked.

Before the other one could reply, Jega turned around. With an apologetic look at Pavel, he did something to the puppy that Theo couldn't see. The animal's head slumped forward.

Pavel's jaw dropped, and his eyes went wide and wild. He barely croaked out "You …" before Diva clamped her hand over his mouth.

Her whispered words came out more like a hiss. "He's not dead. Just unconscious. Now shut up."

When she removed her hand, Pavel's eyes remained wide and his mouth open as he looked at her. He nodded and closed his mouth. His eyes glistened with unshed tears as he stroked the puppy's head.

The soldiers had advanced, their footsteps stealthier. Their breaths came out as pants, like an animal on the prowl. Another sound. Sniffing. They were close.

Theo clenched his hands into fists. *Why can't I control my dragon powers? I could transform and burn them all to ashes.*

In front of Theo, Zima nudged Jega. The younger Kuker gave a single nod.

Jega raised one arm and held his hand straight out in front of him. A ball of blue flames burned and swirled in his palm. He pivoted his hand until his palm faced the cave entrance. In a movement so swift Theo would have missed it if he had blinked, Jega brought his hand back, then thrust it forward. The blue ball shot out like a bullet and landed farther down the slope. It blazed like a tongue of fire from the ground.

The soldiers stopped, barely feet from the cave according to the sound of their footsteps.

"Do you see that?" one asked. "A blue flame."

"Treasure." The other one's panting changed from hunt to lust.

At the mention of treasure, Theo didn't have to ask Jega what he had done. Even in Selo, people believed that a blue flame flashed three times over a location where buried treasure was hidden.

"We can't," the first said, his words sounding reluctant.

"Let's mark the spot now and come back later."

"I don't know …"

Jega raised his hand again and slowly lowered it. The blue flame flickered and shrank with his motion.

"Look," the first soldier cried out. "If we don't mark the location now, we'll never be able to find it again."

"But …"

While they spoke, Jega hurled more blue flames, scattered farther away from the cavern.

"Look at them all." The pitch of the first soldier's voice rose. "I'm going. You stay here if you want."

Hurried footsteps pounded away from the cavern.

The other soldier remained. Rocks clattered as he must have been shuffling his feet. Then, his footsteps faded.

Theo would have smiled if he hadn't been so nervous. The soldiers were in for a surprise when they returned and discovered nothing there. Not only that, but they wouldn't be able to accomplish their task in one night.

Where real treasure was hidden, a talasum, a spirit, guarded the location. The spirit was created in a ritual where the person who buried it sacrificed an animal to protect his loot. He cursed anyone who tried to dig it up. This talasum could be bribed to relinquish his hoard, however. But first, the soldiers would have to use a sieve to spread an even layer of flour or ashes on the ground where they saw the blue flames. Then, they'd have to return the next night to see what type of animal footprints the talasum left. If they sacrificed the same type of animal, they would free the talasum and be permitted to uncover the treasure without being cursed. As there was no treasure here, the soldiers would make two trips to this location for nothing.

Theo hoped the soldiers would stay occupied long enough for him and his friends to avoid detection.

It seemed like hours later when the commander at the top of the ravine called his troops back. The two soldiers on their path ambled past, laughing and speaking words about how wealthy they were going to be. Neither stopped to check the cavern.

A while longer after the sound of marching had faded, Theo squirmed. *It must be safe to leave now.*

Diva likely had the same thought. She twirled in the small space, turned into a dove, and flew from the cavern.

Theo fidgeted and counted the seconds until she returned.

In moments, she appeared as herself at the entrance. "All clear."

After escaping the soldiers, they proceeded down the ravine and arrived at the river. Or what had once been one. Now only a trickle of water flowed over the stony bed. Theo looked up the path they had made down the steep slope. Along with the multitude of boulder-created paths, hundreds of dark holes dotted the terrain. It would have been impossible for Zlo's soldiers to have searched them all.

Mraz got off the cart. "We need to be on the other side, so we'll cross the river here. It'll be easier than farther north where the river is still flowing." He led the oxen across, got back into the cart, and continued following the river north.

"Oh, my aching feet," Pavel said as he sat and removed his sneakers and rubbed the soles of his feet. "I have to rest a while."

Zima sneered and walked past. "Humans are so weak and fragile."

Following him, Jega gave a sympathetic shrug.

Pavel opened his mouth, but Theo covered it. "Don't say anything. Compared to them, we are."

The puppy, now recovered, growled and nipped at Theo's hand.

"Ow!" He drew it away. "I wasn't hurting Pavel. He's my friend."

"You're not human either," Pavel grumbled as he put on his shoes and stood. "That's why he doesn't like you. I'm the only human here, so he feels safe with me."

"Pavel, I'm …" What could he say? He was human? No, he'd been brought up as one, but he'd have to accept he wasn't. Would that make Pavel stop being his friend? Pavel's response to him hurt, but they'd have to sort this out later. They needed to continue the mission now. "C'mon. Let's catch up with the others. At least now we'll be walking on a flat path."

Her eyes sad, Diva looked at the two of them, but kept her mouth shut. Theo was glad she didn't interfere. Pavel would likely have snapped at her, too.

# Chapter 18
# Friendship

THEY WALKED ALONG the river's edge another couple of hours in silence, with only the sound of the cart thumping over rocks and the oxen's heavy feet thudding against the ground. Theo was tense, looking from side to side the entire way. He thought he saw a raven following them, but it was too distant even for his improved vision.

When they reached a branch of the river that flowed freely, Mraz raised a hand and halted the cart. "We'll rest here a while. Have something to eat and drink before we continue."

"Finally." Pavel moaned, looking down at the puppy. "I'll let you out so you can have a drink and do your business."

He put his backpack and Theo's bow on the ground before he unzipped his jacket and set the puppy down. While keeping an eye on the animal, he removed his sneakers and socks and soaked his feet in the water.

Theo set his backpack, quiver, and sword down and settled on a rock next to Pavel. "You know I'm your friend, right? I can't change the fact I'm not who we both thought I was before."

Pavel shrugged, still not looking at Theo. "Yah, I know. It's just … everyone here can do fantastic things. Everyone except me."

"That's not true. Look at all your inventions." Theo dug in his backpack and pulled out the laser that had stunned the red creatures. "None of the rest of us would have thought to make something like this. And look how successful it's been, both in Selo and here at Vida Fortress."

"Yah, but that's not the same as superpowers."

"No, it's better." Theo lightly tapped Pavel's shoulder. "Because you have a super-brain, Einstein."

Pavel beamed. "Well, maybe. But, still …"

Theo tensed. *Here it comes. Questions I don't have answers for.*

"Nobody here needs me, or wants me, the way they do you," Pavel said with sadness. "Not even Diva."

"I do. And …"

Pavel held his hand up. "It's more than that. When this is all over, where will you stay? Selo or Dragon Village?"

"I …"

"I know." Pavel sighed and cast his eyes to the ground. "You haven't figured that out. I just don't know where that leaves me in your list of priorities."

"You'll always be my friend. My best friend. No matter where I am. No matter who I am."

Pavel looked up, his eyes swimming with unshed tears. "But you won't need or want a human friend when you'll have the love and respect of all of Dragon Village."

"That's not true." Theo wrapped an arm around Pavel's shoulders. "You're like a brother to me. I'll always need you and your inspiration. Not to mention, your inventions."

"Even if they don't work?"

"Especially when they don't work."

"Hope I'm not interrupting." Jega seated himself on the other side of Pavel. "I'd like to apologize to you, Pavel. I didn't have time to explain what I was going to do. I didn't hurt the puppy."

"I know. It's okay, but don't be surprised if the puppy tries to bite you. Oh, where is he?" Pavel looked around and found the animal curled up, sleeping by a bush.

Jega stood. "Perhaps I should catch a fish, so we can do a friendship ritual."

"Friendship ritual?" Pavel said.

"With a fish?" Theo added.

Jega grinned. "As in, cook it and eat it."

Theo and Pavel laughed.

The Kuker grabbed his spear and stepped onto a stone in the river. He bent and stirred his hand in the water. "Ah, I think there's something under this rock."

Jega pushed it aside, and reddish-purple tentacles poured out of the cavity. Before he could react, the creature's limbs tangled around his shoulder.

"Jega!" Zima screamed and rushed past Theo, who sat frozen to the spot.

Zima tore at the tentacles, ripping them off his brother. Every time he removed one, another squeezed itself around Jega.

"Theo!" Pavel shouted as he dug in his backpack. "Put your Pavel-o-paralyzer on high power and come help."

As Pavel pulled out his spare laser, Theo shook himself out of the shock of the sudden attack. He turned the switch all the way up and joined Pavel, who was already slicing off the creature's tentacles. Diva had changed into a hawk and was tearing at the creature as well. Mraz stood by with his spear aimed at the monster.

"Be careful not to touch Jega with the beam," Pavel warned Theo.

Theo aimed at a tentacle that was reaching for Jega. The creature let out a loud squeal as the laser burned through the tip. Purple ooze fell in globs into the water. Theo and Pavel cut off more limbs until the creature dropped into the now purple-tinted water and disappeared as quickly as it had arrived.

Diva turned back into a girl and pulled out an ointment from her pouch as Zima helped his brother out of the water. Jega gripped his shoulder, his face contorted with pain.

"Here, sit," Diva ordered. She applied the ointment to the wounds. "It'll heal quickly."

"Thank you, all of you." Jega let out a pained sigh. "I guess I learned a lesson. Don't turn over stones when you're not sure what's under them."

"We're glad we could help," Pavel said.

"No fish today, I guess. We'll have to settle for whatever Mraz brought and do our friendship ritual another time." Jega held out his hand to Pavel. "You're full of surprises. May I see that device you used?"

"It's my Pavel-o-paralyzer." Pavel handed the gadget to the Kuker. "It stuns things. Or in this case, cuts through them."

Jega examined it. "Marvelous. Simple but effective."

"Glad you think so." Pavel threw a victorious look at Zima. "Your brother didn't want to try."

"Hmmmph." Zima stalked away.

Pavel wore a wide grin. Theo smiled, too, glad for Pavel's triumphant moment.

AFTER THEY ATE AND RESTED, they left off traveling along the river and continued for another couple of hours toward the Kukeri sanctuary. Here, Mraz said his goodbyes.

"I must secure *Lamia's Bible* where no one will find it." He held the purple bag close to his chest. "It's possible Zlo needs a spell written in here to complete his ritual tonight. Even if he doesn't, we don't want its other secrets to fall into his hands. It's essential I stay with the book until everything is safe once more in Zmeykovo. Zima will take over leadership and driving the oxen."

"Take the human with you," Zima said. "This is too important a mission for him to mess up."

"Enough of that talk," Mraz said with a stern voice. "Pavel stays with your team. You'll need all the help you can get."

Theo groaned. No one could keep Zima's temper in check. Not Jega. Not Diva. And certainly not Theo himself. Only Mraz. Theo chastised himself for not listening more carefully to their discussion the other night, so he would have known Mraz was leaving. But the sword had captivated Theo, mesmerized him. Even now, he could feel its power pulsing through the scabbard.

"Oh, just great," Pavel muttered.

Theo was certain it was for the same reason he was concerned. Zima would be intolerable.

Mraz either misunderstood or intentionally ignored their discomfort. "Don't worry. Your next stop is at the lake, and that's only about a half hour's walk from here. Rest well. The last part of the trip will be over rugged terrain."

"My poor feet." Pavel moaned. "I guess we should get going. The sooner we move, the quicker I can sit."

"Do I need to carry you?" Zima sneered and let out an exaggerated sigh.

Pavel folded his arms across his chest and stood tall. "No, I'm fine. I can walk by myself, probably faster than you."

Theo looked away, at the path in front of them, blocking out the duel of words between his friends. He took a few steps forward. "Hey, Pavel, you coming?"

The walk to the lake was pleasant and quick as Mraz had said. Trees and shrubs were scattered throughout the area, and the cool breeze refreshed him. Best of all, the way to the lake was flat, so the walking wasn't strenuous.

As they drew closer to their destination, Theo's shoulders slumped. "Oh, no."

Pavel squinted and pushed his glasses closer to his eyes. "What do you see?"

"Something red on the beach. More creatures, I think." Couldn't they have a peaceful moment before they had to confront Zlo?

"Maybe not." Diva pointed to a figure that had risen and was waving.

Theo, Diva, and Pavel left the Kukeri brothers and slow-moving cart behind and hurried to the lake. Ruslana greeted them from a rock she had taken over, her tail swishing in the water.

"Are you escaping Dimana again?" Theo asked as he gave her a big hug.

"That I am." She laughed, but then became serious. "I barely escaped from the bay this time. Zlo's forces are out in numbers now, looking for you."

"We already ran into one group." Theo shuddered. "Thanks to Jega's power of fire, we managed to escape." He told her about the encounter and what Jega had done.

"Brilliant." She smiled. "He's my favorite Kuker."

"And you're my favorite Rusalka." Jega strode up behind them and bowed.

"Where's that obnoxious brother of yours?" Ruslana asked. "I hope you left him behind at the sanctuary."

"Alas, no." Jega over-exaggerated a sigh. "He trails behind and will be here momentarily."

"Fun's over, I guess." Ruslana prepared to jump into the water.

"Wait." Theo grabbed her hand. "Don't leave. You can ignore him."

"Ignoring Zima is like ignoring a crab clinging to your tail." Ruslana pursed her lips. "I really should return home. It's safer under the water than here on land."

"All right." Theo hated his friends having their freedom of movement taken away. Tonight would tell what their future would be. "I need to ask you something first. Have you heard of golden tear pearls? It's something Zlo needs to perform his ritual."

"Golden tear pearls?" Ruslana rubbed her chin, then shook her head. "Sorry, it's unfamiliar to me." She gave him a hug. "Good luck. We're all counting on you to beat the beast."

With that, she flipped her tail and dove into the lake.

"If no one else is hungry, I am," Pavel said. He sorted through his backpack and retrieved a large plastic bottle, only this one had been cut and the top repositioned inside the base in the opposite direction.

"What's that?" Jega asked.

"It's my Ribotron. It's to catch fish."

Diva looked at it with curious eyes. "I'll go gather fruit while you fish with your strange drinking device."

"I must stay here and see how this works." Jega sat on the rock Ruslana had vacated.

Pavel grinned. "It's easier and safer than running your hand through the water and getting stung by a red creature. This will actually capture several small fish, rather than a large one, but we'll need at least one if we want to do your friendship ritual."

Jega laughed. "We will, indeed. Explain its mechanisms, please."

"This is usually used when you're stuck somewhere with no food and no other way to catch fish."

"And do you always carry it around with you in case that happens?"

"No." Pavel shook his head. "Unfortunately, in our world, people throw these bottles around, and you can find them littering the ground practically anywhere. This model is only the first draft, my travel-sized fish catcher. I plan to add more bells and whistles later."

"I'm afraid those items won't work well under water," Jega replied.

"Not *real* bells and whistles," Pavel said. "That just means more features."

"I see." Jega nodded. "Proceed, please."

"As you can see, this is a larger version of the water bottles Theo and I have." He held out his plastic drinking bottle and demonstrated as he spoke. "I cut the top off here where it's the same size as the bottom. Then I cut off this smaller part that we drink from, so the hole is large enough for the fish to swim through. After that, I turn the top part around and insert it into the bottom section until it fits snugly. Fish find it easy to enter, but not to swim back out."

"So simple, yet this catches fish, you say?" Jega held out his hands. "May I see?"

"Sure." Pavel handed over his Ribotron.

Jega examined the gadget all over. "Surprisingly light and simply marvelous. How does it work?"

"Before I insert the top, I put something inside to attract the fish. Could be bait or even something shiny like white rocks."

"Why are there all these holes on the top?" Jega poked his fingers into them.

"Those are to make sure the fish trap stays underwater. Plastic, as you mentioned, is light and so it floats," Pavel said. "When it's all put together, you place it into the water. Against the current is best, so the fish naturally swim into it. It's a good idea to put it tight against rocks, too, so it doesn't get swept downstream. And best of all, this one has a rope attached, so I can pull it out later and not worry if red creatures are in the water."

"Would you be willing to trade for this?" Jega asked.

"Trade?" Pavel paused a moment. "I'm not sure this is worth much of anything. It's easy to make, and plastic bottles are everywhere."

"But not here."

"Okay, sure. Or I could just give this one to you."

"No, I'd like to give you something in return."

Pavel shrugged. "Sure. Why not?"

Jega removed the tooth necklace from around his neck and a silver horn attached to his side. "Will these do for a trade? The teeth are from a wolf that attacked me ages ago, and this is a rhyton, my drinking vessel."

"Wow! Yah. Sure. They're awesome. Worth way more than a discarded plastic bottle, though."

"Not to me." Jega handed over the items. "Now, let's eat and celebrate friendship."

Jega placed the Ribotron into the water as Pavel had recommended, and soon several fish had made their way inside. Pavel started a fire and cooked the fish, and Diva laid out the fruit, nuts, and berries she'd gathered. They sat on a large, flat stone. Even Zima joined them when he arrived and had unhitched and fed the oxen.

Theo had been so busy he hadn't had a chance to admire the place they stopped. The lake jutted up next to the mountain, and a stream of water poured out of a crevice in the rocks, darkening the gray stones. Away from the beach area, trees lined the shoreline. Ripened fruit colored their branches red, yellow, and orange. The beach itself held white sand, and large flat stones were scattered around, making a great place to have a picnic.

Or a final meal.

As they finished their food, a light rain fell but quickly dried up. In the sky, a colorful rainbow broke through patches in the dark clouds, as if telling the two moons that their reign was soon to end.

"Queen Zunitza is protecting us with her spirit," Diva said and looked at Theo. "Do you know of your mother's connection to the rainbow?"

"No, I'd—"

Before he could finish, Zima shouted. "Pack up, everyone. We've wasted enough time. Let's get going."

Jega got up and went to help Zima re-hitch the oxen.

"I'd like to hear it," Theo said.

Pavel poked his head between the two of them. "Me, too."

The three friends picked up their possessions and followed the Kukeri brothers.

Diva began her tale. "We call the rainbow Zuna. Our queen was named after it. For that honor, Zunitza was the first Samodiva to make our belts, woven from threads in all the colors of the rainbow: red, orange, yellow, green, blue, indigo, and violet."

"The belts make you … ah, Samodivi even more beautiful." Pavel blushed as he spoke.

Theo smiled, glad his friend was back to being Diva's admirer. Pavel still clung tight to the puppy, though. Perhaps now it was more to protect the animal in this dangerous place than it was out of mistrust of everyone else.

Diva gave Theo a knowing look. She, too, must have recognized the change in Pavel.

"Do you have stories about where the rainbow comes from originally?" Theo asked.

"Yes, our people believe that Tangra, the god of light and the sun, created the rainbow to reassure us that he wouldn't flood the world. The gentle glow of the rainbow is a sign that he hasn't withdrawn his blessing from our land."

"Like the rainbow after Noah's flood," Theo added.

"I don't know this Noah. Perhaps you can tell me about him."

"It's similar, about God promising not to flood the world again," Theo said. "But I'd like to hear more about your rainbow stories, if that's okay."

"Sure." Diva returned to her tale. "The rainbow drinks water from the clouds."

"That must be why it appears after a storm," Pavel said, "because it's gulped down all that water."

"True," Diva said, "But that's not enough to make it full. When the heavenly moisture is gone, the rainbow bends down to earth to drink from a spring, a river, or the sea."

Pavel removed his glasses and cleaned them on his shirt. As he put them back on, he said in his most Einstein-like way, "I'm going to invent something to help me find the ends of the rainbow."

"Really?"

"Yes, really."

Diva smiled. "The place where the rainbow drinks is secret, and it's difficult to trace the ends of her colorful belt. To find it, look for the silver cup she drinks from. She leaves it near the spring."

Pavel beamed. "Great. Thanks for the tip. I'll be rich when I find all the treasures there, and then I can really be an inventor."

"That all depends," Diva said. "If the treasures you're looking for are knowing what your future holds and making all your wishes come true, then good luck."

"Oh." Pavel scrunched up his face. "Maybe I don't want to know my future. Look how much trouble knowing his fate has been for Theo. I'll stick to inventing more practical things."

Theo nodded. "I agree. Don't get sucked down that hole. Anyway, Diva, thanks for telling us about the rainbow."

"My pleasure."

They walked around the perimeter of the lake for perhaps another hour. Not far ahead the flat landscape turned into jagged rocks, climbing high into the sky. The huge assembly of rocks resembled grotesque, deformed monsters, with gaping holes for their eyes and mouth. Some sneered as if saying, "How dare you cross our boundaries?" Others growled, ready to devour those who trespassed. Theo hoped these weren't the remnants of the Ispolini, but he feared they likely were. They formed a border around what must be Kaleto.

They had arrived.

Only a few more hours until midnight, and they still had to pass the monstrosities to reach the fortress. And once inside, if they made it through the gate, they had to find and stop Zlo. Theo rubbed his pounding head. How were they going to possibly succeed in so little time?

*I can't think that way. We overcame many obstacles to defeat Lamia as a team. We can do the same with Zlo.*

When they reached the towering rocks, Zima stopped the cart near a small cavern. He and Jega unhitched the oxen and let them graze on clumps of grass. They pushed the cart inside and loaded themselves with rope and weapons.

Zima smirked at Jega. "So, brother, my plan or yours?"

Jega straightened his back. "We could do both, but since it's better to stay together, let's try your plan. We don't have much time."

"Agreed." Zima pounded his spear onto the ground. "Everyone, fill your water vessels, have a quick bite to eat, and leave your possessions in the cavern. Take only what's essential to fight or travel. The rest of the way in will be rough going."

Theo and Pavel placed their backpacks into the cart in the spot the weapons had occupied. They each took a quick drink and filled their bottles.

Pavel looked longingly at the bow he carried. "Can I really use this?"

"Yes, of course." Theo removed the quiver and handed it to his friend. "You'll need these first, though."

"Is there anything special or magical I need to know to use it?"

"No," Theo said. "You know the techniques. I just practiced a lot what Diva taught me."

"In three words," Diva said, "Focus. Focus. Focus. If you know how to shoot, you'll be fine."

"Just watch out for the cobra." Theo laughed.

"What?" Pavel juggled the bow. "It'll turn into a cobra when I use it?"

"Just kidding." Theo tapped the bow. "It only hissed at people it didn't like."

They rejoined the group, and Zima glared at Pavel, who had the puppy secured in his jacket. "That creature is not essential. Leave it here."

"No." Pavel took several steps back, clutching the whining animal. "He'll be afraid and might get lost."

Theo touched his friend's shoulder. "He could die if you bring him with you."

Pavel shook his head repeatedly. "He's my friend. I'm bringing him. You wouldn't leave a friend behind, would you?"

"Fool, you'll be the death of us all," Zima spat out, then turned his back on Pavel. "All right. We chose the eastern gate, because it's the most difficult to reach. It's less likely they'll be expecting us here. There could be one guard or many. We won't know until we get there. Be prepared for anything."

Diva spoke up. "I can tell you how many. I'll fly ahead and survey their numbers."

"Good thinking." Zima gave her a nod of approval. "We'll continue forward while you do reconnaissance."

Diva spun on her heels, forming a funnel of white and pink light from which a falcon emerged. She flew high above the stone formations toward the fortress.

Pavel watched until she disappeared. "If I had taken my drone, we could have studied every inch and taken pictures. And Diva would have been safer."

"Drone?" Jega scratched the back of his head. "What type of bird is that?"

"It's an aircraft. A bird made of iron and steel."

"I see. A steel bird, like we have a bird of fire, our golden bird."

While Diva was familiarizing herself with the fortress layout, Zima said, "She's a warrior. She'll be fine. Let's move out."

The Kuker strode forward toward the tall stone giants. They made their way through tight paths between the stony outcrops. Beyond the monsters, they used mountain climbing gear, or the Kukeri equivalent of it, to ascend lichen-covered boulders. The way upward grew easier in a few areas where a previous explorer or warrior must have hewn stone arches through the massive rocks. The dankness inside them reminded Theo of the path up to the Stone Forest in Selo.

When they reached the end of one archway, they came out into open space. Ahead of them lay a wooden bridge. Zima had stopped there waiting for them.

"The Samodiva is returning." He pointed toward a descending falcon. "We'll wait for her report."

Theo panted and placed his hands on his knees as he bent over to regain his breath. Pavel looked just as worn out, leaning against the boulder they had crawled through. His friend rubbed the puppy's head while the animal tried to lick his face.

Diva circled above, as if looking for them or checking out the surroundings more. Soon, she glided in their direction, landed on the ground, fluttered her wings, and returned to her girl form.

Theo felt a tinge of jealousy. Diva was a master of her craft. It seemed so effortless for her to shapeshift when she needed to perform a task. "I wish I could manage my powers like you do and get my wings when I need them."

"You will be able to, Theo. It takes time to get to know ourselves. Sometimes if we're not careful, our strength can work against us."

Zima stepped closer. "What did you see and learn, Samodiva?"

Diva threw back her shoulders and stood straight, the way a human soldier would do when addressing a commanding officer. "Hundreds of soldiers with spears and cannons guard the battlement. The central entrance and the western one are well-guarded, but the eastern one is less secure. Only two soldiers are positioned there."

"That's encouraging news." He gave Pavel a smirk. "I was correct after all, human." He turned back to Diva. "Anything else?"

"Inside the fortress several more guards are positioned near another gate," she said. "That must be the entrance to their underground passages, and perhaps where they're keeping Zmey."

Theo's heart raced. He hoped his father was safe and … alive. As much as he wanted to rescue Zmey first, he knew his father would tell him to protect Kosara and the Firebird.

Zima's voice cut back into Theo's thoughts. "And you're certain the bird was correct? This is where those witches came?"

"Yes." Diva nodded. "The Youdi's wagon is near the underground entrance. They're here, wandering around with their wicked smiles."

"Wonderful." Zima strode toward the bridge. "Let's finish this."

The two Kukeri brothers stepped onto the rickety wooden bridge wide enough for one person to cross at a time. They marched forward and soon disappeared around a bend. Theo approached the entrance. The slats were rotten and missing in places, the handrails worn and splintered. The entire structure looked ancient and ready to fall apart.

"I can't," Pavel whispered behind Theo.

Theo turned around. Pavel's face had paled. Theo knew Pavel had to be thinking about the bridge he had got stuck on during their first trip here.

"It'll be okay," Theo said. "This one doesn't sway over a ravine."

"And," Diva added, "more than one person can cross at a time. Theo can go first, you can be in the middle, and I'll be behind you."

Theo stepped onto the bridge and looked back. Diva was nudging Pavel forward. Theo breathed a sigh of relief as they started across. He took slow steps to make sure Pavel could keep up. When Theo rounded the bend where the Kukeri had disappeared, all he saw was more bridge. It appeared to go on forever, winding through and over the boulders. One step at a time, he reminded himself, and they'd be across. After many turns and upward twists, the path straightened. Up ahead, Zima glared at them.

"About time," the Kuker said, just short of shouting.

Theo stepped off the bridge. "We—"

Zima got in Theo's face. "I don't want to hear it. I'm tired of putting up with your friend." He marched off once more.

"Sorry about—" Jega started, but Zima cut him off with a command to get moving.

Theo turned back to the bridge. Pavel had collapsed onto the ground, breathing heavily. "Ow! You bit me," he yelled. "Sorry, I didn't mean to squash you."

The puppy wiggled and squirmed and escaped from Pavel's jacket. The animal ran through a narrow opening in the rocks.

Pavel shouted, "He's gone! My puppy's gone."

Zima turned around as Pavel scrambled to his feet and squeezed through the rocks.

"Pavel, come back!" Theo shouted into the crevice.

"I told you that animal and your friend would be a problem," Zima said. "Leave them to get what they deserve. We have more important people to rescue." With long strides, he continued toward the fortress.

Theo was torn. They had to save Kosara and the Firebird and find Zmey, but he couldn't leave his friend alone either. Pavel had just made a point that the puppy was his friend, and he wouldn't abandon him. Theo shouldn't hesitate to do the same for his friend, and yet he did. Was Pavel right? Did his friend not rank high on Theo's priorities? Decisions shouldn't have to be so difficult to make.

Theo decided he didn't have to choose. He could protect everyone, or try to. They still had time until midnight. He'd go after his friend first.

He stepped toward the opening. "Diva, will you tell the Kukeri where I went?"

"No, I'm coming with you." She tossed her curly hair around. "It's not much farther to the gate. Zima and his attitude can wait. Friends stick together."

They both pressed themselves through the rocks. Pavel was nowhere to be seen. Theo called to him but received no response. Their voices echoed in the darkness. They must be in a cave.

"Diva, where do you—?"

A tight grip over his mouth smothered Theo's remaining words. He kicked backward and dug at the hands that grasped him, but to no avail. His mind went fuzzy, and his body slackened. Moments before his world went black, Diva squeaked somewhere near him.

# Chapter 19
# Under Evil's Spell

THEO WOKE TO DARKNESS. A cloth bandaged his eyes. He moved his hands to untie it but discovered them bound behind his back. The odor of burnt tallow filled the area where he had been left. Another smell permeated the area, too. Sweat, grime, and blood.

"Hello, anyone here?" he called. "Pavel? Diva?"

A fist punched him in the stomach. As he bent over in pain, a sharp metal object stabbed him in the shoulder.

He breathed in someone's hot, foul breath as a voice close to his ear hissed, "The Lord Zlo needs your blood. He'll see you soon to begin the ritual."

Footsteps thudded away and a door slammed shut with a clang.

A cackle came from across the room. "Join the club."

"Baba Yaga?" Was she a prisoner or a guard? "Are Diva and Pavel here?"

"He he. Ho ho." She cackled again. "Nope. Just you, me, and Jabalaka relaxing in this fine resort."

He breathed a sigh of relief that Diva and Pavel had escaped. But Jabalaka was here? He wouldn't have betrayed them all, would he, and be in this together with Baba Yaga? What would he get out of it? A voice in his mind whispered, "His life."

"Jabalaka, can you untie me?"

All he received for an answer was a groan.

"How about you, witch, can you untie me?" He had a few seething words to say to her, but first he wanted to look her in the eyes.

"Nope. Do it yourself. I'm having a steam bath." Once more she cackled.

Theo struggled against his restraints. Now that he was more alert, it felt like rope binding his wrists. When he tugged on it, the rope moved only a short distance. It must be tied to something. He felt around with his hands, touching a round beam, possibly a pole. He kicked his legs. Those remained free.

"How can I get out of this?" he grumbled.

"*Use your powers,*" a voice spoke to his mind. It wasn't his mother or Shar. Who else had a direct connection to his thoughts?

Theo closed his eyes, even though he couldn't see. He let his mind relax. How could he do this? Love and righteous anger, his mother had told him, were keys to transformation. He thought about all the sacrifices Zunitza had made to keep him safe, even giving him up to have someone else raise him. His heart felt her pain and ached with a desire to avenge her.

Tears burned his eyes, and soon heat shot through them. The intensity was too much to endure. He opened his eyes. The cloth binding him began to smolder. He inhaled smoke, but it didn't irritate his throat. He stared at the material more deeply. It crumbled until two holes appeared in front of his eyes.

*Am I really doing this?* He turned his eyes to the side, and more cloth burned away into ashes. In a short time, he had burned enough that what remained fell from his face and settled around his neck. *I wonder if I can shift into a dragon, too?* He concentrated harder, but nothing more happened.

"Bravo. I'd clap, but I'm a bit constrained."

"You!" Theo turned toward where the witch's voice came from. Instead of sitting in a mortar as he was used to seeing her, she was locked in what looked like a whiskey barrel. Her head poked from the top, her hands stuck out of holes that allowed only her fingertips to touch, and her scrawny, crooked legs protruded from the bottom. Chains bound the contraption to a wall.

He looked at her with disgust. "Serves you right, whatever you did, you treacherous old witch. You play both sides. It's bad enough you tried to poison the deer, and you stole *Lamia's Bible* and sold it to the Youdi. But there was no reason to abduct Boo and then give him to the Youdi."

Baba Yaga sneered. "That bird was so stupid and afraid of his shadow. I couldn't train him. He was of no use to me. Even my Kotka didn't like him. I was glad to be rid of him."

"He's my friend, not a thing you can treat as your possession."

"Maybe you should pay me for the food I gave him then. Room and board."

"Kidnappers don't get rewards. You're just a selfish old witch."

"Little do you know what's really happening here. You're angry, but Lord Zlo doesn't take kindly to things not going exactly his way." She jerked her head toward the other side of the room. "At least I didn't displease him as much as Jabalaka."

Theo looked where she indicated. Chains strapped a groaning man around the outer edge of a slow-moving metal wheel that looked like a millstone. Torn clothes and red welts covered his body, and his head tilted to the side. Under the wheel, reddish-purple creatures squirmed in a tub filled with a green liquid. Theo watched in horror as the man dipped head-first closer to the wiggling tentacles. They wrapped around his body, slapping his face and exposed skin, and he screamed. The torture continued until the man had passed from beneath the wheel to the other side as he rose to the top.

The screams subsided to moans.

"That's Jabalaka?"

The one time Theo had seen the man he had looked the way Lamia had cursed him: a foot-high, round frog-man, with flippers for feet and webbed hands. The only part that remained of that creature was the tuft of reddish-blond hair now matted with blood and sweat onto the man's head.

Jabalaka had been kind to Theo. The man didn't deserve this punishment. Theo seethed with anger. "Zlo will pay for this."

Two strong hands gripped Theo under his armpits. Whatever it was had long claws that wrapped around Theo's chest.

A voice behind him said, "You can tell that to him personally. He requests your presence."

The creature removed one hand and released Theo from the pole, keeping his hands tied. It squeezed Theo as it pushed him down a long corridor and shoved him through an open door at the end.

The room looked like a cathedral, with a high, arched ceiling. Instead of exuding peace and beauty, though, gloominess and evil settled over the expanse. Arches lined the walls, with twin torches blazing in sconces from them. In the middle of the room, a black cloth covered an object about four feet high and just as wide. Something else lay under the covering, causing it to buckle in the center.

Dim light pierced an image in a stained-glass window at the other end of the room, casting its reflection onto the elevated portion of the cloth. As the creature behind Theo prodded him forward, the image in the window became clearer. A rosette formed from seven skulls encircled a large ruby-red dragon's eye. Etched dragon wings spanned both sides of the rosette, and above it glowed an image of the two moons, red and blue facing each other.

A cloaked figure, his face hidden in the shadows, was seated on a carved stone throne beneath the rosette. At his side stood a warrior covered with black metal armor and a helmet. Antlers protruded from the sides of the helmet, and a long snout with a gaping hole like an anteater jutted out the front. Icy-blue, bulging eyes glared out from underneath. The parts of the creature that armor didn't concealed were covered with thick black hair. The monstrous being held a bow with an arrow aimed at Theo.

Seven stones steps encircled the throne like the tiers of a pyramid. A Youda Theo had never seen before stood to one side of the steps, and the Karakonjul Bor Stobor stood on his four horse legs on the other. He clutched the handle of a weapon that lay tucked under his hairy arm. Lined up next to him were seven knights dressed in black armor, each holding a spear like a scepter. On their heads they wore iron helmets from which snake figures jutted out.

The cloaked figure rose, and torch light flickered off of the silver embroidered along the edges of his garment. The others around him bowed as he descended the steps and approached Theo.

Theo quaked, despite his resolve to be brave, as what he assumed was Lord Zlo stood before him. Although Theo had encountered plenty of unpleasant and dangerous creatures in Dragon Village, everything about the man before Theo screamed evil. It wasn't Zlo's looks so much that terrified Theo, although the man was scary looking. With scarred skin as dark as night and red eyes glowing like a full moon, he looked like a fossilized zombie. Deep furrows lined the man's brows, and his cleft chin couldn't have been born by nature. Former battles must have left the deep gouge there. Theo had seen stranger looking beings, like the warrior standing next to the throne. But it was the darkness that radiated off of Zlo like heat waves on concrete in summer that made Theo lose his confidence.

Even so, Theo managed to speak, his voice raspy. "What do you want with me … Zlo?"

"Hello, Theo." The man walked behind his captive. "I'm glad you know who I am. Introductions are so tedious, don't you think?"

Zlo's voice, like his appearance, sent shudders down Theo's spine. It wasn't raspy or guttural. It was deep, too deep, and soothing, like being put into a trance. But the tone wasn't meant to induce calmness. It was like a viper striking to paralyze its victim before devouring it. Theo imagined that was what Satan's voice would be like to those he promised the world to in exchange for their souls.

Theo licked the inside of his dry mouth. "You won't win. We'll defeat you."

"We?" Zlo made his way to Theo's front. The evil being waved his hand around the room. "I don't see anyone here to assist you."

"They'll come." Fear seeped into Theo's pores. Would they find him in time?

"Unlikely." Zlo continued to circle Theo. "I've been watching you since you defeated my servant Lamia. You're incapable of doing anything on your own. Always one of your friends or the other to save you from yourself. From your mistakes. How many times have you almost gotten them killed? The Fates may have told you that you're a hero, that you've been chosen to be a ruler, but they were wrong. You're nothing."

Zlo droned on, making Theo sleepy. *He's right. I'm nothing. My friends are the real heroes.*

"I don't know why Lamia thought she could persuade you to join our side." Zlo stood in front of Theo again, his eyes searing into Theo's soul. "Or, more importantly, why she would have even tried. You're no leader. All you are is an unimportant little boy."

"An unimportant little boy," Theo repeated, his eyes drooping.

"Even this," Zlo said as he reached his dark, clawed hands toward Theo and fingered the burnt cloth. "You call this power? True power lies in the soul, not in a few party tricks, as you'd say in your world."

"Yes, just party tricks," Theo mumbled. "Not power."

"Even my second-in-command, Radan, has more power than you. Look at him. Don't you agree?" Zlo raised Theo's head and forced him to gaze toward the warrior who stood by the throne.

Theo nodded, words becoming difficult as his throat tightened.

"I raised Radan as my own child." Zlo's words went on, soothing, calming, intoxicating. "I gave him strength and taught him how to be a warrior. He's grateful and happy, delighted to be my charge and friend."

"Grateful," Theo managed to squeak out.

"Even your father's trusty Knights of Light knew which was the winning side and vowed allegiance to me. Now they're my Knights of Darkness, ready to do my command."

"Your command."

"All this could have been yours if you'd been faithful to Lamia. You could have been a true soldier, a true hero."

The voice drove Theo deeper into his subconsciousness, telling him to remain there forever, wallowing in his failures.

"*Fight him, my beloved son.*" Zunitza's words floated gently around Theo. "*You've never been a failure. Being a hero means working with others. Only those who want glory and control desire to do things on their own.*"

"*Yes, fight him. Wake up,*" another voice joined in. "*The land is dying and needs your help. Your friends need you.*"

Theo walked around in the hazy fog of his mind. "*How? How can I save myself? Zlo's too powerful.*"

"*He's not more powerful than you,*" Zunitza said. "*Believe in yourself. Overcome your fear.*"

"*And rely on your friends to help you,*" the other voice was now screaming at him. "*Be fearless. Only your fear is preventing you from succeeding. Hold onto your dreams and your desires.*"

Theo fought back, pain searing his mind as he loosened the threads of Zlo's control. "I. Am. A. Hero." He forced the words from his lips.

A lightning bolt shot through the mist. The fog slowly lifted, revealing dark stones beneath his feet. The smell of burning torches and the flickering of their light returned to his senses. Theo stared at black-booted legs in front of him. He lifted his head, stared Zlo in his glowing red eyes, and repeated, "I am a hero."

"But you weren't enough of a hero to stay at home, were you?"

"What do you mean?" *What game is Zlo playing?* "My friends were in trouble. I came to help. That's what a hero does."

"You fell for my trap." Zlo's tight-pressed lips turned into a triumphant smile.

"Trap? I've managed to escape from your soldiers, until now."

"Ah, yes." Zlo rubbed his chin, his smile growing larger. "That was rather clever, but I can't take credit for that deceit. That was all Bor Stobor's doing."

Theo looked at the Karakonjul. The creature barked and wagged his horse's tail.

"Oh, no." Theo's muscles went rigid. "Not the puppy?"

"That's right." Zlo let out a sinister laugh. "Your Samodiva friend warned you that the Karakonjul was a shape-shifter, but you ignored her good advice. That cute little puppy your friend adored so much is my servant."

Theo groaned. His thoughts should have been on planning how to escape, but all he could feel now was the pain—and shame—Pavel would likely suffer for being fooled.

"Bor Stobor couldn't wait to help." Zlo gloated. "Promises of allowing him free reign in your world all year was a great incentive. I like to reward my servants for success. He's tired of his kind being restricted from entering for only a couple weeks after the winter solstice when the portal between his world and yours weakens. Once I unleash my terror, that portal will remain open always, and he'll be able to make your world his home forever."

What other terror was Zlo planning on unleashing? Theo couldn't let this happen. Even if his friends weren't here to help, he could do something. Anger arose in him. The need to protect. A burning sensation surged within his chest, and his blood boiled with power. He gave a tug, and the rope binding his hands snapped.

"I'll never let that happen," Theo shouted as he rushed toward Zlo.

Quicker than Theo could take another step, Zlo had nodded to his warrior, Radan.

A sharp pain pierced Theo's chest as an arrow struck him, then dissolved into black smoke. Invisible hands held him in place. He struggled in vain to free himself.

"Don't burn out your power," Zlo said. "The more you fight it, the quicker the poison courses through your blood and the stronger the paralysis becomes. I've had plenty of time to practice on your father to perfect the formula."

"You won't win." Theo spat out the words through tight lips.

"But I will." Zlo's glowing red eyes reflected Theo's hopelessness back to him. "And it was rude of you not to let me finish."

Theo wanted to shoot Zlo with one of his own poisoned arrows and tie him to the wheel of torture he was inflicting on Jabalaka.

Zlo laughed as if reading Theo's mind. "Bor Stobor has kept tabs on you and your friends the entire time, passing on information to my other servants, the ravens. The birds followed you every step of the way, keeping me aware of where you were."

Zlo paced the room, his voice growing angry. "They told me how you deceived two of my soldiers with your illusions of treasure. You had a good laugh thinking how funny it would be when they returned to dig up the non-existent treasure, didn't you?" Zlo stopped pacing and cast his angry glare toward Theo. "The laugh's on them. The ravens delighted in the flesh of those soldiers—while they were still alive."

Bile rose in Theo's throat, and he wanted to gag. He had to free himself from this paralysis, so he could stop this monster.

"Oh, is that too delicate for your hero's stomach?" Zlo laughed. "But let me now finish what I started to tell you, how you fell into my trap. The puppy isn't the trap I set for you. That's not why I think you're clueless."

Theo remained silent, not wanting to know how else he'd failed.

"No, I'm talking about my slugi, what you like to refer to as 'red creatures.' Did you really think they were how I planned to take over the world? By polluting the human's water sources? That's only a small part of what I'm going to do."

"How …?" Theo felt Zlo's penetrating glance trying to take over his mind again.

"I needed you here," Zlo screamed in Theo's face. "Without you, my plan would have failed. I purposely sent them and allowed the Rusalki's messenger to get through. I knew you'd come if your friends summoned you."

"No!" Theo squeezed his eyes tight. Zlo must be lying.

*I didn't fall for his deceit. I didn't.* Yet in his heart, Theo knew everything Zlo said was true.

"Enough of this chatter. It's almost time to begin the ritual. But for that, I'll need something from you."

Zlo's bony black hand reached out and ripped the medallion from around Theo's neck.

# Chapter 20
# The Ritual

Was the evil lord going to use Theo's medallion to open a portal between the human and supernatural worlds, the same way Theo had used it to open a portal to Dragon Village? That was the only reason Zlo could have wanted the medallion, wasn't it?

A nagging sensation thrummed at the back of Theo's mind. Someone was trying to communicate with him, but Zlo's poisoned arrow had muted Theo's dragon capabilities. He had to discover another way to prevent that demonic creature from performing the ritual. Theo struggled mentally and physically against his invisible restraints to no avail. He was frozen to the spot, able only to watch.

Zlo strode toward the center of the room and stopped by the object covered with a black cloth. "The time is near. Prepare for the ritual."

Radan marched forward, bowing before his master. "What about the boy?"

"No time for that." Zlo turned his head and shot his evil glare at Theo while he spoke to Radan. "When we're through, he can be chained with his father in the deepest dungeon. I should kill them both, but they'll suffer more without family, without subjects, without this land they love so much. Zmey doesn't mind the darkness now, and neither will his son when we're finished with him."

*What horror has Zlo inflicted on my father? And what's he going to do to me?* How was Theo going to stop this ritual? He concentrated harder on trying to rid himself of the poison.

A fragment of a voice broke through to his mind. "*Use Sa—*" Then it was gone. Scattered like ash in the wind.

Sava? Was he supposed to try to contact her? But how?

In front of Theo, Zlo delivered orders to his servants. "Prepare the altar. Bring the girl and the offerings."

Radan removed the black covering from what Theo now knew was an altar. In the center stood an elevated round table around which three marble balls, each the size of a baseball, their tops indented, rested in a carved hole. The light from the two moons coming through the dragon-eye window revealed a sun engraved in the stone table. A star shape like Theo's medallion had been carved into the center of the sun. Instead of the entwined dragons, this one held the IYI symbols like the ones that had appeared on the cover of *Lamia's Bible* after Theo had inserted a key to unlock the book.

"No, I won't do it," a female voice echoed around the room.

Theo averted his eyes from the altar to where the Knights of Darkness carried two cages, one large and one small. A black covering concealed what lay inside, although the hissing and mewling from the smaller one indicated its captive was likely Kotka, Baba Yaga's cat. The men set the cages onto the floor near the altar. Behind them, two other knights escorted a girl dressed in white.

*Diva.* They had captured her after all. Theo wanted to scream for her to fight, but she walked in on her own. The guards, with heads slightly bowed, hovered close, but didn't touch the girl or force her forward. Were they showing her respect and reverence? Or did they fear her?

As the girl approached the cages, the torches lit her pale face, which was almost translucent. Her hair was snow-white, and symbols of the sun and moon decorated her garment. The aroma of sweet honey filled the room. The prisoner wasn't Diva; it was Kosara. Theo hoped that meant the guards hadn't captured Diva or Pavel.

Zlo nodded toward the cages, and a Knight of Darkness removed the covering from the smaller one. Kotka flew around her enclosure, hissing and banging like a madman against the bars with her purple wings. The knight covered his eyes as he withdrew the cloth from the larger cage. A blinding golden light illuminated the room.

*The Firebird.*

When Theo had seen the bird before, sitting in the sacred Znahar Tree, the Firebird had lost its song, and had not glowed so brightly. Now, its multicolored feathers burned like the fire it was named after. Imprisoned, it once again refrained from its song. How Theo longed to hear it.

Zlo stretched out his bony hand, pointing at Kosara. "Priestess of Bendis, Guardian of the Firebird, watch now while I destroy the messenger to the gods and retrieve its sun pearls."

Kosara stamped her foot. "Don't! You'll kill the soul of Zmeykovo."

"Exactly." Zlo approached the cage and opened the door.

Sparks shot out of the evil lord's hand as he touched the Firebird. Whistling like shooting fireworks penetrated the room, and thousands of glowing sparks scattered around the cage. The Firebird shed tears and burst into flames. His light went out, like a fallen star. All that remained was a pile of purple ashes covering the bottom of the cage. Zlo dug through the ashes and gathered three golden pearls as large as hazelnuts.

Theo choked back his grief. The golden tear pearls. The missing part of the prophecy. That was the reason Zlo had needed the Firebird.

"You killed him!" Kosara didn't wipe away the streams running down her face. "Your time will come, and you and all of your servants will pay. The bird will be reborn, even stronger, and your end will come. The soul of the land will make you suffer. Tangra will destroy you once and for all."

Zlo turned his glowing eyes toward the priestess. "Your spirit god will soon be within my power. Then I, not he, will have dominance over everything." He motioned to the Youda. "Let us now begin. The moons are about to align. Witch, bring me the blood and the silent water." He cast his gaze around the room, making eye contact with everyone. "A painful death to anyone who now dares to speak."

The room went eerily silent. Even Kotka ceased screeching.

The Youda returned moments later carrying a bowl and two vials, which she set on the altar in front of Zlo. She backed away, her head bowed, and returned to her dark corner of the room.

Kosara kneeled by the open cage, remaining silent, and removed a gold-embroidered bag from the folds of her garment. She pulled out a wooden egg and opened it. Inside the hollow cavity, she collected the ashes of the Firebird as if entombing the bird for its eternal rest. She returned the egg into her bag and hid it away, but remained seated, her head bowed, by the now-empty cage.

Zlo barely gave Kosara a glance as he prepared for his ritual. Theo imagined he didn't care if she took ashes from a dead bird. He had the ingredients he needed to bring his monstrous malevolence into the world.

The evil lord opened the back of Theo's amulet and removed the Y-shaped key, placing it into the middle of the sun on the altar in the carved-out spot.

He lifted one vial of blood, raising it so the glow coming from the dragon-eye window shone on it. "Blood of power. Blood of a young Samodiva on the verge of gaining her full abilities. Use that power now to bring my desires to fruition."

He poured the blood into the I to the left of the Y.

*That's why the Youdi needed Diva, for her blood.* Theo struggled again against his invisible restraints that kept his mind and body bound. *I have to free my dragon powers.*

"*No,*" the voice in his mind said, breaking through for a moment. "*Use Samodiva power.*"

Zlo raised the second vial of blood, letting the glow from the two moons shine on it. "Blood of life. Blood of a young dragon lord on the verge of gaining his full abilities. Use that power now to grant life and freedom to those I choose."

He poured the blood into the I to the right of the Y.

Theo retreated into the recess of his mind, this time unaided by Zlo. He wandered through the thick, heavy fog. "Mom, can you hear me? How do I use Samodiva power?"

A weak reply came. *"Remember Lesh?"* The voice faded, and Theo found himself back in the fortress.

Zlo nodded to Radan. His servant grabbed Kosara from behind and slapped his hand over her mouth. He dragged her toward Zlo. She struggled as Zlo seized her wrist and scratched it with the claw of his little finger. He held her hand over the sun on the altar. Drops of blood appeared like dew and ran down into the letters.

Raising his arms toward the dragon eye, Zlo chanted, "Blood of purity. Blood of immortality. Desecrate the pure. Perpetuate the evil. White Light destroy. Darkness prevail."

Zlo nodded to Radan again, and his servant pinched the side of Kosara's neck. The priestess ceased struggling and went limp in the warrior's arms. He dragged her back to the cage and dropped her beside it.

*"Hurt me, not the priestess."* The words formed in Theo's head, but didn't pass his lips.

He focused on returning to his mind, where he could talk to Zunitza, if that had been her. Nothing happened. What did she mean? Lesh was the giant vulture Theo had defeated. He didn't use any Samodiva power then. He had tried to twirl like Diva once, hoping he'd shift, but nothing had happened. He repeated the words to himself again. *"Use Samodiva power"* and *"Remember Lesh."*

Then he recalled what happened.

It wasn't *his* Samodiva power that had been used. It was Diva's. She had been wounded, badly, but she'd healed herself.

*Can I do that, too?*

Zlo had said he'd tested the poison on his father, a dragon, but would it have the same effect on a Samodiva's power? Theo focused his thoughts on forcing the poison from his body.

Zlo lifted the bowl of silent water, letting the glow of the moons sparkle in the liquid. "Silent water. Hear now my commands and obey. Give birth to all manner of evil. Bring forth my demonic hoards, to plunder, to devastate, to conquer the world."

He poured the water over the sun. The blood in the crevices swirled around, mixing, tinging the water pink.

Theo wanted to scream. *I'm going to fail.*

"*Come on, Theo,*" a voice whispered, "*You can do this. Relax. Concentrate. Like arrow-shooting lessons. You are powerful.*"

He took a deep breath and held it. *Focus. Focus. Focus.* He slowly released his breath while he concentrated on only the poison. He found it, a purple residue clogging his veins.

"*Good,*" the voice said. "*Separate it. Push it toward the surface.*"

Theo pulled it out, piece by piece, until his blood ran clean. A tingling started in his chest and radiated outward. His lips moved, but sound refused to come.

*Can't fail. Have. To. Try. Harder.*

Zlo placed a golden pearl into each of the hollowed-out holes of the marble balls. As light from the window passed over them, a swirling purple-black mass pulsed within the pearls.

"Let evil reign," Zlo shouted as the light from the two moons merged through the pupil of the dragon's eye and shone directly onto the **Y**.

A beam shot out of the rays of the carved sun on the altar. The light spun like a funnel and formed an arch made of two crowned snakes. Their tongues darted in and out, finally joining. Flames erupted from their mouths, which formed into a soccer-sized fireball, swirling above them.

The evil lord thrust his claws into two of the pearls and chanted, "Come forth, demonic forces."

The golden pearls burst, and sulfuric odors spread throughout the room. The mists swirled, forming grotesque shapes. They performed their demonic dance in the air, changing shape as the smoky fibers formed and reformed into one hideous creature after the other.

Zlo threw up his hands toward the dragon-eye window. "Go. Gather strength. Prepare for battle."

The mist swept upward, passing through the fireball. A thick dark form exploded from the other side. Twisting limbs, screeching mouths, were all mashed together like a rat king. The giant, grotesque mass shot through the black dragon pupil. There, in the window, they swirled and pulsed, with incessant shrieking.

"*No,*" Theo shouted, but the sound came out barely a whisper.

The evil lord thrust his claws into the remaining pearl and shouted, "Arise, my faithful servant."

The golden pearl burst, and the mist shot toward Kotka. The cat screeched like a demon from the underworld and pounded her wings on the metal bars of the cage. The mist wrapped itself around the animal, twirling, squeezing, faster and faster. Black smoke spewed out of the cat's mouth, mixing with the purple-black mass from the pearl. With one final screech, Kotka fell to the floor of the cage, panting.

The purple-black mist continued to spin as if possessed by demons. It undulated like a snake toward the dome of the chamber, twisted into a spiral, and dove into the midst of the fireball. Purple light flooded the ball. It spun and spun, expanding with each rotation. The purple flames moved so fast the ball no longer seemed to be moving, except for the flicker of purple light—and its growing girth.

The light fragmented into a myriad of blinding pieces. In its place, spinning above the altar, an enormous purple crystal floated. Like the fireball, it spun faster and faster. It shattered with a loud crack. The explosion hurled thousands of particles into the air.

"No," Theo screamed, his words finally finding voice. He closed his eyes as the glass needles tore at his face.

Silence permeated the room.

Theo shook his head. He could move.

Glass particles splashed onto the floor. He opened his eyes and froze.

A giant dragon eye stared at him.

He had failed.

Lamia was alive.

# Chapter 21
# Battle for Control

Lamia, the three-headed dragon Theo had killed last year had been reborn, larger and more powerful than before. Black lines streaked through the once-golden scales that covered her body and the red ones that lined her underbelly. She lacked the all-seeing third eye on her middle head, the eye Theo had pierced with the silver arrow to destroy the monster. Even if he had his bow with him, he wouldn't have been able to kill her again that way. The silver arrow had disappeared after it entered the beast. He would have to find a new way to put an end to her, this time forever.

In a puff of black smoke, Lamia changed from dragon into the half-woman, half-snake appearance Theo had first seen her. Her pointed ears stuck up from beneath her golden hair, now also lined with black. Dark, reptilian eyes betold the coldness of her demeanor.

She slithered toward him, the way she had during their first meeting, and curled her lizard tail around his legs. Once more, she ran cold fingers, more claw-like than before, along his chin. "I'm so glad to see you again, dear nephew, but you don't look pleased about our reunion."

Zlo held out his hand to Lamia. "Come, my pet. Your get-together will have to wait. We must visit your brother immediately. He has something you need so you can remain in this realm."

"Just let me teach him one lesson."

"Now!" Zlo commanded.

Lamia dissolved into mist and appeared at Zlo's side. She hissed toward Theo. "Soon. Not much longer, and I'll deal with you, my brother's mongrel offspring, who thinks he's a dragon. You'll suffer the fate you deserve."

"Yes, yes, I'll leave him for you, my pet." Zlo stroked her chin. "Right now, we're wasting time."

"We could bring him to his father now," Lamia said. "That would cause them both great pain."

"There's no time. We must hurry." Zlo glanced at the merged moons. "Besides, I want the *hero* to see the destruction he's failed to avert."

The evil lord turned his glowing eyes toward Theo. "When the moons have drawn apart and become two once more, my demonic hoards will have grown to full force and will be released into your world."

Zlo gave one last command as he began to dissolve into mist. "Radan, do what you must to keep the boy here until we return."

Lamia focused her eyes on Theo. "There's no escaping, nephew. The fortress is secure. I'll be back for you." She, too, dissolved into mist.

The two black forms slipped out through the door.

Radan nocked a poisoned arrow and pointed it at Theo, while Bor Stobor and the Knights of Darkness maintained their positions. The Youda had disappeared, or at least had hidden from view.

Theo's heart raced. *How can I beat them? I don't have my father's sword, my sword, or any other weapon.*

"*Theo, together we can defeat them.*" The voice inside his mind was now free and recognizable.

"*Diva? Where—?*"

"*No time for questions. I've been with you the entire time.*"

Something small tickled his ankle. He looked down. A white mouse poked her head out of his pants leg.

"*Listen,*" she thought to him. "*I've been watching. Bor Stobor has your sword. I'll get it from him and throw it to you. Be ready when I shout, 'Now!'* " With that said, Diva the mouse scurried across the room.

Theo wanted to see what Diva was doing, but he didn't dare look that way, fearing someone in the room would discover his friend. He didn't have to wait long. Bor Stobor shrieked and his horse's hooves clattered against the floor. Next to Diva, the Karakonjul lay on his side, his four legs twisted, bones sticking out. The beast howled and thrashed his tail.

"Now!" Diva, once more transformed into girl form, hurled the sword and scabbard toward Theo.

The weapon spun like a silver star, shooting off sparks as it soared across the room.

Theo grabbed the cold silver handle with both hands. *Give me strength, Zunitza.*

Radan let fly the arrow, but Theo withdrew the sword from its scabbard and struck the approaching weapon. The arrow burst into a myriad of shards, which flew in all directions across the room.

More knights from outside the room rushed in, their own swords and lances drawn.

Kosara moaned and sat up, rubbing her head. An evil grin spread across Radan's face and he ran toward the priestess.

Theo shouted, "Diva, don't let him touch Kosara," but Diva had already sped across the room to stand in front of the priestess. She held her stance, an arrow aimed at Radan's heart.

"Knights of Darkness, don't just stand their gawking." Radan waved his arms in the air. "Capture them. All of them."

The warriors within the room rushed toward Diva and Kosara, while the ones by the entrance ran in Theo's direction.

"Stop!" Theo pointed his sword at the ones coming his way.

The weapon lit up with a silver-purple light. Theo almost dropped it, startled by the change. He gripped it tighter and drew an arc around the men. A ray of light shot out, engulfing the warriors. The men froze mid-step.

"Theo," Diva yelled.

The other warriors were almost upon Diva and Kosara. Theo swiveled and shot out a beam of light toward the attackers. They, too, froze like statues. One more time, Theo pointed the sword at Radan and froze the beast.

Theo looked at Diva and Kosara. "The moons are pulling apart faster than they came together. We have to stop them!"

The dragon eye in the rosette flickered like a lighthouse. The blackness of the pupil had expanded since the ritual, already filling half the eye as if the demons within were pushing it open like a doorway. Hundreds of twin red orbs blinked from within the swirling mass. The light from their stares illuminated the floor, making it look like blood. Theo touched a spot next to him to reassure himself that it was only light and not a sticky substance.

What exactly had the prophecy said? He chanted the words: " 'Sword of father. Sword of victory. The unborn hero wields its might. A bloody rose it must pierce.' "

The red dragon eye had to be the "bloody rose." He stood, aiming the sword at its center.

"Let's do this." He stared at the eye the way Diva had taught him to shoot an arrow. Focus on where he wanted the weapon to hit. Relax his muscles. Concentrate on the target until his vision tunneled on that location. Release the weapon when that's all he could see.

The instructions clear in his mind, he stretched his body back and threw the sword at the rosette with all his might. The tip gleamed like lightning and spun like a drill. Seconds later, the blade slammed into the middle of the dragon eye.

Time seemed to slow with the sword stuck in the middle of the pupil.

*It didn't work. If the eye's not the bloody rose, then what is?*

A spark spat out of the rosette followed by loud thunder. The glass shattered.

"Get down!" Theo shouted and covered his head as the dragon eye and skulls circling it exploded like a grenade.

Fragments of red, black, and white glass scattered throughout the room. The altar shattered. Demons gathering within the eye shrieked loud enough Theo imagined they could be heard in the underworld. The mass of black inside shot out of the window and spread out into black streaks, heading in all directions throughout Dragon Village.

Then an eerie silence filled the room. Theo jumped to his feet, helping Diva and Kosara up. "We have to get out of here before Zlo and Lamia return. Diva, protect Kosara while I look for a way out of here so I can free Jabalaka."

Kosara rose. "The room they kept me in adjoins the torture room. They wanted me to hear the screams so I would do their bidding. You can get to our friend that way, but you can't escape from that room."

"Thank you, Kosara." He rushed toward the back of the room and found a door.

The hinges squeaked as he pulled it open. He peered around the corner. No guards occupied the room. A groan came from Jabalaka, who was on his way downward, toward the red creatures, slugi Zlo had said they were called.

Theo rushed into the room and found a lever next to the torture device. With all his strength, he pushed it to its upright position. The wheel stopped moving.

"Jabalaka?" He touched the man lightly on his face. "I'm here to free you."

The one-time frog man's eyes opened. His mouth moved, but only a raspy sound came out.

"Boy, don't forget about me."

Theo whipped around toward Baba Yaga. He drew in slow, steady breaths and controlled the tone of his voice, forcing back his anger. "You don't deserve to be free. Learn to take a side, you traitor. Maybe your cat will help you."

"Kotka?" Her hands trembled in the restraints.

"Yes, your cat's alive, no thanks to you."

"I didn't—"

"I don't have time to hear what you did or didn't do." Theo turned his back on her and looked for a way to remove the chains binding Jabalaka to the wheel.

The witch cackled. "But I'm sure you'll have time to see what I have. Something I know you want."

Anger bubbled to the surface of Theo's skin. He wouldn't look. Whatever it was had to be another of Baba Yaga's tricks. He had to free Jabalaka. Strength surged through his arms and claws and scales burst out over them. He tore at the chains, and they shredded. As quickly as they had appeared, the dragon features disappeared. Theo held onto Jabalaka as he slid the man off the wheel.

"Can you walk at all," Theo asked as he wrapped one arm around the man's waist.

Jabalaka nodded.

"I know you want this," Baba Yaga said with a taunting voice.

Theo couldn't resist the temptation and turned to look. In the witch's hand dangled his medallion.

"How'd you get that?" It had been on Zlo's altar before the fighting began.

"I still have tricks in my bag, boy." She cackled again. "Release me if—"

The next moment her mouth fell open, and she looked at her empty hand. Theo blinked rapidly. His legs tingled and his hands trembled, but he waved the medallion so the witch could see it. One moment he had imagined rushing the witch to retrieve it, and the next, he had seized his medallion from her. One more dragon power developing.

Baba Yaga shook her head. "I see you're becoming your father's son. He would help me, so you—"

"Save your breath," Theo said as he helped Jabalaka out of the room and slammed the door behind him.

Diva met him. "Theo, we have to hurry. More Knights of Darkness are pounding at the door."

Theo ran into the room. Debris from the destroyed altar had been piled against the heavy door. Even so, it buckled in with each *thump* from the other side.

"I've blocked it for as long as I could," Diva said, "but the Knights of Darkness will break through soon. We have to get out of here. I looked for a way to escape, but it's like a prison. The only way out is through the door or through—"

They both said "the broken window" at the same time as they looked at the gaping hole above the throne where the dragon eye used to be. It was large enough for them to escape through—but too high to climb.

"Do you think you can shift?" Diva asked.

"I have to. Can you take Jabalaka while I try?"

Diva nodded and carried the injured man to rest on the throne.

Theo concentrated on shifting. *Hurry, hurry*, he told himself. Pain spread all over his body, and the bumps beneath his arms expanded.

*Thump, thump, thump.* A loud crash came from the doorway as the pieces of broken altar went flying. The door slammed open.

"Not so fast, nephew." The monstrous Lamia appeared under the frame. Behind her stood more Knights of Darkness, armed and ready to attack.

Jabalaka screeched from the throne. By the time Theo looked that way, the injured man had somehow reached the shattered window and was already halfway out.

"Stop! You'll die." Theo took a step forward.

Jabalaka looked back. Fear etched his face, but sadness also. He glanced once more at Lamia and shuddered, before he tumbled out the window and disappeared into the darkness without a scream.

Theo spun around and advanced on Lamia. "Look what you did. He's so terrified of you, he'd rather jump to his death than face you again."

Lamia laughed. "He was always a weak fool."

"You'll pay for his death."

He swung his sword at Lamia's gold-and-black-striped body. The blade bounced off without making a scratch. Theo struck her again, trying to remain upright.

"A new toy, nephew? Zmey's sword can't hurt me, a blood relative." Lamia laughed, then her face twitched in pain.

Lamia wrenched an arrow from her shoulder. Blood flowed, then trickled, and the wound healed. The dragon-woman twisted around, glaring at Diva, who held her bow with another arrow aimed at Lamia.

"You!" Lamia shrieked, scales erupting on her face. "I should have made sure I'd killed you the first time, Samodiva."

"Try your best now, oh pretend queen." Diva mock-bowed and returned to her warrior stance in front of Kosara.

"You dare challenge me? Knights of Darkness, seize them!"

Theo pointed his sword in the direction of the newest arrivals and froze them. Then he swung his sword back toward Lamia.

*Maybe the laser will freeze her, too.* He held the tip pointed against her throat.

"Even your sword's rays won't hurt me. I have new powers." Lamia stroked a belt she now wore. On it, a white dragon and a golden one, formed a figure eight. Each dragon was eating its tail. She rose higher on her serpentine tail and bared sharp canine teeth. "You think you can protect yourself and your friends. I'll kill them and send you so far inside your own mind that you'll remain there forever, locked in your pain and memories."

The dragon-woman dissolved into mist and appeared next to Diva. Lamia swung her tail at the Samodiva, hitting her in the chest. Diva crashed into the cage holding the cat and fell onto her back. Undeterred, Diva pressed the bow to her chest, ready to shoot.

The cage toppled over, and the cat flew out. Spitting and hissing, Kotka rushed at Lamia and dug her claws into the dragon-woman's face.

Lamia roared, pulled off the cat, and tossed her into the air. The flying creature returned, claws out. While Lamia fought with Kotka, Diva shot the dragon-woman in the stomach with another arrow, then got to her feet and returned to Kosara's side. The Samodiva aimed a third arrow at the dragon-woman.

Lamia snarled as she pulled out the arrow. She grew even larger, and her sharp teeth gained ragged points. The cat yowled and retreated, fleeing through the open door. Lamia snapped her clawed fingers. A black whip appeared in her hand. She cracked it toward Diva and Kosara, capturing both in a snare. Diva tugged at it like a wild cat, but it held her tight.

"Never underestimate me. This lovely weapon is my favorite, a whip made from my darling mother's skin." The vertebrae of

Lamia's snake tail twisted as she approached her captives. "Little woodland nymph, you'll pay for wounding me."

Theo looked around the room for something else to attack Lamia with. Black smoke appeared in front of him. Zlo's burning eyes shone from its midst. The evil lord gained form and reached out his bony hand to seize the sword from Theo.

"So, you decided to return, did you? You're too late. I destroyed your portal." Theo held a defensive position and stabbed toward his foe.

Zlo laughed as he once more dissolved into black mist. "You'll never win."

Theo felt a cold breath behind him. He spun around, facing Zlo again. Theo focused on the black figure with blazing demon eyes fixed on him. Never would Theo have imagined he'd find himself in this situation. Fighting a demon with a sword given to him by the sisters of Fate. Having the destiny of the world depend on him.

*It's now or never. Time to send this monster back to the evil realm he comes from.*

Standing his ground, Theo plunged the sword toward the dark, tall figure of Zlo, but the demon once more dissolved into the shadows.

"Enough of these children's games. No more hide-and-seek." Zlo's voice came from the throne. "You have no clue whom you're trying to fight. I'm eternity. I'm the master of the black forces."

Zlo shot out rays of light from his eyes toward Radan and the frozen Knights of Darkness. They all stumbled forward. "Lamia, I give you leave to finish these insignificant creatures. Just keep the boy alive—for now."

Lamia drew her whip tighter around Diva and Kosara and sneered at her enemy.

Theo remembered Zunitza's words and pushed aside his fear. He imagined Zmey's might and power and his mother's loving smile. A surge of strength, fire, and anger pulsed through him. Flames shot through his hands, and his wings were born. His legs thickened, and metal wrapped itself around his chest. His shoulders expanded, and his wings stretched. He breathed fire toward Radan and each group of Knights of Darkness from his dragon mouth. The knights all dropped to their knees, while Radan stopped mid-step.

Theo approached Lamia. A spark of fear crossed her face, and she took a step back, dropping the whip. She narrowed her eyes to slits, and a wicked smile broke out on her face as she slithered toward him. "Your strength may be increasing, nephew, but it'll never compare to mine."

*"Even though I'm your brother's son, you don't deserve the title of aunt. After I get the rest of my friends to safety, I'll come back to kill you again, this time forever."* Theo sent the thought to Lamia.

He flapped his wings, and the torches in the room blazed with a blue light. *"Diva, go. Will you look for Pavel, the Kukeri, and your sisters? Make sure they're okay and tell them what happened. I'll be right behind you."*

Diva nodded. She twirled, changed into a falcon, and flew out the window.

Theo lowered his body to the floor. *"Kosara, get on."*

Without waiting for a second invitation, the priestess climbed onto Theo's back, and he flew out the shattered rosette.

Theo thrust out his wings, soaring upward, past the fortress and toward Cherna Mountain. The Znahar Tree lay to the south. He climbed over the crest of the mountain, the air cooling his body, relaxing his muscles after the intensity of the battle and his confrontation with Lamia. It felt good to fly again. He hoped the thrill of it never wore off. His mother was right. He had power within him. All he had to do was overcome his fear.

# Chapter 22
# Born from the Ashes

KOSARA'S BODY TREMBLED, her grasp on Theo's back tight. She leaned closer to his ear and spoke two frightening words. "Lamia's coming."

Theo pivoted in his flight to look back. Lamia, in her three-headed dragon form, had crested the mountain. Theo resumed his course, thrust his wings with more force, and accelerated. The Znahar Tree wasn't much farther. He would make it there before Lamia, but then what would he do to protect Kosara?

Descending with smooth circles, Theo landed near the majestic tree. A chilling silence greeted him. His heart ached for the state of the once-beautiful site. The tree's branches stretched out like hands cracked by time. Silver heart-shaped leaves, now withered, no longer produced their melodious music. The pool at the base of the tree's roots had lost its golden hue and was filled with nasty red creatures.

After Kosara slid from his back, Theo shifted into boy form. He stood to the side as the priestess withdrew the myrtle egg from her embroidered bag and laid it in a carved hole in the tree's trunk. Theo thought that was a good resting place for the Firebird's ashes.

Over her face Kosara lowered a red-and-white veil. She danced like a butterfly around the tree, her legs barely touching the withered grass. Her sweet voice sang a chant.

"Tangra, Tangra!
The bird was flying
And prayed to God –
Give us, God, a little rain,
To revive the life
To revive the land.
Give it to us, Zuna,
To preserve the land,
To revive the Sun,
To preserve the good.
Help us defeat the demon,
Tangra, Tangra."

From the depths of the dark clouds sprang a horseman glowing like solar flares, followed by two fiery lions. As the image passed over the crown of the tree, his golden spear scattered light and thunder across the sky.

"Tangra." Kosara kneeled, and Theo followed her gesture.

A wet drop fell on Theo's nose, then another. He lifted his head toward the refreshing, gentle rain, letting it splash down his face. A flock of white birds squawked as they flew overhead, seeking shelter. The sky filled with a bouquet of intense bright colors. As the rainbow unfolded, its radiance merged with the glow from Tangra's light, and covered the area like a protective dome.

From the hollow, where Kosara had put the myrtle egg, flew a featherless bird the size of a dove. It spiraled around the trunk, and a funnel of flames blazed from its body. As the bird approached the crown of the tree, it became larger. It grew feathers, its tail extended, and light from its new feathers illuminated everything around it.

Theo sucked in a quick breath. "The Firebird." The messenger to the gods had been reborn.

The branches of the tree moved as if from a breeze. Lizards, ladybugs, and crickets crawled on the trunk. The branches crackled and buds popped along the bark, bringing forth lavish silver, heart-shaped leaves. Their music lifted toward the heavens as if in praise for their restoration.

The slimy red monsters, the slugi, in the pool of water surrounding the tree screamed as they shriveled and became red water lilies. Goldfish poked their heads to the surface, and frogs began a serenade. The resplendent Firebird spread his blazing golden wings, sprinkling light all around, and joined in with his own exquisite song.

Theo remained speechless. It was mesmerizing. He'd never heard anything so divine.

A loud roar interrupted the idyllic moment. With outstretched wings, Lamia appeared above their heads.

Theo grabbed his sword, ready to battle the beast.

Flames spewed from the monster's mouths. Lamia beat against the light shield, but every time she touched it, sparks and thunder repelled her.

Kosara touched Theo's shoulder. "The dragon cannot reach us. Zuna and Tangra protect us."

"I don't want to hide from her." His muscles tight, Theo kept his eye on Lamia. "I'll defeat her once and for all."

"You're not ready. You need your full dragon powers. Be patient. Your time will come."

The dragon circled several times, eyes glowing with anger and hatred. She crashed into the shield once more, then, with the roar of a wounded animal, flew away, likely to her master's lair, but not before she sent a message to Theo.

*"I'll return, nephew. I'll find you and your friends no matter where you are. Zlo's army of demons will destroy you and every living thing in Zmeykovo. My master will find a way to open a portal between our worlds. Then we'll kill your family and all mankind."*

THEO REMAINED WITH KOSARA as the day wore on, and darkness of night gave way to the light of day. The glorious sun had reappeared, and the black clouds had dispersed.

Eyes closed, he sat beneath the tree, relishing the warmth. A poke on his cheek startled him, and he opened his eyes. "Boo, my little friend."

The magpie said, "Waak," then flew away to chase a ladybug crawling on the tree trunk.

Another familiar sight made Theo's heart glad. Pavel rode Whirl toward the Znahar Tree. Behind him, Diva, Jega, Zima, Sava, and Ula approached as well on Sur and his herd of deer. All his friends except Jabalaka had survived.

Pavel was the first to jump from the deer and run to hug his friend tight. Diva waited near the Kukeri and her sisters, adjusting the strings on her bow. She stood tall like a soldier and held the others back, allowing Theo and Pavel a moment alone.

"I'm so glad you're okay, Pavel. I didn't know what happened to you when attackers surprised us, when the puppy …" Theo stopped. How could he explain to his friend that the puppy was a lie and had been the Karakonjul all along?

"Tell me about bad surprises." Pavel stood with drooped shoulders as he stared at his hands. "Diva already let me know about Balkan. I let my emotions take control of my reason. Very unscientific. All of you were right. I can't believe how stupid I was."

"You weren't stupid. And it's never wrong to protect someone you love." Theo grasped his friend's shoulder, and Pavel looked up. "You made me see how the most vulnerable need us the most. If we can't take care of them, without controlling them, we shouldn't be leaders."

"I'm not a leader." Pavel sighed. "I'm not the heir to Dragon Village."

"No, you're not heir, but you *are* a leader. And more importantly, you're my best friend. If or when I ever have to rule this place, I'll need you helping me make decisions."

"You will?" Pavel's face lit up. "You can count on me. You might have wings, but I still have a lot of ideas for new inventions. I'm sure I can find ways to help you protect people here and even in Selo if we need to. We're in this together."

"Yes, and, if you're willing, I'd like you to look after my mom and Nia when I can't be in Selo."

"Uh, sure, but Nia's able to do that."

"Okay, you two have had enough time." Diva squashed her way in between Theo and Pavel. "As Pavel said, we're in this together. All of us. Now, we have to join the Kukeri and my sisters and decide how we're going to stop Zlo and Lamia."

Diva dragged the boys over to the others, who appeared to be in a heated debate.

Zima paced and shouted, "No, we have to restore Zmey to the throne before doing anything else. We need a true leader."

"But, it's imperative we secure all portals to the human world," Sava countered. "Theo closed the one Zlo tried to open, but it won't be long until the evil lord discovers or creates another one."

"Theo prevented the demons from entering the human world, but now they're loose in Dragon Village," Ula said. "What's our plan or priority for dealing with them?"

Jega stood back from the others, shaking his head.

"Hey, everyone," Theo shouted, and the arguing stopped. "We can't just focus on one and not the other. We can form teams again, the way Mraz had us do. I, for one, want to find my father. We all need his wisdom and guidance, and I need him to help me understand my powers. I won't stop trying until I rescue him and we stop Lamia and Zlo forever."

He might not be the "true leader" Zima wanted, but Theo had learned that it was important to listen to the needs of each person on his team. As his powers grew, he couldn't try to force his way of doing things onto others. If he did, he would end up like Zima, believing that only one solution existed. Each one of them had their own passion to protect Dragon Village. He hoped he could extend that passion so they'd give all they had to defend the human world as well. Theo needed all of them to work together if they wanted to succeed.

"Theo, look." Kosara appeared in the midst of the group, interrupting his thoughts.

He looked to where she pointed at the Znahar Tree. Beneath the branch on which the glowing Firebird sat was a bud, nestled in a wreath of pure silver leaves, a sign of hope.

The Golden Apple!

# About the Author

Ronesa Aveela is "the creative power of two." Two authors, that is. Nelly, the main force behind the work, the creative genius, was born in Bulgaria and moved to the U.S. in the 1990s. She grew up with stories of wild Samodivi, Kikimora, the dragons Zmey and Lamia, Baba Yaga, and much more. She's a freelance artist and writer. She likes writing mystery romance inspired by legends and tales. In her free time, she paints. Her artistic interests include the female figure, Greek and Thracian mythology, folklore tales, and the natural world interpreted through her eyes. She is married and has two children.

Rebecca, her writing partner was born and raised in the New England area. She has a background in writing and editing, as well as having a love of all things from different cultures. She's learned so much about Bulgarian culture, folklore, and rituals, and writes to share that knowledge with others.

Connect with us at www.ronesaaveela.com.

Be sure to follow us on Kickstarter for extra goodies when we launch new books: https://www.kickstarter.com/profile/ronesa-aveela/.

## The Story Continues...

Discover what happens next in Theo's adventures in *Dragon Village Ouroboros*: https://books2read.com/DV3-Ouroboros.

## Dragon Village Series

1) *The Unborn Hero of Dragon Village*

2) *Dragon Village Firebird*

3) *Dragon Village Ouroboros*

4) *Dragon Village Golden Apple*

5) *Dragon Village Colobar*

## Special Offer

Would you like to learn more about folklore and mythology? Sign up for our newsletter and receive a FREE supplement to our "Spirits and Creatures" book series. To download the article about a malicious water spirit, Vodyanoy or Vodnik, use this link: https://BookHip.com/VFVPQJ or find the link on our website.

## Further Reading

Discover more about the dragons and other creatures in this book in our nonfiction series called "Spirits and Creatures." Available in ebook, paperback, and hardcopy formats from your favorite retailer. You can also request your local library to carry a copy.

Household Spirits – https://books2read.com/household-spirits

Rusalki – Slavic Mermaids – https://books2read.com/rusalki

Dragons – https://books2read.com/dragons-aveela

Baba Yaga – https://books2read.com/babayaga

More to come…